The Awakening of
George Darroch

THE AWAKENING OF GEORGE DARROCH

Robin Jenkins

WATERFRONT

in association with the Glasgow Herald

To the students, staff, and black squirrels
of Glendon College, Toronto

First published by
Waterfront Communications Ltd
in association with the Glasgow Herald
34 Bernard Street
Edinburgh

Copyright © Robin Jenkins 1985

The publisher acknowledges subsidy from the Scottish Arts Council
towards the publication of this volume.

Jenkins, Robin, *1912–*
   The awakening of George Darroch.
   I. Title   II. Glasgow herald
   823'.914 [F]   PR6060.E5194

ISBN 0 86228 112 1

Typeset by Witwell Ltd., Liverpool
Printed and bound in Great Britain by
Redwood Burn Limited. Trowbridge, Wiltshire

FOREWORD

Between the years 1834 and 1843 various events took place throughout the world important enough for history to have recorded them. Some still stir our imaginations today. Slavery was abolished in all British territories. Queen Victoria ascended the throne. Britain acquired Hong Kong. Charles Dickens published *The Pickwick Papers* and *Oliver Twist*. The Boers set off on their Great Trek across the River Vaal. A British army was decimated in Afghanistan. But history has dismissed in a few dry lines an event that took place in Scotland and was considered by those who played a part in it as the most momentous in the history of their country since the Reformation. They were convinced that it would be an astonishment and inspiration to Christians everywhere and above all to their descendants. Alas, today both in Scotland and abroad it is quite forgotten. In a recently published book, giving a year by year account of events of consequence, among the entries for 1843 the Great Disruption is not mentioned. We are told that the *News of the World* began publication and that a statue of the late Lord Nelson was hoisted to the top of a column in Trafalgar Square, but about the soul-shaking Disruption not a word.

What was this great issue that vexed the ministers of the Church of Scotland and their congregations so sorely for ten years? It had to do with religious freedom. In 1834 the law of the land stated that a landowner could impose any minister he pleased on a church that stood on his land. The Kirk at last protested. At its General Assembly it passed a Veto Act, giving congregations the right to set aside ministers imposed on them whom they considered unsuitable. Test cases followed. The Scottish courts and eventually the House of Lords, composed mainly of English Episcopalians, decided in favour of the landowners. The Veto Act was declared invalid. The politicians made it clear to the ministers that so long as the Kirk remained Established it must obey the laws of the country respecting the rights and privileges of landowners. The only escape was by breaking away from the Establishment. Many ministers boldly advocated that drastic course: they were the Evangelicals. Others, the Moderates, prudently urged acquiescence, pointing out that those who broke away would sacrifice church, manse, stipend, and status. Ministers in those days sometimes had as many as twenty children. They had all seen, in the slums of the cities, how poverty and destitution could degrade and corrupt.

Matters came to a head on 18th May 1843 at the General Assembly in St Andrew's Church, Edinburgh. Up to that day it was not known how many ministers would stick by their pledges and come out or how many would renege and stay in. The Marquis of Bute, who was to be the Queen's Commissioner, was advised by his aides the night before that no more than thirty would come out. It was one thing to make exalted vaunts about upholding the Crown Rights of Christ the King, it was quite another to face the prospect of being evicted from your comfortable manse, you and your large family, and having to find shelter in some leaky cowshed, with only the charity of well-wishers to supply your needs. It would be little wonder therefore if most of the switherers came down finally on the side of good sense, conformity, and safety.

PART ONE

CHAPTER 1

The manse was hushed. In his study Father was once again asking the Lord for reassurance. It was amazing how so mild-mannered a man should have such passion when praying.

His sons, dark-haired Arthur aged seventeen and fair-haired James two years younger, in their room above the study, could have made out every word if they had strained their ears. They did not take the trouble. They had heard it all many times before. Besides, they did not sympathise with their father in his agony of conscience. They thought that he had no right to run the risk of causing his family to become destitute and homeless, in order that he could keep what he called a promise to Christ the King but which was only a promise to himself.

In the colliers' rows a few fields distant from the manse, and in the weaving town of Cadzow two miles away, they had seen what poverty meant: scabs and hollows of hunger, rags, disease, deformity, and filthy hovels.

Their father and those ministers who shared his views had justice on their side, for the Government in London, composed mainly of Englishmen who were Episcopalians, ought not to have dominion over the Presbyterian Church of Scotland, but the issue did not seem to the two boys important enough to give up kirk, manse, stipend, and status for.

Nor did it seem so to the majority of Church of Scotland ministers, including their Uncle Robert, their mother's brother, himself the incumbent of a kirk in Edinburgh three times the size of their father's; nor to their mother, although she had not

3

said so and never would, for being a Christian wife she placed her husband above criticism. In any case she was not well, being with child again for the fifteenth time.

When Uncle Robert came tomorrow, to plead with their father for the last time not to take part in the threatened disruption, his nephews hoped that he would succeed, otherwise their own careers would be jeopardised.

In the autumn Arthur was to enrol as a student of law at Edinburgh University. Money would be needed for his upkeep and fees.

James was intended for the ministry. He had no objections but was resolved to be like Uncle Robert, living comfortably and preaching judiciously, with a church that had titled people among the congregation. Blue-eyed and pink-cheeked, James was like his father in appearance but not in nature. He bore grudges and did not forgive easily.

"I promise you, Arthur" he said, "if any minister takes Father's place and comes into our house, and if his children ride their ponies in our paddock or fish in our stream, I shall pray that they all go to hell."

Arthur was amused. As a future minister should, James believed in a hell where sinners were roasted, but he also liked more immediate and visible torments for anyone who offended him.

Arthur himself thought it childish to believe in hell or heaven, or in a God that handed out punishments or rewards, like a spiteful schoolmaster.

Alone in her attic bedroom their dark-haired ten-year-old sister Mary lay stretched out on her bed, with her eyes shut, her hands pressed together under her chin, and her toes pointing upwards, in the posture of the stone lady in Craignethan Abbey. Pretending to be dead, she was trying to empty her mind of all images and thoughts, and her body of all sensations. It was not easy. Sometimes her nose itched, sometimes the soles of her feet, and now and then she could hear from next door happy yelps of laughter from her sister, eight-year-old Agnes.

4

Through the open window buzzed a belated bumble-bee. Unlike Agnes, who went into hysterics if one came too near her, Mary was not afraid of bumble-bees and trusted them. If you did not harm them they would not harm you, and they did good by pollinating the flowers. In her mind echoed the chant of the village children: "If a bumbee stung a bumbee on the bum what colour would the bumbee's bum be." She was careful not to smile: not because the song was rude and as the minister's daughter she should not smile at rudeness, but because she loved to be serious. Taking her hands from her breast she waved her arms up and down like wings. She imagined she was a bee. She felt very small and furry. She hid in the blossoms of the gean tree and sucked their honey. Her mouth was filled with sweetness.

Fair-haired Agnes thrust her head out of the window, cocked to the side like a bird listening for worms. Then she skipped back to the bed where six-year-old Sarah, also fair-haired, nursed her cloth doll. "He said —." But Agnes never really heard what her father said when he was praying, it was the way he said it that she always found so funny.

In any case Sarah wouldn't have understood. She had been born an imbecile. She was never cross, as Agnes herself was so often, never curious, like Mary, and never talkative, like three-year-old Jessie.

But Jessie was not saying anything tonight. In her cot, in her sisters' room, where she liked to sleep, she was hot and flushed. John had looked like that before he died, last December when there was snow on the ground.

Agnes went over, put her hand on her little sister's brow, and sighed, as she had heard her mother do.

In the large stone-floored kitchen Mrs Barnes the housekeeper was talking to Mrs Strachan the wet-nurse, who was giving suck to eleven-month-old Matthew. In the scullery Bella the maid was washing and drying dishes.

5

They were discussing the mistress's health.

"Correct me if I'm wrang, Mrs Barnes, but this'll be her fifteenth, won't it?" said Jeanie Strachan. "It's hard to keep coont. Three miscairragies, four weans buried, and anither yin sickening. If you ask me, the meenister's worried aboot losing his kirk, but he should be a lot mair worried aboot losing his wife. Forty-four's gey auld to be haeing anither wean, especially for a woman as delicate as her."

Bella keeked in. A collier's daughter, aged sixteen, she was thin and stunted, with wizened face and knowing eyes. "Some women in the village shop were saying that if the mistress was to dee the meenister wad mairry again withoot losing ony time."

Mrs Barnes turned her face aside. Bella and Jeanie exchanged winks. They knew she was having her wee secret smile. She often dreamed of being the minister's second wife, but she had little chance, not just because she wasn't a lady, her father being only a joiner, with his own business true enough, but because she had a neb twice as big and a chin twice as long as they should be, and besides she was thirty-six. The minister would go for some younger and prettier widow, like Mrs Wedderburn.

"They were saying it was religion did it," said Bella slyly.

"They were ignorant and foul-minded to say any such thing," said Mrs Barnes, sternly. "And I don't allow talk like that in my kitchen, Bella Stewart."

"Just the same," said Jeanie, "he didnae get a' thae weans by praying."

Jeanie had four herself and had not much enjoyed their begetting. Sometimes Strachan couldn't wait till he had washed off the pit dirt. She could see herself enjoying it fine if it was done as the braw wee minister would do it, politely and daintily, but just the same as thoroughly as any collier or ploughman twice his size, judging by the results.

"Whit Bella was saying aboot religion could be true," she said. "Look at a' the weans meenisters hae. Mr Saunders had ten."

"Mr Jarvie's got nane," said Bella.

"There's a reason for that," said Jeanie.

She and Bella laughed coarsely. Mr Jarvie had a belly on him like a pregnant mare.

"That's enough of such talk," said Mrs Barnes. "If you're finished, Bella, get off home and make sure you're back tomorrow at six sharp. They'll all be up early. Mr Drummond's coming from Edinburgh."

"He'll hae something to say aboot his sister being bairned again," said Jeanie. "He was angry enough last time."

"That's none of your business, Jeanie Strachan."

"If you wait till I've ta'en the wean up to the mistress, Bella," said Jeanie, "I'll walk hame wi' you."

Mrs Barnes knew that on their way to their hovels they would invent outrageous things about her and the minister. Well, let them. She loved the gentle little man and given the chance would make him a lot happier than his sickly wife ever had. Already his wee lassies looked more to her for affection and help than to their mother.

In the matrimonial bedroom Mrs Darroch lay quietly weeping. She did not want to waken Baby Matthew in his cot by her bedside. She was careful too not to let tears flow copiously. Her husband must not notice her distress when he came in. She felt weak and unclean, as if the baby in her womb had died and was rotting. Now and then she felt stabs of pain. She was terrified that she would die and leave her children motherless. She was worried, too, about Jessie.

After a long bout of prayer George seemed to need to use her body to give his own peace and calm. She did not understand why, for his explanations were strange and confused, not fit for a Christian wife to hear, but it was her duty to submit and she had always done so, though never gladly. She could not help thinking however that he ought to abstain while she was with child. Sometimes she suspected that it might have been his making use of her body while she was carrying Sarah that had caused the child to be born feeble-minded.

These were woes so private that she would have kept them hidden from God Himself if she could. She must try to hide them from Robert when he came tomorrow.

She was not quite asleep when George crept in but she pretended to be.

Except for his sighs, caused, he would say, by spiritual exhaustion but also, she thought, by self-pity, he undressed quietly, climbed into bed, and lay still, too close to her.

He was her husband and the father of her children, those alive and those dead and the one still to be born, and she loved and honoured him. Yet as she lay with her back turned and felt him begin to fidget she knew that, if he did not leave her alone that night she would, in a part of her that belonged only to herself, hate him.

It was not poor Margaret's fault, but her husband would have been happier lying on a coal bing, in a place of smoking desolation. There, faith would have a chance of bursting into flames as the hot dross sometimes did, and he would be able to feel that he was in the divine presence, about at any moment to look on the glorious face of Christ the King.

That expectation, without which life for him would be unbearable, was, alas, never more remote than in his marital bed. The many disappointments and humiliations suffered here had not led to humility, which could have been fruitful but to barren frustration and sterile self-disgust.

Margaret had been brought up to look on the physical obligations of marriage as unavoidable evils. He had read once, in a book of missionary travels in Africa, of a practice some tribes there had of mutilating the genital parts of women, so that intercourse caused pain instead of pleasure. It was the same with Margaret and most other women of her class, except that it was their minds which had had the operation.

During their honeymoon, in the small Highland town of Callander, at the entrance to the Trossachs, in walks along the river banks and through the woods, he had described to her with enthusiasm how the joining of their bodies in married love should be the holiest of communions. He had not been able to explain it clearly, for it was a mystical conception and the authors he quoted were rather obscure, but even so there had

8

been no reason for her to be revolted, as if he had been uttering obscenities. From then on she had lain under him more rigid and arid than before.

As a divinity student, he had been aware that locked up in him was a reservoir of spiritual power which would be released if he ever belonged to a truly liberated Kirk which put Christ the King first in all things, and also if he was married to a beautiful woman who found in his body the same reverence and joy that he did in hers. Then he would be able to gladden the sorrowful, strengthen the faith of doubters, rescue the poor from their degradations if not from their hardships, make merciful the hard-hearted, and even in some measure heal the sick or at least alleviate their pain.

Had he not, only yesterday, in the twentieth year of his ministry, with the fervency of his prayers allayed the fever consuming Mrs Wedderburn's little girl, Maud? The young widow's soft white hand in his, and her adoring eyes, had given him the inspiration he needed.

But it was not cheerful, swift-footed, blue-eyed, red-cheeked, and auburn-haired Annabel Wedderburn, who reminded him of roses and violets, homely flowers, that he desired. No, it was grave, slow-moving, brown-eyed, dark-skinned, and spicy-breathed Eleanor Jarvie, whose beauty was exotic and mysterious, redolent of frankincense, pomegranates, and the cedars of Lebanon.

All his colleagues, whether Evangelicals like himself or Moderates like Robert Drummond, would condemn him. They would call it the deadliest of sins for a minister of Christ to lie beside his ailing pregnant wife and yearn for — they would say lust after — another woman, who was also his friend's wife. They would say that Margaret's twenty years of aversion was no excuse for him, nor was John Jarvie's obesity, which made sexual congress impossible, an excuse for Eleanor. In older stricter times they would have been burned or stoned to death.

He was considered timorous, by his sons, by his brother-in-law Robert, by his brother Henry the sea-captain, by Sir James Loudun, chief heritor of the parish, and by most men in his congregation; and perhaps so he was in many things; but for the

9

beatific joy of lying in Eleanor Jarvie's arms he would, he thought, give up not only kirk and manse but wife and children too.

Long ago, as a boy of ten in search of Christ, venturing into the part of Greenock where ear-ringed sailors and their doxies lived, he had looked through a pend and seen a handsome, black-haired swarthy woman stripped to the waist washing herself in a wooden bine, golden in the sunlight. Catching sight of him she had smiled and lifting up her large shining breasts in her hands had offered them to him.

He thought of Eleanor offering him hers and lo, his body was roused, ready for the rapturous celebration of love which he had dreamed of often but never once had experienced.

Suddenly Margaret said, irritably: "Do you want to use me, George?"

The callous word shocked him. "Use you, my dear?"

"That is what you do, you know. I am very tired and do not feel well."

"I am very sorry, my dear. Is there anything I can do?"

"You can let me go to sleep."

"I thought you were asleep."

"I have been worrying about Jessie. Did you go up to see her?"

He had forgotten. "No."

"I hope at least you included her in your prayers."

He had not.

"I hear you prayed like a Trojan for little Maud Wedderburn."

Who had described it so disrespectfully? Surely not Annabel.

"That is what Mrs Wedderburn told me."

He sighed. "We shall both pray for Jessie tomorrow, by her bedside."

"I hope she has recovered by the morning. You have to be in Cadzow early to meet Robert's coach from Glasgow."

"It is not expected to arrive till eleven o'clock." He hoped before that to pay John Jarvie a visit and see Eleanor. Last time he had called John had been confined to bed. His heart was cracking under the strain of his enormous weight. There had

10

been other visitors. Darroch and Eleanor had had to be very careful.

"Good-night, George." She moved still further from him, to the edge of the bed.

"Good-night, Margaret."

It amazed him that though she had nothing but repugnance for that part of his body with which love was made she knew its ways.

CHAPTER 2

At breakfast there was excitement because Uncle Robert was coming from Edinburgh.

"Will he bring us presents?" cried Agnes.

"You should think of giving, not getting, my pet," said her father.

"I've got nothing to give," she said, scornfully. "If he brings me a box of sweeties I can share them, can't I? If I've got nothing how can I share it? Nobody wants a share of nothing, do they?"

"No need to shout, Agnes," said her mother. "I have a headache." She was still worried about Jessie who was too ill to get out of bed.

Agnes let out a scream and covered her eyes. Sarah's nose needed wiping again.

Arthur and James looked away. They thought Sarah shouldn't be allowed at table. She put them off their food. She plastered porridge all over her face, and all too often those yellow snotters appeared at her nose. Sometimes, too, she messed her drawers.

Sarah's father said bravely: "Will you do it, Mary, or shall I?"

"I'll do it, Papa." Lovingly Mary cleaned her sister's nose with the cloth she kept for that purpose.

Tending the table, Mrs Barnes felt sorry for her master. She was sure few other ministers with serious religious matters on their minds had to put up with this kind of nonsense. Agnes was a delightful wee girl but there were times when she needed a spanking. As for her brothers, a thrashing would do them good too. Look how they blamed their father for everything, even for poor Sarah's dirty nose. Mary was the only one who helped him. It was always she who looked after her daft wee sister, wiping not just her nose but her bottom too. If she didn't look out she would still be doing it when she was an old woman. She would have no life of her own. Perhaps that was why she was always talking or thinking about death.

If God gives me the chance, thought the housekeeper, I'll see to it that Mary isn't sacrificed.

Here was Mary though, being morbid again. "I was dead last night," she said. "In a dream."

"We don't want to hear about your silly dreams," cried Agnes. "I don't believe them. You just make them up."

"Agnes is right, Mary," said her mother. "We don't really want to hear."

"Yes, we do," cried Agnes, changing her mind. "Did you go to hell?"

"I think it was heaven. It was full of bumble bees. I was a bumble bee myself."

"Oh, that's stupid," shrieked Agnes, "Did you see John? Was he a bumble bee? Isn't she stupid, Mama?"

Mrs Darroch sobbed, with her handkerchief, now found, at her eyes. John's name was still fresh on the tombstone in the kirkyard.

"Did you see a bumble bee that buzzed very loudly and called itself Napoleon Bonaparte?" asked Arthur. "Historians would be interested to know. The French think he is in heaven, but the British are sure he is in hell."

"Did you see one that buzzed wisely and called itself David Hume?" asked James.

"I tell you, she's just making it up," yelled Agnes. "You shouldn't listen to her. Bumble bees don't go to heaven, do they, Papa? They've got no souls."

Her father smiled. He knew that his sons, and many others, thought he had no humour. He did not have a great deal perhaps, for even as a child he had been serious-minded, but he did have enough to join in his children's fun-making.

"Why should they not?" he replied. "They are useful,

13

harmless creatures."

"They're not harmless at all," cried Agnes indignantly. "One stung me. I thought it was dead and I picked it up and it stung me on the finger."

"Was God a bumble bee, Mary?" asked Arthur.

Mary nodded

All children, thought her father, were born pagans. Mary had remained one.

"Who knows? Perhaps He is," said Arthur. "Does it say anywhere in the Bible, explicitly, that God is not a bumble bee?"

"You'll go to hell for saying that, Arthur Darroch," cried Agnes.

Mrs Barnes soothed the excitable little girl. "Mary's just having a little fun. Anyway, isn't it time you got ready for school?"

"I want Sarah to come with us today," said Mary.

"I don't," cried Agnes. "She can't do anything. she just scribbles. She makes a stink. They all laugh at her."

"No, they don't," said Mary. "They wouldn't dare. She likes being with us. I'll look after her. Say she can come, Mama."

"It is for your father to decide, Mary.'

He shrank from having to make decisions about Sarah. This was because he thought it must have been to chasten him that the little girl had been sent into the world with a mind that, unlike a kitten's or a puppy's, would never develop.

Many times Mrs Barnes had prayed to be given the right to share his anguish.

"Let her go, Mr Darroch," she said. "The dominie told me he doesn't mind having Sarah. He said she has a good effect on the other children."

"Because she makes them see how fortunate they are," whispered Mrs Darroch.

"I don't think he meant that, ma'am. She's so sweet-natured that they all feel peaceful in her presence. We know that ourselves, don't we?"

But, alas, though Sarah was smiling contentedly her nose needed wiping again. They all watched in silence as this time her father did it, using his fresh white handkerchief.

14

CHAPTER 3

Arthur and James had long ago satisfied themselves that their finding fault with their father was not breaking the Fourth Commandment; on the contrary, it was showing how concerned they were for him.

They could easily see in him reasons why Sarah was an imbecile, and congratulated each other on having escaped that terrible inheritance.

In many ways he was still childish, having outgrown neither the simpleness which kept Sarah from being able to wipe her own nose, nor the habit of confusing reality with fantasy, which in a little girl like Mary was natural but in a man of forty-one was an indication of permanent immaturity.

In the carrying out of physical tasks he was, as the local people said, fushionless. If his shoes were muddy he would insist on cleaning them himself but would make such a poor job of it that Mrs Barnes or Bella had to do it all over again. When the pews of the church were being repaired he had assisted the carpenters. Behind his back they had had to repair his repairs. He was the worst driver of a horse and trap the boys had ever seen. He never kept his eyes on the road, so that one or other of the wheels was constantly in danger of slipping into a ditch.

His very handsomeness was an embarrassment to his sons. No man's hair should have been so fair, soft, and wavy: it was the envy of all the ladies. His complexion, too, was ladylike, being smooth and pink without a blemish. Only five-foot-seven inches in height, he was small-boned and lightly built. He took a child's size in boots and gloves. Old Lady Annie, mother of Sir James Loudun, and aunt of the Marquis of Cadzow, once at the door of the kirk compared her hand, twice the size, with the minister's.

Arthur and James would not have wanted him to have an enormous belly like Mr Jarvie, minister of St Margaret's in Cadzow, or a big purple nose like Sir James, or a stiff shaggy beard like Farmer Cuthbertson, but they would have preferred him not to be quite so slim, quite so delicately nosed, and quite so fluffily whiskered.

Though as a Christian minister it was his duty to be benevolent, he seemed unable, like other ministers with double his stipend, to be so in intelligent moderation. If a beggar came to the door, he was not content like other Christians to send them on their way with a pokeful of crusts. He had them in and given a hot meal, even though it meant his own family going without. Once every week he visited the colliers' rows, taking with him food and clothing, as well as tracts and prayers. He contributed to a mission in Cadzow that dispensed soup and homilies to the poor. He had taken on old John Cairns as gardener-and-groom, though he was almost crippled with rheumatism. In all this bountifulness his sons saw an element of conceit. He was as foppish in his good deeds as in his dress.

He suffered from the handicap of not having been brought up in a genteel, cultivated household. Grandfather Darroch of Greenock had been a self-made ship's chandler who spoke broad Scots and drank ale at the dinner table. Of his two other sons, Andrew the oldest had fallen heir to the business and could be seen any day in his shop wearing a striped apron like a workman, while Henry the youngest had become a sea-captain, sailing to far-off places like India and China. On his last visit to Craignethan manse ten years ago he had offended his sister-in-law by a remark about the bare bosoms of Javanese women.

Sir James Loudun could use language as crude as an ostler's without seeming ill-bred, whereas their father who spoke courteously even to the colliers' sluttish wives or prostitutes in Cadzow could never quite overcome the defects of his uncouth

16

upbringing. He showed it mostly by being too anxious to spare the feelings of inferiors.

Fortunately, their other grandfather, the Very Reverend Robert Drummond, one-time Moderator of the Church of Scotland, had been a gentleman and a scholar. Arthur and James complimented each other on taking after him.

As for their father's intended secession from the Established Church they would not have minded if he had been a leading figure in the campaign like Dr Chalmers or Dr Candlish instead of an obscure follower. All that he and his family were likely to get out of the "noble and historic struggle" was misery, whereas Dr Chalmers and the other leaders would win fame and honour, not to mention fortune, for they would deliver speeches up and down the country which thousands would pay to hear, and publish books which thousands more would buy.

In any case, they could not take seriously their father's magniloquent claim that he was defending the "Crown Rights of Christ the King" against the tyranny of the State. Impressive orators like Chalmers could rant out cant evangelical phrases like "the temple must be purified" and be acclaimed as sages and martyrs. Not so their father: he was too lacking in spiritual force and too ornamental in appearance.

As a preacher he did well enough for a small country parish where the stipend was lower than average and where the congregation consisted of tight-fisted tradesmen and shopkeepers with businesses in Cadzow and homes in rural Craignethan, coal-mine officials, grieves and gamekeepers, farmers and farm labourers, and domestic servants, most of them semi-illiterate or worse. He had the sense to stick to safe platitudinous moralising, delivered in a voice which, provided it did not become impassioned, was quite euphonious. Certain extravagant notions he had regarding the scope of a minister's responsibilities he prudently kept to himself.

There was one aspect of him that for their mother's sake they did not care to talk about.

One hot summer afternoon, three years before, during the school holidays, when Arthur was fourteen and James twelve, they were trespassing in the grounds of Hairshaw House, watching deer and birds through pocket telescopes given to them by Uncle Henry the sailor, when they caught sight of one of the grooms from the Big House, a big dour brawny fellow called Saidler, who had once been publicly rebuked for getting a woman with child, and one of the maids, a black-haired good-looking girl called Mysie Laurie, whom Arthur had often admired in church. They were forcing their way through brackens as tall as Saidler himself to a grassy space in the midst. Mysie did not seem very willing for he had her by the hand and was dragging her. Arthur and James, among the branches of a lime tree, had a good view restricted only a little by the dense leafage. They did not dare speak, however, for though the pair now embracing were almost a hundred yards away sounds carried far in the silent wood. If Saidler had caught them peeping he would have climbed the tree and assaulted them, for he was known to have a violent temper. Sir James kept him on because he was expert with horses.

Mysie could not have been altogether unwilling, having come to this lonely place with a man notorious for wenching, and having already received so much encouragement Saidler was not going to let her deny him now. So as the boys watched through wavering telescopes he suddenly tired of her protests or entreaties and pushed her down on to the grass. Still on his feet himself he began to pull off her white drawers, so roughly that they could be heard ripping. He tossed them aside and, dropping his own breeches, threw himself on top of her, pushed up the skirts of her dress and petticoats, and then, with no more resistance from her, rammed into her what could not be seen from the tree but could easily be imagined. Still visible though was his bare arse, strong as a bull's and spotted with red plukes. His thrusts were slow at first, with pauses, for enjoyment not for rest, but soon they became faster and faster until with a shriek of triumph — or did it come from her? — he completed the race and lay still, on top of her, heedless of the horde of flies that had gathered. Arthur and James in the tree were pestered with them too.

Saidler soon rose, returned her drawers to her, and offered to help her put them on. He seemed very pleased with himself. She,

18

with a display of modesty ludicrous in the circumstances, turned her back on him while she rearranged her dress.

Before she was quite ready he led the way through the brackens back to the path. He did not wait to help her but let her fend for herself. They were in a hurry. Perhaps they were on duty soon.

It had all taken little more than ten minutes.

In a state of excitement Arthur and James had shouted witty and lewd remarks about the fucking they had just witnessed, but when they had got home and had seen their mother's sick face and swollen belly — she was big with Jessie at the time — they had realised that their dainty little father must be as lustful as the big groom with the plukey arse.

Their condemnation of him had been all the more vindictive because they had known that it was unfair. What Saidler had done to Mysie and their father to their mother, many times, was necessary if the human race was not to die out. It was done by the highest in the land: Prince Albert did it to Queen Victoria. It was done by every minister in Scotland, to their wives, or if they were widowers, like Mr Ramage of Cadzow, to their house-keepers, according at any rate to Stephen Ramage, a fellow pupil of Mr Brodie's Academy for Young Gentlemen, who claimed he had watched them at it, through a keyhole. It was sanctioned by God within marriage, and it had resulted in what to Arthur and James were the most wonderful things in the universe, their own existences.

All that was true but nevertheless their father was not to be forgiven.

CHAPTER 4

Driving into Cadzow, Darroch, as always, was greatly comforted by the company of his sons, despite their frequent warnings to him to look out. They were so smart and intelligent in their school uniforms of red jackets, brown trousers, and black shiny hats. Mr Brodie their headmaster had prophesied that Arthur would be a Judge of Session one day and James a Moderator. It was true they were critical of their father, but surely it was the nature of young men to criticise their elders. If it was not so how could there be change and progress? As an advocate Arthur would one day fearlessly defend those persecuted for speaking the truth, and James as a minister would help to bring about what his father could only dream of, that in a Christian country no one would go hungry, no one would be homeless, and no one need despair.

He was glad that though times had been difficult, with deaths in the family and not enough money, he had done all he could to ensure that their childhoods were as carefree as possible. He knew they were at present apprehensive about the effect on their careers of his forthcoming resignation from the Established Church. He had not been able to store up any money but he was not too proud to ask their uncle Robert Drummond to help them. When they were established in their professions they could pay him back. Also, if it was necessary, he would appeal to his own brother Henry, who was still unmarried and well-off. Henry was too manly to be spiteful. He would never hold it against his nephews that their mother had more or less ordered him out of the manse. He had left with a cheerful laugh, not a sulky brow.

In spite of Margaret's new pregnancy, and Jessie's fever, and Sarah's imbecility, and Agnes's excitableness, and Mary's morbidity, Darroch was confident that there was ahead of him a share of the glory that would come to Scotland when many of its ministers, himself one of the humblest, walked out of the Established Church for principle's sake and formed the Free Church of Scotland. There would be ringing of bells in heaven itself.

One wonderful consequence of his having to abandon Kirk and manse in the service of Christ the King would be his dependence on relatives, friends, colleagues, parishioners, and even strangers. By succouring him and his family they would be given an opportunity to please Christ. In Craignethan and beyond there would be an upsurge not only of Christian faith but also of Christian love.

They were now rattling past Hawthorn Bank, the house owned by young Mrs Wedderburn.

Thinking of Annabel, Darroch felt more uplifted still. Now that she was over the worst of her grief at the death of her husband two years ago she showed every sign of having a merry heart. She had confessed to him, winsomely, that what she disliked most about being a widow was having to sleep alone. She let him hold her hand longer than other young ladies did. She understood better than they that his motives were pure.

Margaret called her a flirt, too fond of teasing young men, like Arthur. He had replied that it was innocent dalliance.

"I hear little Maud Wedderburn has recovered from her fever," said Arthur, rather hoarsely: he suffered often from sore throats. "Some medicine the apothecary in Cadzow sent did her good. Perhaps it would help Jessie too. You should call in and get some, Father."

Darroch smiled. It had not been the apothecary's coloured water that had cured Maud: It had been his own earnest praying, side by side with her mother, their elbows touching. Prayer would cure Jessie too. That it had not cured John, or Robert, or Margaret, who all had died, and had not prevented

21

Margaret's three miscarriages, was because his faith at those times had been too weak. It was stronger now.

"Maud wasn't as ill as Jessie is," said James.

His father turned to look at him in alarm. "But, James, Jessie is only a little fevered, as Maud was. She has been like that before and quickly recovered."

"Please keep your eyes on the road, Father. John did not recover. When I went up to see Jessie this morning she did not know me. I think she is going to die."

Darroch's heart sank. Was poor Margaret to undergo all that sorrow and anguish again?

"James is right, Father," said Arthur. "And Mother too is not well."

"You are both in pessimistic mood this morning."

"She should not be having another child, Father," said James. "Did she not almost die having Matthew?"

"Did the doctors not say she should have no more children?" said Arthur. "I think you should send for a doctor from Edinburgh to attend her. Uncle Robert would pay his fee."

"What good did Edinburgh doctors do Sarah?" asked James, scornfully.

They had come, three of them, the most learned and experienced in their profession, bearded, looking wise and capable. They had measured Sarah's head, examined her tongue, poked into her ears, tasted her urine, pressed her skull, peered into her eyes through instruments, and in the end announced their verdict: she must have sustained some brain damage either in the womb or at birth. No cure was known. A miracle was possible but unlikely. For telling what was already known they had charged large fees. Uncle Robert had paid half.

"We are not a lucky family," said Arthur, bitterly.

But to believe in luck, good or bad, thought his father, was to disown Christ. Surely nothing happened without His contrivance. If he caused His creatures to suffer it did not mean that He had ceased to love them.

Do I really believe that with all my soul, wondered Darroch, gazing at his horse's tail. Am I being wholly sincere when I say to grieving parents that their child's cries of pain and untimely

22

death were part of God's purpose, which would be revealed on Judgment Day?

"If you're rich," added Arthur, still bitter, "like the Louduns it must be much easier to endure misfortunes."

"If you're rich," said James, "you have no misfortunes."

But that was not so. Sir James, though the owner of Hairshaw House, the vast mansion visible through the trees, had had three children dead in infancy and nowadays could scarcely walk because of gout or sit because of piles. Moreover, he had a shrewish wife who ordered him about.

Though its exterior was grim, with its many small turrets and windows, Hairshaw House was magnificent inside, with French furniture, Chinese carpets, and ceilings painted by Italian artists. One such painting, the largest, showed a voluptuous woman, a goddess, lying on a bank of flowers and being nuzzled by fawns no more naked than she. A band of shepherds gazed at her in awe. One, rather smaller than the rest, was fair-haired. He too was naked. It seemed to be to him that she was holding out her hand. Whether by accident or intention his organ of love had been painted as not quite at rest. It looked as if her grave gaze was having this effect on him. In the distance was a city of shining towers, blue lakes, and green trees.

When Darroch had last looked up at that painting he had seen the goddess as Eleanor and himself her chosen swain.

It had been Sir James who, twenty years ago, thanks largely to the influence of Margaret's august father, had presented Darroch to Craignethan parish, against Lady Loudun's wish, for she had had a nominee of her own, a genuine gentleman, whose father owned land. From the beginning she had treated Darroch like a servant, hired not to scrub her floors or tend her table or cook her food or groom her horses or plough her fields or manage her coal mines, but to preach obedience and submission to all her other servants who performed those tasks. Sir James occasionally had begged Darroch not to be too upset: Grizel pushed him about too. But Sir James himself was not pleased that Darroch intended to join the seceders and therefore quit Craignethan parish church. He did not like change. There was no necessity for it. The world was fine as it was. In the past, he had pointed out, the Louduns of Hairshaw had been staunchly Presbyterian: one of them, Alexander, had been killed fighting for the Covenanters at Bothwell Brig, not many miles away. Sir James was proud of his ancestry, but he was of the opinion that the brutal past, when Christians slaughtered Christians, was best forgotten.

Old Lady Annie, Sir James's mother, had championed Darroch. "A very pretty sermon, Mr Darroch," she would say, "and very prettily said. But when are we going to hear whit you really think and no' whit you ken we want to hear? I'm shair there are thochts in that handsome heid of yours wad surprise us a'."

She was dying now and might be dead before Sunday when he was going to make public for the first time some of those surprising thoughts.

"I was asking, Father," said James, "if you were going to consult Sir James again before you finally decide to come out."

"I have a master greater than Sir James whom I have consulted many times, James."

"Yes, Father, we have heard you."

"With His help I shall decide."

They then arrived at the gates of Mr Brodie's academy. (Fees twenty guineas a year, equal to a farm-worker's annual wage, and a fifth of Darroch's own. Robert Drummond paid James's.)

"Remember the medicine for Jessie, Father," said Arthur.

"Thank you for reminding me, Arthur."

"Tell Uncle Robert that we are looking forward to seeing him," said James.

"I shall certainly do so, James."

Then, in conversation with fellow pupils, they went through the gates. He gave them a last wave but it was not returned.

CHAPTER 5

Just outside the town he passed a group of barefooted, ragged, very dirty children, carrying bundles. There were eight of them, five boys and three girls. The oldest was a girl about fourteen, the youngest a boy about four. Their furtive manner and unkempt black hair indicated that they were Irish, whose parents had come to Scotland to scrape a living howking potatoes and had stayed to do all kinds of hard menial work for very low pay. Local people, though taking advantage of them, showed them no sympathy, saying that they ought to go back to Ireland where their Papist religion and unChristian habits belonged.

Darroch stopped his trap and called to them. They looked back suspiciously. They were more accustomed to rebuffs than invitations. The fourteen-year-old girl, whose hair came below her waist, slowly approached.

"Whit do you want, Mister?" she asked, in an Irish accent.

He took some coppers from his pocket and threw them. Shame made his aim careless. Some fell in the ditch.

All the children rushed to search frantically. One held up a dead bird that he had found.

"How many did you fling, Mister?" cried one.

He had not counted. "Six pennies, I think."

They had found only five. They renewed the search.

"Never mind," he said, throwing another.

It was picked up by the girl. She came close to the trap and held on to the wheel. She was already a woman, as he could see

25

through the sparse rags. Her face, oval and thin, would have looked beautiful in an austere way had it been washed, and if she had not had to live so harsh and degraded a life.

"You've got bonny hair, sir," she said, with a leer.

Her sisters and brothers, even the little lad of four, were looking on in expectation. Never before had he seen on such young faces not only acceptance of evil but hope that evil succeeded.

She was soliciting him. A doubt struck her. "You're no' a priest, are you, sir?"

A priest in these parts was a Roman Catholic minister. "No, I am not," he replied. "I am a minister of the Church of Scotland."

That didn't matter. He could be solicited. "I could come to your hoose, sir," she said.

"Where are your parents?"

"She's deid and we don't ken whaur he is. He was always drunk, onyway. For a shilling, sir, I'd dae onything you wanted."

She was not offering to wash dishes or polish boots.

"I've done it for lots o' gentlemen."

He could not resist asking: "Not here in Cadzow, I hope?"

"Here and a' ower. Backwards or frontwards, it's a' the same to me."

"These are terrible things you are saying, my child."

"I'm no' your child, you fancy wee cunt," she cried. She went on to scream even worse obscenities.

Hurriedly he drove on. He felt inexpressibly sad.

What ought to be a beautiful and holy act was everywhere profaned, by venality, coarseness, and viciousness. Instead of liberating and purifying the spirit it darkened and defiled it.

To avoid thinking about the depraved child and his inability to save her he thought about Roman Catholicism. Though he had the conventional Presbyterian distrust of it he secretly envied it its pageantry and colour, its encouragement of mystery, and its belief in miracles and saints.

Presbyterianism was grey, bleak, and cold, like a wintry moor. It made of love a duty. It deprecated joy. It sought truth only in gloomy places. It required its ministers to be at all times sober and cautious, in dress, speech, thought, and aspiration; whereas he loved imagining himself in robes of crimson and gold, delivering mystical and impassioned addresses, in a glorious cathedral. Instead, for twenty years he had had to preach dull sermons to dull people in a square box of a kirk with stumpy steeple and mean little windows. Small wonder that in Covenanting times it had been used as a prison.

In a few weeks a rainswept hillside might be his tabernacle.

He would rejoice. He would then have the inspiration to look on depraved children and not be overcome by the evil possessing them. He would drive it out and bring them back to Christ.

CHAPTER 6

In Cadzow he quartered his horse and trap in Murdoch's stables in the east end of the town. He found the way blocked by a crowd of workmen listening to a burly grey-haired fellow haranguing them from an upturned barrel.

It was a narrow wynd with on either side typical Scotch houses for the working-class, consisting of single-ends or one room-and-kitchens, built of stone as thick as that in Edinburgh Castle. The privies and middens were at the back but even so the cobbled road in front was littered with filth including human excrement.

Women with hostile haggard faces watched from doorsteps. Some held babies. Other children clung to their skirts.

The revolutionary turned and saw Darroch sitting in the trap. He took off his tammy and bowed. It was not so much a mocking as an ironic gesture.

"Consider this, sir," he cried, in a strong, clear voice. "Twa weans are born, at the same minute. From the womb, from the hands of God you would say, they issue so much alike that their own mothers have difficulty distinguishing one from the other. But one is the son of a rich man and has silken cushions to lie on and gowns of fine Egyptian cotton to keep him warm and servants to tend him hand and foot and a carefully chosen wet-nurse to give him suck. The other is the son of a weaver without work, living in a single-end, in this very street if you like. He has bare boards for a cradle, rags for clothing, a milkless mother to suckle him, foul air to breathe, and rats to bite him. Why should

28

this be so, in a land that calls itself Christian? I have asked many people that riddle, sir. I have asked judges, magistrates, landowners, lawyers, and manufacturers. Now I ask you, a man of God. Can you give me an answer, sir?"

Suddenly, as if his accosting of Darroch was the excuse they were waiting for, a troop of policemen armed with staves came rushing round a corner and began to deal out vicious blows. Darroch saw and heard a skull being cracked: blood flowed. He cried out in protest but moments later was too taken up with pacifying his horse Blackie which reared and neighed in alarm.

A sergeant bellowed that they were obstructing a public place and so were committing an offence for which they could be arrested.

Those cowed and frightened men were only too anxious to get away unhurt. As they fled they protected their heads with their hands.

The meekness of the poor always astonished Darroch. There were so many of them and their situation was so desperate that they might have been expected to rise up in fury and tear to pieces their oppressors and exploiters, among whom he himself would be included. Had they not done so in France, just fifty-four years ago?

If a man's children were starved and he saw food in plenty in shops but had no money to buy any, what force was it that kept him from stealing? Was it fear of imprisonment and disgrace? Partly, yes. Was it that years of insufficient food and living in squalid conditions had broken his spirit? Yes, that too. Was it from thousands of years ago the voice of Moses forbidding theft as being against God's commandment? Yes, no doubt, for the poor of Scotland were well acquainted with the Word of God. But was it not above all the promise given them by Christ that if they endured meekly they would one day be rewarded with peace and plenty?

The atheistic agitator would have jeered at that advice. At the moment though he had himself to look after and was doing it boldly and vigorously. When two policemen tried to seize him he struck their hands away.

He would have been taken, however, if a number of the

women, two of them still carrying their babies, had not rushed at the policemen, clawing, kicking, and even biting. One, white-haired and toothless, shrieked: "Rin for it, Jerry!" Another who was yelling "Offeecious cunts!" got a fist in her mouth. Blood spurted.

It was a scene which should never have happened in a town that had six Christian churches.

A policeman was bent over, groaning and clutching his privates. Those women knew where a man was most vulnerable.

Drink as well as poverty and hate was to blame. Gin-shops outnumbered the churches by ten to one.

In the melée Jerry, as the old woman had called him, made his escape.

The sergeant held Darroch's horse. "Sorry you got mixed up in this, Mr Darroch."

"Who is he, sergeant?"

"Name's Taylor, sir. Jeremiah Taylor, ca'd Jerry for short. Frae Glesca, as you'd expect. Famous troublemaker. He's been in jile before and he'll be again, as soon as we get a warrant. He's a cunning devil. Whit he says stops short o' sedition or inciting to revolt."

"Are these women always so fierce?"

The sergeant grinned. "Juist aboot. But there was a nasty murder here yesterday, in Mercer's Lane, that's maybe got them a bit fiercer than usual. A woman, a prostitute, cut her ain lassie's throat and then tried to cut her ain. She did a thorough job o' the first, for the lassie's deid, but she bungled the second. So she's in jile noo wi' fower doctors trying to save her so that she can be hangit later."

"Dear God! What age was the girl?"

"Twelve. She was following in her mither's footsteps, if you see whit I mean. Weel, things seem to hae quietened doon, so it's safe for you to go on your way, sir."

"Thank you, sergeant."

Darroch drove on. He had tears in his eyes. They were all he could offer the afflicted woman who had killed her own child. He could have offered prayers too but as an answer to Taylor's riddle they did not then seem adequate or appropriate.

A part of him had always believed that radicals like Taylor were dangerous and must be suppressed, not only because they stirred up sedition and provoked violence, but also because their gospel of materialism could, if it took hold and spread, corrupt the whole world.

Another part of him, more private, saw them as the true heroes of the age, risking their lives and liberty on behalf of the weak and deprived. In their vision of the future they promised the masses food, houses, work, schools, votes, and self-respect. Christ's promise contained all those things too and universal love besides, but it could only be kept if His ministers showed more active compassion and spoke out more courageously against society's manifest injustices, and did it soon, otherwise they would be ignored, deservedly, not only now but for all time. A brave new Free Church was more urgently needed than Dr Chalmers knew.

CHAPTER 7

Some ten minutes later he was walking through the prosperous part of the town on his way to St Margaret's manse. Here, among the well-stocked shops and fine buildings, there were no rioters or fierce women or ragged children. Men lifted their hats to the little minister from Craignethan, young maids giggled and hung their heads, mature women smiled and were pleased when he smiled back. He was known for his charitableness towards the poor, though he had seven children of his own to provide for, out of a meagre stipend. Mothers who had lost children and thought themselves inconsolable had been consoled by Mr Darroch's sweet smile and sincere voice.

Nevertheless if these people, whose good opinion was valuable to him, had known that he was on his way to St Margaret's manse, not so much to comfort his sick friend as to look with desire on his friend's wife, they would have shunned and despised him. Like Robert Drummond's their morality was limited by lack of imagination. They could never have been made to understand that if ever he looked upon Eleanor's naked body it would be with reverence.

As he stood on the manse doorstep, hat in hand, a voice, in the depths of his mind, spoke to him, so still and small that he could not be sure what it was saying, but he knew that it was the voice of truth and therefore the voice of God.

Eleanor opened the door. For a few moments the contrast between his ethereal image of her and the solid reality disconcerted him.

Her jet-black hair flowed over her shoulders: the parting in the middle gleamed. She was wearing only a rather grubby white nightgown. Her feet were bare and, alas, not as clean as they should have been. He had heard scandalised whispers that she did not wash as often as she ought for so tall and ample a woman, and it was probably true, but then how often had Leah washed? Where Annabel Wedderburn gave forth a scent of roses Eleanor smelled of spicy food, wine, and stale sweat. He had never found it repelling.

"You are just in time, George," she said.

He thought something must have happened to her husband. If Jarvie fell he could not get up unaided.

She led the way into the house. She never hurried. Some said it was because her mind was torpid from excess of wine, others were of the opinion that it was because she was too heavy. Darroch himself saw it as stateliness. The goddess in the painting would never have been impatient.

The house was dark and stuffy, with the windows shut and the curtains drawn. Eleanor kept no resident servants. A woman came to redd up, that was all.

She did not take him to her husband's bedroom but into the parlour. In its midst was a tin bath, illumined by rays of sun. Some water was already in it.

"Would you mind filling it for me, George?" she asked.

If it had been Annabel he would have suspected that she was teasing him. Eleanor was never frivolous.

Draped over the backs of chairs was an array of woman's clothing, all new as far as he could judge: petticoats, drawers, camisole, all white, and a black dress fit for a queen in mourning.

The hot water, with a film of coal dust over it, was in a huge iron pot on top of the hob in the kitchen. Six times he filled a pitcher and emptied it into the bath. Despite his care his shoes got splashed and his sleeve dirty.

At any moment someone might come to the door: the cleaning woman, the doctor, a church official, or a tradesman; or poor John Jarvie might come blundering in.

"Thank you, George, that should be enough."

"I shall go and see how John is," he said, hoarsely.

"I shall tell you how he is, George. He is dead."

He was astounded.

"During the night. The doctor said it could happen any time. He was prepared."

Her calmness frightened him. He fled, to find out if it were true.

The bed had had to have its legs reinforced. On it, his face covered by a white sheet, lay Jarvie. Darroch touched his brow. It was icy cold.

Darroch wept.

In his imagination he heard the wheezy sad voice: "George if I had children, like you, I would put their welfare and happiness above all else. Do not, George, be misled by your dreams."

At divinity college he had been stout but not inordinately so, and very pious. He had been married once before to a pretty young woman who had died giving birth: the child had not survived. When, some three years later, he had married Eleanor Volpetti, of Italian descent and Roman Catholic background, his friends had been amazed and concerned, though she had brought with her a considerable fortune, her father having been a well-to-do wine merchant in Edinburgh.

The doctors had said that his obesity was caused by a malfunctioning of glands which had made him overeat enormously, but it had always seemed to Darroch that grief and disappointment had played their part.

Darroch wiped the tears from his eyes and went back sadly to the parlour. He knocked. "May I come in?"

"By all means, George."

He entered, and received the biggest shock of his life. Eleanor, as naked as the goddess in the painting, stood smiling at him.

It was the first time he had seen a woman's naked body but few, he realised, were as magnificent as Eleanor's. His visions of her had not done her justice. Beside her the goddess was fat and commonplace. Eleanor's breasts were large, white, and round, her belly substantial but not gross, her waist narrow, her hips wide, and her thighs strong and splendid. The hair covering her

34

most sacred part was black and shining, like the small snails that came out after rain. The entrance to the place of love was as awesome as he had imagined it to be.

As a Christian minister and her husband's friend he had to lower his eyes, as poet and visionary he had to look his fill.

Just then were heard in the distance angry shouts. Police and rioters were clashing again.

It was a reminder of the censorious, hypocritical, cruel, and callous world.

He lowered his eyes. "I beg your pardon," he muttered, and withdrew.

'Don't go away, George," she called. "I want you to let Dr Grant, and others, know that Jarvie's dead. But give me an hour or so to wash and get dressed. Wait in the library. Take your pick of the books. Jarvie wanted you to have them."

He crept away to the room which John had called his library. It contained thousands of books. Among them were Bibles in many different languages.

Darroch tried to pray but had to give up. He tried to read the Bible but had to give that up too. Memories of Eleanor's body kept breaking into his mind. He could not keep them out.

He was afraid, too, that he would be too late to meet Robert's coach.

At last she came. It was hard to believe she was the same woman who had met him at the door in the grubby nightgown. The black dress suited her superbly. Her old stoop was gone: she now carried herself very straight. Her hair was built up like a crown. She had put on perfume, not rose- or lavender-scented, but musky and strange, suiting her personality.

"You can go now, George, and tell them. I want the remains put in the church, as soon as possible."

He would have offered to pray with her but was afraid she would refuse.

She showed him to the door. "I shall go to Italy, George."

"Italy?"

"Where the sun shines and sinners are more honest. Please give my regards to Mrs Darroch."

CHAPTER 8

Because of the pain which had been attacking her all that morning more and more severely, Mrs Darroch was glad when Mrs Wedderburn at last left, taking spoiled little Maud with her. She was grateful to the younger woman for bringing the medicine for Jessie, although she had pointed out, and summoned Mrs Barnes to support her, that it would be unwise to give to one sick child medicine which had been prescribed for another. That was the trouble with Annabel, she was kind but in that rash indiscriminate way so peculiar to Glaswegians. For a widow she laughed too readily and loudly, skipped when she should have walked sedately, favoured gaudy clothes (she had once confessed a fondness for coloured drawers!) covered her person with gewgaws, as often as not wore no hat, had Maud's hair done up in elaborate ringlets which encouraged nits and, worst of all, flirted shamelessly with young men, so that poor Arthur for one blushed whenever she spoke to him. At twenty-four she had the ambitions of a girl of fourteen; for instance she was eager to travel to far-off lands like heathen India, and that morning too, as on most of her visits to the manse, had blethered a great deal about George's brother the sea-captain, wanting to know when he was coming to Craignethan again and urging Mrs Darroch to invite him. Her interest, alas, was increased and not diminished when she was reminded that he was given to coarse language, as one in his profession was bound to be. She had rattled off silly questions, little caring that they were offensive to her hostess. "Had he ever flogged mutineers? Did he have one eye like Lord Nelson? Did he wear earrings? Had he ever said anything about beautiful native women who wore flowers in their hair and little else?" Mrs Darroch had had to reprove her several times but it had made no difference. Mrs Darroch had realised however that all that bright chatter could have been to keep her mind off Jessie's illness and her own.

Therefore, as from the window of her sitting-room she watched her young neighbour, clad in white, red, and green, being chased among the laburnums and lilacs of the manse garden by Maud dressed in the same flower-like colours, she envied and blessed the good-hearted bold young woman who had said that going home by the road was dull so she was going across the fields. Warned about the bull, she had cried, "Oh, a bull's always contented when he's got his harem about him."

Mrs Darroch herself had not been as carefree as that when she was twenty-four: she had had one child dead and another miscarried by then. But there had been a time when she too was lively and high-spirited, as Robert could testify.

Feeling another stound of pain, she had to creep to a chair and sit down, with her handkerchief in her mouth to smother any screams that might emerge involuntarily. She waited for the redhot sword to be withdrawn, as thank God it had been up to now, after a minute or so. The time would come very soon when it would remain in and she would die. Before that happened she must do all she could to safeguard the future of her little girls. When Robert came she would beg him to renew his promise to help them. He was a good man and a loving brother, and he would keep his word, whatever Bessie his wife might say. What was more important, however, was to try to make sure that George did not marry some young, pretty, irresponsible woman like Mrs Wedderburn (though *she* was more inclined to laugh at George than be enamoured of him) who would not cherish the girls as they deserved and needed, especially Sarah. Nothing was more certain than that George would marry again, but it must be to some mature, sensible, kindly woman not likely to have any children of her own and able therefore to expend her love and care on his. Not many such women existed.

Fortunately there was one at hand: Mrs Barnes. At thirty-six she was not above child-bearing age, but since she had not become pregnant during her six years of marriage when she was younger it was not likely that she would now. The girls were fond of her and she of them. Her sympathy for Sarah was not maudlin, stupid, and insulting, like Mrs Strachan's or Bella's, or Lady Loudon's: it was clear-sighted and intelligent. She knew what was to be done and would do it resolutely. The two boys, particularly James, might object because she was not a lady, but they would quickly come to see that her usefulness far outweighed her social inferiority.

George himself was the difficulty. He would think Mrs Barnes not comely enough to be his wife. Also, though of plebeian origins himself, he would not wish to marry a joiner's daughter unless she was young and beautiful. She did have, however, something that would appeal to him, probably more than beauty of face. She had a strong and shapely body. Her being from the common people would have the advantage that she would be able to allow him liberties that no genteelly nurtured woman ever could.

These thoughts caused the minister's wife as much pain in her mind as the disease did in her womb, but she endured them for her children's sakes.

Mrs Barnes of course had to be consulted.

Stooping, with her hand on the place where the pain was, as if to placate it, Mrs Darroch pulled the cord that would ring the bell in the kitchen and bring the housekeeper. Then she sat down and waited, hoping she would not faint.

Soon Mrs Barnes was at the door, knocking softly. She came in, wearing the loose black dress that had been supplied her. As was its purpose, it tended to conceal her very fine figure.

She saw at once something was badly wrong. "What's the matter, ma'am?" she asked, greatly alarmed. "You look very distressed."

"I'm afraid I am not well, Mrs Barnes. I have a terrible pain here."

"We should have asked Mr Darroch to fetch the doctor."

"It wasn't so bad when he left. In any case, there is nothing a doctor can do."

"Don't say that, ma'am. If Dr Fairbairn can't there are others in Edinburgh and Glasgow with mair skill that can."

"Mrs Barnes, would you please make sure there is no one listening at the door. I have caught Bella and Mrs Strachan eavesdropping before now."

"They are both in the kitchen, ma'am."

"Please make sure. What I have to say to you must be very confidential."

Mrs Barnes went to the door and opened it quickly. No one was there. She listened. She heard Bella singing down in the kitchen. Jessie was now in her parents' room, on that same landing. The baby's cot had been taken down to Mrs Barnes's room beside the kitchen, so that she could look after him during the night. She heard no noise from the little sick girl. Jessie seemed to be sleeping peacefully, thank God.

Mr Barnes returned and stood before her mistress. "It's all right, ma'am, there's nobody there, and Jessie seems to be asleep."

"Thank you, Mrs Barnes. Please sit down. No, here, where I can see you."

Mrs Barnes sat down. It was the first time she had been invited to do so in her mistress's presence.

Mrs Darroch looked at her and imagined her sitting there, not as a servant but as the mistress, in a handsome dress. She would suit the part well. She had no presumption now, she would have none then.

"Mrs Barnes, there is something I want to say to you, something so private that I must ask you to promise never to repeat it to anyone."

"I promise, ma'am. But should you not be lying down and resting?"

"Not even after I am gone."

Mrs Barnes moved her feet nervously. "Please don't talk like that. You will get well again. Think of your children."

"I am thinking of them. I think of them all the time. This child within me has already died."

39

"If you think that, ma'am, you must be seen by the doctor this very day."

"There is nothing the doctor can do for me. I know I am going to die soon. Therefore what I am going to say to you is more important than my seeing a doctor. When I am gone I would like you to take my place."

Mrs Barnes blushed. "I don't understand, ma'am."

Mrs Darroch realised then that so intimate a conversation ought not to be conducted as if between mistress and servant but rather as if between equals or even friends. They should be using Christian names. She was not sure what Mr Barnes's was. She asked.

"It's Jessie, ma'am, same as your wee girl's."

"Will you please let me call you Jessie? I want you to call me Margaret."

"Just for this once then."

"If you wish, for this once. I want you, Jessie, to marry Mr Darroch after I am gone. For my children's sakes. I know you would take good care of them."

"That I would."

"They know you, Jessie, they like you, they trust you, they would quickly accept you as their mother."

Mrs Barnes had tears in her eyes. "It's the pain, Margaret, that's making you speak like this."

"So it is, but I know what I am saying. My mind is clear. Would you have any objections to marrying Mr Darroch?"

After a long pause Mrs Barnes whispered: "No."

"Few women would take on the responsibility for four little girls, one retarded in her mind, and an eleven-month-old baby."

"I would gladly take it on." Mrs Barnes's voice had become quite hoarse. "But would not Mr Darroch, if he was going to marry again, choose someone younger than me, and bonnier, and better bred?"

"Yes, Jessie, he would, if he could find someone like that willing and able to take on the responsibility of the children. I do not think such a paragon exists." She could not keep bitterness out of her voice.

After another long pause Mrs Barnes murmured: "He may

never ask me to marry him, Margaret."

"He must be persuaded that it would be in his children's interests and therefore in his own. I am sorry, Jessie, if I seem to have no concern for your interests. I am being very selfish but I cannot help it."

"I would do the same if I were in your place, Margaret."

Mrs Darroch gazed at the other woman's face and saw it as plain, to the point of ugliness indeed, but also earnest, devoted, intelligent, and trustworthy.

"Jessie, like myself you are a Christian woman. I would not bequeath my children to you if you were not. What I am going to say is bound to offend you deeply."

She wondered if Jessie has already guessed. She had been married. She had been in bed with a man. She knew what men would give their souls for.

"I intend to ask Mr Darroch to sleep in the small back room downstairs."

It was separated from the kitchen by a small corridor.

"I shall tell him it is because I wish to have little Jessie beside me while she is ill."

Mrs Barnes kept fingering her wedding-ring. She said nothing.

"I find this exceedingly painful to say, Jessie, and you will find it just as painful to hear. The blame, if there is any, must be mine, not yours. You must know that you have my sanction and my blessing."

She had not noticed the pain in her body for the past two or three minutes. Either it had eased or had been absorbed by the greater mental pain caused by this proposal she was about to put to Mrs Barnes.

"I want you, Jessie, to put Mr Darroch into a position where he would be obliged to marry you. It would have to be done before I die. Afterwards would be too late."

Mrs Barnes turned pale. She touched her bosom, in nervousness perhaps, but there could be some deeper reason.

"I have shocked you, Jessie."

"Yes, Margaret."

"You will not do it?"

41

"I will do it, if I can."

They looked into each other's eyes. No more needed to be said.

"I should have reminded you, Jessie, that if Mr Darroch keeps to his resolution to come out of the Established Church in order to join Dr Chalmers and the Evangelicals, he will be without a manse or a church or a stipend."

"He will keep to his resolution, Margaret. It is very important to him."

"You speak as if it is also very important to you. Do you take the side of the Evangelicals?"

"I take Mr Darroch's side."

"Today is the 4th. The Assembly is on the 18th. We could be evicted any day afterwards. Lady Loudun will see to that." More bitterness. The pain in the body returned. "I shall be dead by then. It will all be left to you, Jessie."

Weeping, Mrs Barnes went and sat down on the sofa beside her friend and embraced her. Mrs Darroch was weeping too. How could they continue as servant and mistress when they had just made a compact that would, whether it was kept or not, bar them from heaven?

CHAPTER 9

Robert Drummond stepped down from the stagecoach into the sunlit cobbled square of Cadzow and took deep breaths and stretched out his arms, like a man accustomed to the best of everything, including space and air. The coach had been stuffy and a lady passenger had objected to the window being opened. He had humoured her, though other passengers had grumbled. He considered himself a gentleman first and a clergyman afterwards, and dressed to look more like the one than the other; but it was as a man of the world that he attended to the urchins who clamoured round him, offering to carry his bag for various sums from a penny to sixpence. He picked out the one whose price was the lowest. This was a lad of about twelve, smothered in rags too big for him, especially the baggy breeks and the cap that came down over his eyes. The other boys looked on him as a halfwit, and in a way he reminded Drummond of George Darroch, though George was always as dapper as a chaffinch. This gawky boy had the same knack of not noticing that he was being laughed at.

There was no sign of George who had promised to meet him. He did not mind. He could always arrange with the landlord of the inn to have him conveyed out to Craignethan. It would save him from the terrors of George's driving. It would also enable him to spend half an-hour or so in the inn enjoying a tankard of cool ale and a little harmless badinage with the wench with the red cheeks and the well-displayed (and well worth displaying) bosom, if she was still employed there.

"You, lad, that said a penny, what's your name?" he asked.

"Erchie Blackwood, sir."

"What does your father do, Archie?"

"He's got nae faither," jeered one of the other boys.

"He's a bastard, sir," said another.

Archie looked crestfallen.

Drummond approved of people who were ashamed if they had good reason to be: he would go out of his way to help such people. Archie of course couldn't help being a bastard, but Drummond liked morality to be on a firm sure basis. George was always floundering in morasses of doubt. How much simpler for everyone if Archie was ashamed of being a bastard and everyone liked him for being ashamed.

"Well, Archie, I'm going across to the inn yonder for a refreshment. What I would like you to do for me is to take care of my bag and at the same time look out for the gentleman who was supposed to meet me here."

"How will I ken him, sir?"

"He's a minister, Archie, though he may not look like one. He is small, very neat, with fair hair, and fair whiskers."

"Sounds like Mr Darroch of Craignethan," said one of the older boys.

"It *is* Mr Darroch of Craignethan."

"I don't think I ken Mr Darroch, sir," said Archie, "but I'll recognise him frae your description, sir."

"I'm sure you will, Archie. Just tell him that Mr Drummond is waiting for him in the inn. If you do that and look after my bag you will earn yourself sixpence."

"Oh, thanks, sir."

His disappointed rivals traduced him.

"He'll forget, sir. He's no' very bright."

"He comes frae Mercer's Lane, sir. They're a' murderers and whures that come frae there."

"That's no' true," protested Archie. "It was juist Mrs Cooper cut her lassie's throat, sir, yesterday. She was drunk. Naebody else has murdered onybody, no' for a while onyway."

Here were matters so unsavoury as to be best left alone.

44

Just then a gang of rough-looking fellows marched across the square.

"Wabsters, sir," explained Archie. "They're angry because they've got nae work. Some o' them hae been fechting wi' the police."

Waiting until the desperadoes had gone Drummond went over and entered the inn, which he knew from previous visits. To his delight the buxom lass was still there. Her neat ankles were clad in red stockings, and her bosom was generously exposed. The difference between him and George was that he could see a woman like this and be content to chaff her and tweak her cheek perhaps or even nudge her soft rump, and leave it at that, whereas George would blush and simper over her as if she was the Duchess of Buccleuch. The provoking thing was that most women, from serving-wenches to duchesses, or at any rate the aunts of marquises, seemed to find him irresistible. It was not really surprising. A sex that made a to-do about buying a hat or a bunch of ribbons was likely to make a fuss of such a fanciful, little man.

He was ordering his ale and having a close view of the fine breasts when George came in, at a trot.

Drummond had never seen him so dishevelled. His housekeeper must be dropping her standards. He was agitated too.

"Sit down, George. Better late than never. As you see, I'm comfortably ensconced."

"I'm very sorry, Robert. I was detained. You see, my friend John Jarvie died during the night. I had to fetch the doctor and the undertaker."

Drummond received the news calmly. "So his heart broke at last. See how lucky you are, George, keeping so slender. I'm the one should take alarm. But you must have a glass of wine to steady your nerves. I think wine's more your drink than ale." He called to the barmaid: "A glass of Madeira for my friend. Well, it should be a warning to his spouse."

"What do you mean, Robert?"

"Isn't she on the fat side herself? I've always thought of them guzzling their way together through vast heaps of buttered baps and cream cakes. So a title has been relinquished. I wonder who

45

now is the fattest minister in the Church of Scotland. I should think Mr Petrie of Portobello would be well to the forefront."

Drummond felt genial. He had been confident before that the offer which he had brought, and which according to Bessie only a madman would refuse, would be accepted by George with a minimum of palaver. He was even more confident now, seeing George made so squeamish by this whiff of mortality, a pretty rank one it was true.

The ale and wine were brought. Drummond treated himself to another peep at those luscious orbs, the owner of which treated herself to rather more than a peep at George's flaxen locks and dimpled cheeks. She devoured them with her gaze.

Drummond took a long draught of ale.

"Well, George, how is my dear sister?" he asked.

The sip of wine that George had taken seemed to have turned to vinegar in his mouth.

"Well, George?"

"She is with child again, Robert."

"Good God!" cried Drummond, so loudly that other guests looked across at him. He clutched the tankard as if he was about to smash his brother-in-law's bowed head with it.

"Dr Fairbairn says that with care and rest she should come through it safely," murmured George, having the impertinence to defend himself.

"What else could he say? That you have killed her? For that, George, is what you have done. Care and rest, you say, when what you have in mind is to have her and her children flung out into the fields like cattle beasts. Unless of course you have given up all that nonsense."

"I have not changed my mind, Robert. I cannot."

"Rubbish. It is as easy as sneezing. Dozens of ministers with convictions as sincere as your own have done it, and dozens more are doing it every day."

Perhaps now was the time to put forward the unrefusable offer, which would make further discussion of this kind academic; but Drummond, angry at the news about his sister, wanted to rub George's nose in the mess he had made, like a kitten that persisted in pissing in corners.

46

"I would have thought, George, no man of sense and decency would throw away his livelihood if he had seven children to provide for, and a wife in very precarious health."

"My family will be provided for, Robert."

"Ah, so Sir James is standing by you, and also the majority of your congregation? You have received assurances to that effect?"

"I have asked for no assurances. This Sunday for the first time I am to address my people on the subject of the forthcoming Disruption."

"Your brothers then have offered financial assistance?"

"I have not approached my brothers for help."

"Who then is going to provide? I hope you are not depending on me, George. My resources are limited."

"I am depending on Christ, Robert."

This was the thing Drummond hated most about the Evangelicals, their apparently humble but really most arrogant way of speaking as if the Creator of the universe was at their beck and call. Christ the King they called Him and then expected Him to serve them like a lackey.

Just then an altercation broke out.

A man with a blue bonnet had come in and sat down in a corner. The landlord had at once appeared and was now speaking to him in a low voice. Evidently he was asking him to leave, but the fellow was unwilling. Suddenly the landlord lost his temper and snatching the bonnet off the table threw it towards the door. Then he appealed to his other customers.

"Excuse me, ladies and gentlemen, but this man's a known troublemaker. His name's Taylor. I don't want him in my inn."

Taylor was a cool one, in spite of his grey hair and tired face. He sat where he was, as if he owned the place. He was the sort who would cut the throats of rich men or, rather, incite others to do it and claim that it was being done in the interests of social justice. Though he looked composed and humorous, he was a fanatic and therefore dangerous. Like George, indeed.

George turned and looked at him. Taylor smiled and bowed his head.

"Do you know him?" asked Drummond.

"No."

"He thinks he knows you."

"I heard him addressing a crowd of workmen this morning. He saw me listening."

"Preaching bloody revolution, I suppose?"

"What he said Christ Himself would have approved."

Astonishing Drummond even more Geroge stood up and spoke to the landlord. "The gentleman is doing no harm, Mr Syme. Why cannot he be served like any other customer?"

The landlord knew George. "Are you aware, Mr Darroch, he's an atheist as weel and lives wi' a woman that's no' his wife, that's somebody else's wife, and has three weans by her?"

"As Christians, Mr Syme, are we not enjoined not to judge lest we ourselves be judged?"

The poor landlord's face was a picture of indignation, as any sane man's would be when confronted, in and out of kirk, with such specious piety.

"Just the same, Mr Darroch, I've sent for the police," he said.

Taylor stood up, still smiling. "I don't want to cause trouble. If someone will be so good as to hand me my bonnet I shall leave."

"Pick it up yourself," said the landlord.

The other guests sat staring at the bonnet.

George went and picked it up. After knocking saw-dust off it he handed it to its owner.

"Much obliged, sir," said Taylor, bowing. "You are the only Christian in the house."

He went out smiling.

You will not smile like that, thought Drummond, with a vindictiveness not characteristic of him, when they drag you to jail and beat the insolence out of you.

"George, you are a fool," he whispered.

Yes, but there was the sonsy wench staring at George with wide-eyed admiration. Not only was he a bonny wee man, he was also not afraid to live up to his Christian ideals.

Drummond finished his ale and prepared to leave. "I hope the children are all well, George?" he asked, more or less casually.

"Jessie has a fever."

Drummond sat down again. Whatever you do, Robert, Bessie had said to him, don't bring back anything smittal and give it to Isa. She's the only egg in *our* basket.

"What kind of fever?" he muttered.

"She's hot and has a temperature."

"What does the doctor say?"

"He hasn't seen her yet."

"For God's sake, George, why not?"

If Isa had so much as a sniffle or a cough the doctor, a professor at that, was sent for immediately. George seemed to think children were readily replaceable. Well, he had good reason to think that.

"He must see her this very day, George. We'll call on him and tell him so."

"He may be out on his rounds but we can leave a message."

As they were going out of the inn the sergeant of police arrived with half-a-dozen men.

"Is he still here, Mr Darroch?" he asked, eagerly.

"If you mean Mr Taylor, sergeant, he has gone."

"Don't worry, he'll no' get far. We'll get him. Before he gets back to Glesca. There's naebody in this district will gie him shelter."

"Was that a warning, George?" said Drummond facetiously, as they walked away.

They went straight to the doctor's house, with Archie Blackwood behind them lugging the heavy bag. The doctor was out but his wife took the message. She undertook to have him visit Craignethan manse some time that day. She thought it would be about four o'clock.

Then they made for Murdoch's stables.

In view of the offer which he had brought Drummond had resolved to say no more about George's taking part in the threatened secession, especially as he was convinced that it would never take place, but that display in the inn of humbug masquerading as humility provoked him.

"So, George," he said "you are going to depend on Our Lord. Leaving aside the question as to whether or not He actually

49

performed miracles in His lifetime it is highly improbable that He would see fit to perform any now, after so many centuries, and in so inconsequential a place as Craignethan. Do you expect a haystack to be turned into a weather-proof house? Guineas to be made out of withered birch leaves? Angels flocking to the door with food? You are not a medieval saint, George, but a humble member, foolishly disaffected it is true, of the Church of Scotland, which does not believe in saints or contemporary miracles."

George meekly replied: "You and I see things differently, Robert."

That nettled Drummond. "It is your nature, George, to see things simply, like a child in many ways. There need be no harm in that, so long as you do not meddle. Let the deep-thinking philosophical gentlemen get on with the delving and unravelling, and leave the politicking to bigwigs like Chalmers and Candlish, who have the ambition and the intellectual capacity for it."

He was interrupted by Archie. "This is Mercer's Lane, sir, whaur Mrs Cooper cut her lassie's throat yesterday. It's whaur I live."

Drummond glanced up the narrow wynd. A skinny dog licked its sores. A woman wrapped in a shawl sat on a doorstep, drunk. Small children naked from the waist down poked one another with sticks. One crouched, defecating.

It was squalid and noisome, but he had seen as bad in Edinburgh's Old Town.

"Did you know about this woman, George?" he asked.

"Yes. The police-sergeant told me earlier this morning. He said four doctors were trying to save her life so that the law could hang her."

"You think they should just let her die?"

"I don't know, Robert."

"But if she dies it would be suicide, and suicides go to hell. Is that not so, George? Whereas if the law hangs her she could be said to have paid her debt and find mercy."

"What terrible stresses could make a mother kill her own child, in such a manner?"

"Probably she was too drunk to know what she was doing. I can see, George, you want to pronounce us all guilty."

"We *are* all guilty, Robert, more guilty than we know."

"That, George, is the kind of windy statement I do not like. It intends to mean everything, and means nothing."

CHAPTER 10

After the conversation with her mistress, or rather her friend, or to be more accurate still her accomplice, Mrs Barnes found herself in a state of perturbation, though she did her best not to show it. One minute, with her heart sinking, she thought that she had undertaken to take part in a sinful enterprise; the next, with her heart soaring, she felt that she had in front of her a joyful experience which, if it had God's blessing, would ensure that the rest of her life was useful, fulfilled, and happy. To calm her mind she kept busy, checking that Bella and Mrs Strachan had made all the beds and dusted all the rooms, preparing the vegetables and meat for the evening meal, and getting ready the small back room, pretending to Bella and Mrs Strachan that it was for Mr Drummond's use, though she knew he was to occupy Mary's room; Mary was to sleep with her two sisters.

The minister of the parish at the time of the Napoleonic Wars thirty years ago, Mr Darroch's predecessor, fearful of a French invasion, had had strong locks put on all the manse doors, so that his family, which had included four young girls, could preserve their lives and virtue to the last minute. The French had never come and most of the keys were lost, among them that of the small back room. Snibs had been put on other doors, for privacy, but not on this room's. Like all the other bedrooms, except that of the master and mistress, it was barely furnished, though the bed was a fine piece of furniture, having once belonged to Mrs Darroch's parents. As Mrs Barnes put on clean sheets and pillow cases she looked like any conscientious housekeeper, but felt like a bride. She had Bella warm a pan, to remove any trace of damp.

From her own room, through the kitchen, and down the small lobby, it took less than a minute to walk. It could be done very quietly, if the door from the kitchen into the lobby was left ajar, for it was stiff from disuse and made a noise when being opened, and if care was taken beforehand to see that no stools, pails, brushes, or any other kitchen utensils were in the way, to be banged into or knocked over.

In her own room, with only a few minutes to spare before Mr Darroch returned from Cadzow with Mr Drummond, she went down on her knees and prayed, in a corner with her back turned to the mirror. She begged the Lord, if this ensnaring of Mr Darroch was indeed sinful in His eyes — which it might not be, for He saw into people's hearts and therefore judged more justly — not to blame Mrs Darroch, who had been in so much pain that perhaps she had not realised clearly what she was saying, but to put on her the guilt and all the punishment. In her defence she pointed out that although it would not be completely truthful for her to say that she was doing it for the children's sake, nonetheless it was largely with their welfare in mind, for if it succeeded and she became Mr Darroch's wife and their mother she would devote the rest of her life to making them and him happy.

She got up then, gracefully, for she was still an agile, strong woman and looked in her wardrobe for a dress which, while it showed off her figure to advantage, was not too ostentatious for someone still ostensibly a servant. She chose a dark red one. Taking off the black smock, she threw it away. Torn up, it would do for dusters. Giving way to an impulse, though she could hear Bella stamping about the kitchen and Mrs Strachan crooning to the baby, only a door's thickness away — the keyhole had been stuffed with cloth, by a previous housekeeper — she took off bodice and camisole, until she was naked to the waist, and stood in front of the mirror, having tilted it so that though her face could not be seen in it, her throat, one of her finest features, being without creases and wrinkles, could, and also her breasts, as round and firm as a girl of twenty's.

Though they were hers, and she was not usually vain, she could not help being moved by them. They had never had milk in them, and never been suckled by a child. Her body was perfect for child-bearing, with wide hips denoting a capacious womb. Yet she had been married to Donald Barnes for six years and had never conceived. The Lord for His own good reasons had withheld that sweetest of blessings. Perhaps, if she became Mr Darroch's wife, even if it was done by trickery, He would relent and make her fruitful.

Somewhere in the Bible, she thought, among its many stories there must be one resembling hers.

CHAPTER 11

Glad to forget for the time being George's problems, vexatious notions, and present self-piteous sighs, Drummond surveyed with knowledgeable eye the fields through which they were travelling. They did not strike him as being in very good heart, but then the soil in this part of Lanarkshire was stony and clayey, not to be compared for fertility with the acres in his native Midlothian, particularly around Glenquicken. Craignethan was not really a village but a scattered community, with the kirk and the manse themselves isolated, built on high ground so that they had to bear the brunt of the wind and rain, whereas Glenquicken's kirk and manse were right in the village, opposite the large grassy common, with houses all round, not to mention three shops, a blacksmith's, a carpenter's, and a small inn. At £400 per annum the stipend was a good deal higher than average and three times that of Craignethan Parish. Surely not even George would be so great a fool as to turn down such a desirable living, coveted by dozens. Better just the same to tell Margaret first and leave it to her to persuade her quixotic husband. In her womb was an argument more compelling than any words.

When he was young Drummond's ambition had been to be a farmer, not the kind who got his boots covered with sharn and his back wracked with heavy work, but the gentlemanly and scholarly kind who studied the chemistry of the soil, thought up better ways of doing things (like the Rev. Robert Bell of Forfar who had invented a reaping machine), experimented with fertilisers, and produced cattle capable of giving larger yields of milk or a better quality of meat.

He had always felt that there was something not quite manly about being a clergyman. At College he had won prizes (unlike George who had barely scraped through) and thereafter had risen up the clerical ladder — helped it was true by his father's reputation — until he was now established in St Magnus's, one of the most fashionable churches in the capital. In theological and scriptural debates he could hold his own with the astutest brains in the Kirk. His father would have been proud of him. Even so, he still thought he would have found greater satisfaction in acres of golden wheat and herds of sleek fat cattle.

He quoted aloud a few lines from Virgil's *Georgics*, showing off, yes, but also expressing longings not yet extinct.

George, no Latinist, did not understand. In any case he seemed to be lost in doleful thoughts. Luckily the old horse had learned not to heed its master's touch on the reins, and found its own sure way past puddles and pot-holes.

George, he thought, should have been an actor, specialising in sad or romantic melodramas. He had the requisite touch of humbug in him and his appearance was most appropriate. That picking up of Taylor's bonnet and handing it back to him had been a piece of acting. As part of a drama it would have evoked great applause from all the silly women in the audience. Look how the rosy-cheeked barmaid had turned pale with admiration; yet she would look on the public hanging of Taylor without losing colour.

Craignethan had never been a suitable parish for George. It had once been Covenanting country, and the sour dregs still lingered. Blood had been shed in the kirk itself, and in the kirkyard were buried men called martyrs by some, but by Drummond fanatics. In Glenquicken the people were better educated and more cultured, and therefore more tolerant. It was close enough to Edinburgh, only ten miles away, for Arthur and James to live at home when they attended the university. Moreover, though probably nothing could ever be done for Sarah there would be a better chance of her benefiting from ameliorative treatment if she was in easy reach of the centre of medical knowledge.

CHAPTER 12

Drummond could not keep tears out of his eyes when he saw how ill and old his poor sister looked. Her hair had turned almost white, her face was yellowish and shrunken, and there were dark shadows under her eyes. She had tried to disguise her dying state with a pretty pink dress and a Paisley shawl, but within minutes of seeing her brother she was clinging to him and weeping sorely.

She had had too much to bear, four children dead, three miscarriages, and seven children alive, one an imbecile, and a lecherous little charlatan for a husband. He did what he could to console her, assuring her the doctor was coming, patting her head, calling her Meg as he had done when they were children, and whispering that he would look after her and her children.

Little Jessie, she sobbed, was very ill.

God forgive him, he waited, in dread, for her to ask him to go and see the sick child.

"Would you like to see her, Robert?" she asked.

"Of course, Meg, but I am no doctor, you know."

"I've had her brought down to my own room. George has a room to himself, in the meantime."

You should have thrown him out long ago, he thought.

They found Mrs Barnes sponging the little invalid's face.

Drummond was surprised to see her wearing a dark red dress which showed up her handsome figure. But he liked her. She was faithful and dependable.

"How bad do you think she is, Mrs Barnes?" he whispered.

58

He really meant: Do you think she is going to die, like John?

"It's hard to tell with young children, Mr Drummond."

"The doctor is coming this afternoon."

"I'm relieved to hear that, sir."

But she did not sound as if she had much faith in doctors. Neither had he. It was not their fault. The human body was a continent vaster and more mysterious than Africa.

Meg was holding Jessie's hand. The fair-haired little girl did not know her.

"Here is your Uncle Robert, pet, come all the way from Edinburgh to see you."

He stood close to the cot but did not touch the child. He had given Bessie his promise.

"What do you think, Robert?"

"As Mrs Barnes says, it's difficult to tell with young children. But they do recover with miraculous quickness. The doctor should be able to give her something to reduce her fever."

"I hope so. Little Maud Wedderburn was fevered a few days ago. She has since quite recovered."

"So will Jessie, Meg."

"Oh Robert, why must things change?"

"It's called progress, Meg."

"Papa used to dislike change."

"Yes." As a boy he had suffered from his father's rigid conservatism.

"It always seems to be for the worse."

"Not always, Meg."

"Then there is this trouble in the Church. Will George really have to give up the manse as well as the church?"

"Let's go back to the sitting-room, Meg. You must rest as much as possible. And there is something I want to tell you. Mrs Barnes will keep an eye on Jessie."

"Mrs Barnes has her duties to attend to. Shall we stay here a while. We can sit by the window."

"As you please, Meg."

They sat by the window which looked on to the road and beyond to fields and woods. On a fine still day like this the manse's high position was an advantage.

Looking at his sister, what was it that made Drummond think of the murderess in jail? Was it because they were both under sentence of death? The woman had not been tried yet but the verdict was a foregone conclusion.

"What was it you wanted to tell me, Robert?"

"First of all, Meg, let me assure you there will be no division in the Church. The latest estimate is that fewer than thirty will walk out on the 18th and most of those will be begging to be re-instated before the year is over."

"Would they be re-instated?"

"Probably, but not in their old kirks and manses."

"All my children were born in this house."

Yes, and more than half of them had died in it.

"But there is something else I have to tell you, Meg. I think you will find it good news, very good news."

"Have you told George?"

"No, Meg. I wanted you to hear it first. You may wish to tell George yourself."

She was silent. She had shown obstinacy in the past when asked to take sides against her husband.

"You must have heard me speak of Sir Thomas Blaikie of Glenquicken, Meg."

"Isn't he the gentleman whose two brothers died without heirs and so he came into the estate unexpectedly?"

"Yes, Meg. He used to be a member of my congregation. We became good friends. Bessie and I have been his guests at Glenquicken House on several occasions. Glenquicken itself is one of the most charming villages in Scotland. It is only ten miles from Edinburgh. The kirk itself may not be large but it is very well appointed, not at all bare and bleak like Craignethan. It even has a stained glass window, and there is an organ. It is situated in the heart of the village where a church ought to be, not stuck out in the midst of no-where, like Craignethan. The manse is commodious and recently renovated. Its garden extends to three acres and is a veritable paradise of flowers in summer. It is at its best now. The stipend is £400 per annum. The congregation consists mainly of bien, well-educated people. Does not all that sound most attractive, Meg?"

"It does, Robert, but what has it to do with us?"

"The living is now vacant, Meg. Mr Reid who occupied it for the past twenty-six years died last week. Sir Thomas was good enough to consult me. He values my advice. I took the liberty, and the risk I may say, of recommending George, conditionally of course. He could do very well at Glenquicken if he chose to. Sir Thomas and Lady Blaikie both remember having met him at my house. They seem to have been impressed."

She smiled, proud of her husband.

"Has Sir Thomas the power to appoint whomever he wishes?"

"As the owner of the estate certainly he has."

"But is that not the point at issue in this present trouble in the Church? That landowners should not have this right?"

"No, Meg. That is not the point at issue. What has caused the trouble is that some members of the Church, by no means the majority, claim that congregations should have the right to refuse any presentee of whom they do not approve."

"Should not congregations have that right, Robert?"

She had forgotten that when George was presented to Craignethan twenty years ago he had not been universally welcomed. Sir James Loudun, his patron, had had to quash objections.

It would have been cruelty to remind her.

"Perhaps they should, Meg, and if they are all patient they will get it in good time, but it is surely not important enough for the Church to break up over it. George of course would have to change his attitude or just keep quiet and sit still. Sir Thomas is staunchly Moderate."

She covered her face with her hands to hide her tears. "Oh Robert, why could not this good fortune have come to George years ago. It is too late now."

"It is not too late, Meg."

"For me it is. I have seen you looking at me. You know that I have not much longer to live."

"I won't have you saying that, Meg. This change to Glenquicken could be the tonic you need."

61

"But I cannot ask my husband to go against his conscience," she said, weeping.

He had nothing but sympathy and love for her, although she was so wrong.

"There would be no need for him to do so, Meg. All he has to do in St Andrew's Church on the 18th if there is any walking out — and I suppose Dr Welsh and Dr Chalmers may feel obliged to do so having threatened it long enough — is as I have said to sit still and say nothing, like hundreds of others. Better still, let him stay at home and not attend the Assembly at all."

"He is one of the delegates from the Cadzow Presbytery. It is his turn."

"He can pass it on to a colleague. He can give as his excuse his friend Jarvie's death."

"Is Mr Jarvie dead?"

He had not meant to tell her. Death was a subject to be avoided.

"Yes, Meg. It appears he passed away in his sleep during the night."

"Does George know?"

"It was he who told me."

"Why did he not tell me?"

"I think he did not wish to distress you."

"He would be too upset. They were good friends. I liked Mr Jarvie, but I'm afraid I have never cared for her. You know, Robert, she is always so dirty."

"Yes, Meg, I have heard you say so before. Well, will you give George the good news about Glenquicken? It will help to cheer him up. Perhaps it would be a good idea to let Arthur and James know. They will be very quick to see the advantages."

Then Mrs Strachan came in to say that Mrs Barnes had sent her up to sit with wee Jessie for a while.

CHAPTER 13

In the afternoon when his sister was having a sleep Drummond changed into clothes and shoes suitable for tramping a country road and set off to meet the girls coming home from school.

George had gone to pay his weekly pastoral visit to the colliers' rows. He had invited Drummond to accompany him. Drummond had declined, but had not resisted the temptation to tease his brother-in-law.

"Aren't you afraid, George, that you may endanger the economy of the country? Who will dig coal if you make Christians out of coal-miners?"

All the same, thought Drummond, as he strolled along in the sunshine, swishing off the heads of thistles with his stick, he had been expressing a harsh truth. An industrial society could be sustained only if there were a sufficient supply of men, women, and children too, to perform the many exhausting, dirty, degrading, and in the case of colliers dangerous tasks. If these helots, for they were little better, became Christians and sat in kirk among other Christians and took communion, they would very soon think themselves too good for the tending of machines in noisy factories for twelve hours a day or lying on their bellies in the bowels of the earth howking coal. They would want to be treated like Christians. Who then would do all the necessary, soul-destroying, low-paid work? Hottentots from Africa? Hardly, for were not missionaries, more zealous even than George, striving to make Christians of these too?

He could hear Bessie: "It is all very well, Mr Drummond,

being ironical. What if other people take you literally? Did not Dr Cook himself misunderstand you once?"

George always took him literally. Irony was a way of laughing at yourself. That was something George and all the other Evangelicals never did.

He saw some small yellow flowers glistening in the ditch. Were they buttercups or celandines? When Mary was four she had once solemnly explained to him the difference.

He was especially fond of Mary. He had once told Bessie, with not much exaggeration, that he got more pleasure and edification out of little Mary Darroch's remarks than out of any sermon, however eminent the preacher. When she was only an infant she had come to him with a dead butterfly on the palm of her hand. "Why is it dead?" she had asked. It should have been very easy to say why life had been extinguished in so fragile a creature, but looking at the little girl's puzzled eyes he had been struck by the mystery of death, more than he had been at funerals with important men dead and important men mourning them.

When Jessie was born, Drummond, with Bessie's canny approval, had gone to Meg and George and offered to adopt Mary. She would be one less for them to look after, and she would be a companion for Isa. Meg had seemed willing enough but George had put on a show of a father distraught. Mary herself had settled the matter by refusing to leave Sarah, and there had been no question of the Drummonds adopting the little daft one too.

Perhaps, he thought, he had not been as sympathetic as he should have been to George, father of an imbecile child. He would have been heart-broken for years if it had happened to him. He might have had to leave the ministry, for his faith would have taken such a dunt. It seemed to him that being burnt at the stake or even nailed to a cross would have been easier to endure in that they lasted only an hour or two, whereas this agony of having to cherish an idiot child lasted all one's life. George bore it as well as any man could.

A bull roared in the field beyond the hedge. At least he took it to be a bull until he looked over and saw that it was a cow imagining it was a bull. Up on its hind legs it was mounting another cow. He looked carefully to make sure. Yes, it had udders, hardly the right equipment.

As he went on his way the cow bellowed disconsolately. This was a train of thought not proper for an uncle about to meet his little nieces or a minister of the Kirk, but he pursued it nevertheless.

He had always tried to be sensible about sexual intercourse. Many ministers dismissed it as a mere bodily function, to be done and then forgotten till the next time, like other bodily functions, but he recognised that for some men at least it was also an insatiable passion. He knew ministers who resorted to whorehouses: white-haired respectable members of their profession, with wives and grown-up families. If it was known publicly they would be disgraced and excommunicated. He was lucky that "the beast between his legs" had never taken control of him, and also that he had a wife able, without fuss or stress, to put up with what had to be put up with. Whether Bessie ever enjoyed the act he did not know for he could scarcely ask and she could scarcely tell him; but she had never complained and nowadays chatted amicably during it.

George as a lecher did not surprise him. He had known before small slender men reputed to fornicate more than other men twice their size and weight. Did not sparrows go to it oftener than giraffes? It could well be that there was a connection between religious frustration and sexual frenzy. If no other miracle then this would have to do. And certainly a miracle it was, in that its outcome could be a human being, complete with pinkie nails and a soul.

Was there not a case in morality and Christian theology — consider Abraham's handmaidens — for allowing over-passionate men to use whores and mistresses, so as not to outrage their wives' modesty and damage their health? It had been done for centuries among the aristocracy. If kings and dukes could have mistresses with the blessing of archbishops, why could not ministers of the Church of Scotland, with the General Assembly's?

Again he heard Bessie: "More irony, Mr Drummond?"

He was delivered from these repulsive and unworthy thoughts by the shouts and laughter of children.

Round the corner they came, seven of them. Agnes danced in front, chanting: except that she was fair-haired she was so like her mother at the same age, never still and never quiet. He could have wept to see Sarah, such a beautiful child, too contented, too unconcerned, holding Mary's hand.

He made out Agnes's chant: "Six times seven are fifty-four."

A boy about the same age as herself was blubbering and pressing his right hand against his jersey.

Agnes was the first to notice her uncle. She looked up from plucking some docken leaves and saw him. "Uncle Robert!" she screamed and raced towards him, leaving her schoolbag on the road.

Meg, too, had shrieked long ago when she should have spoken quietly, slammed doors or left them wide open, lost bonnets and dirtied clothes, run about with bare feet, fallen and skinned her knees, laughed and cried all at once.

He picked Agnes up. "What's all the shouting about?" he asked. "And what are the docken leaves for?"

"For Tam Hislop's hand," she cried, throwing them down. "He got the tawse for saying six times seven are fifty-four. Did you bring me something?"

"I wouldn't have dared come if I hadn't."

"No, you wouldn't. What is it?"

"Wait and see."

"I hate waiting."

The other children gathered round them.

"Hello, Uncle Robert," said Mary gravely. "Say 'Hello', Sarah."

Sarah went on smiling.

Tam was holding a docken against his sore palm. He looked, alas, as if all his life six times seven would be fifty four. Involuntary stupidity had been punished, not wilful ignorance. The clever were praised, the dull leathered. It was wrong but Drummond could see no remedy. It had been done in his day too. It would be done a hundred years hence.

He put Agnes down and picked up Sarah. He did not heed

66

Agnes's yelled warning that she stank.

"Tam's not good at arithmetic," said Mary.

"He's not good at anything," cried Agnes.

"He's good at making whistles out of cow parsley stalks."

"Cow parsley tastes awful," said Agnes. "Doesn't it, Uncle Robert?"

It had been many years since he had tasted cow parsley.

"Poor Tam," he said. "Maybe I've got something that will take away the pain."

Agnes looked at him anxiously, as if she was afraid he might give Tam the present he had brought for her.

He gave the boy a sixpence.

It did the trick. Tam smiled bravely.

"Say 'thank you'," cried Agnes.

"Thank you," he mumbled.

"Say 'sir'."

"Sir."

They all laughed, including Tam himself, but not Mary, who frowned.

Drummond wondered if she was displeased with him for assuming that money was cure for pain and humiliation. She was her father's daughter after all.

They all walked together along the road.

"Did you see Jessie?" asked Mary.

"Yes, I saw her."

"Is she better?"

"I'm not sure. The doctor's coming today to see her."

"He won't do any good," said Agnes. "He came to see John and John died."

"Has Papa gone to visit the colliers?" asked Mary.

"Yes."

"He said he would take me but he hasn't."

"I wouldn't go there for twenty sixpences," cried Agnes.

"Do any of the colliers' children come to school?" he asked.

"They can't," said Agnes. "They've to work down the pits."

"Not any more. The law forbids it."

"Nobody bothers about the stupid law."

"Are Aunt Bessie and Cousin Isa well?" asked Mary.

67

"Very well, thank you. They send their love."

"Are Isa's legs still fat?" asked Agnes.

Isa had been on the plump side a year or so ago. "I don't think so, Agnes."

"Can she skip? She couldn't last time I saw her."

The truth was he had seldom seen Isa skipping with a rope.

Mary stopped. "I'll have to change Sarah. I thought it could wait till we got home but it can't. You can all go on. You too, Uncle Robert, if you prefer."

"*I* prefer," cried Agnes, racing away.

The four strange children climbed over a stile. Their homes lay across the fields.

"Can I help?" asked Drummond.

"You can hold my schoolbag if you like. But wait till I get out the paper."

The paper, he saw, was *The Witness*. It espoused the Evangelical cause. This was a fit use for it. He must remember to tell his friends.

Sarah just stood and let herself be wiped. Mary did it thoroughly.

She would be doing it all her life. She had made the mistake of showing that she was willing. Such was the perversity of fate — to call it that — that Sarah would probably live till she was seventy.

"You can carry her now, if you like," said Mary.

At once he lifted the chuckling little girl, though he'd noticed his sleeve was soiled.

CHAPTER 14

Agnes's clamouring for the presents to be given out was stilled by the arrival of old Dr Fairbairn in his horse-and-buggy. She ran and hid. He brought Arthur and James with him, having picked them up not far from their school.

He was over sixty, with scanty white hair and a stoop like a hunchback's. Agnes had once exclaimed too loudly that he couldn't be a very good doctor for if he was he'd give himself more hair and make his back straighter. He had jested that he was going to take her away in his wee black bag. She had hidden under her bed till he'd gone.

Mrs Darroch preferred him to the other Cadzow doctors because he had a kind voice and gentle hands; moreover, he was not so keen to bleed his patients. Darroch approved of him because he readily admitted that prayer could be more efficacious than his medicines. He had added however that this might not be so in the future when the causes of disease were discovered. Thirty years ago he had served as a surgeon in the Army, during the war against Napoleon.

He examined Jessie in the presence of her parents and Mrs Barnes. They watched him take her temperature, measure her pulse, look at her body to see if she had a rash, peer into her throat, and listen to her breathing. It was all done with competence, yet he knew that the little girl was very ill, from congestion of the lungs and there was little he could do to help her.

It was an experience he had had hundreds of times — this was the third dying child he had seen that day — and he had learned how to look, not hopeful, for that would have been deceiving the parents, but composed, for after all who knew what turn a fever could take? He had seen children worse than this recover and others not so bad die. In this particular case, though, he found it more difficult to look calm, not only because he was very tired after a long hard day, but also because he had seen with his first glance that the child's mother was herself doomed.

He had warned her husband after the birth of the last baby less than a year ago that another pregnancy might be the death of her. Here was that husband now, hands clasped, eyes upcast, thinking holy thoughts, and yet one night, three months ago, when his poor wife could not have been looking all that seductive, he had wantonly risked her life for a few moments of self-indulgence. It would have been reprehensible, if more pardonable, in a collier or ploughman; in a man of God it was heinous, deserving almost of castration, as that despiser of clergy would have said, the doctor's lifelong friend and ex-Army comrade, Dr John Williamson of Glasgow, now deceased. Yet Darroch, a simpleton among theologians (a breed Dr Fairbairn himself distrusted) had never been known to say an unkind word to anyone or to do anyone harm, except his wife.

As he washed his hands in the warm water supplied by that estimable woman Mrs Barnes, and dried his hands with the towel also supplied by her, he prescribed the treatment for the little girl.

"Keep her warm. Give her plenty of liquids. Sponge her frequently. Change her nightgown as often as necessary."

"Mrs Barnes has already been doing that, Doctor," said Mrs Darroch.

"Good for you, Mrs Barnes. I shall leave a medicine which may help to reduce the fever."

"What is the matter with her, doctor?" asked Darroch.

"Congestion of the lungs, I fear, Mr Darroch. Did she have a chill recently?"

"She was caught in the rain," said Mrs Barnes.

70

"There is usually a crisis. It think it may be soon. We can only pray that it goes well."

"I shall pray," murmured Darroch.

"The apothecary sent Mrs Wedderburn's little girl a medicine which cured her," said Mrs Darroch. "Can you not give us that medicine for Jessie?"

"A coloured cordial, ma'am. Mrs Wedderburn's little girl had a stomach upset, that's all."

"And this is more serious?" whispered Darroch.

"Yes, Mr Darroch, I'm sorry to say it is. Now, Mrs Darroch, what of yourself? How do you feel?"

Her brother, the big brusque minister from Edinburgh, had more or less demanded that he cure her.

"Not very well, doctor," she replied, in a whisper. "I have had terrible pains all day. I am sure the child is dead."

He turned to Darroch. "May I examine Mrs Darroch, sir?"

"Yes, doctor."

The husband's permission had to be asked before the woman's and the examination had to be done with the patient's clothes on and with the doctor's hand restricted to pats and gentle pressings.

She was right: the child was dead. How could it fail to be in a body so enervated? The only way she could be saved was for her body to be boldly cut open and the noxious matter removed. There were surgeons in Edinburgh who had described this operation brilliantly in a book, but they had never attempted it; not because the pain to the patient would have been unimaginably severe but because society would have condemned the surgeons as blasphemous and criminal, especially if the patient died.

He could only tell her to rest and give her a medicine with laudanum in it, which would enable her to sleep and thole the pain. But that was all. It should not have been all. Miscarriages had been happening since the creation of man. They had killed millions of women. Doctors could not say they lacked experience. Yet here in 1843 was another doctor as helpless as Hippocrates.

He went out with Darroch, leaving Mrs Barnes to put her mistress to bed.

They met Robert Drummond waiting outside the front door. He was smoking a pipe.

"Well, doctor?" he asked, sharply. "How is my sister?"

"The child is dead, Mr Drummond, but it is still in the womb. Usually nature expels such noxious matter, and we must pray that that is what happens."

"And if it does not happen?"

"Then it is in God's hands, Mr Drummond."

"I mean no disrespect, doctor, but are there not doctors in Edinburgh, more eminent in their profession, who could do more for her?"

"If there are you should send for them without delay."

"Could she make the journey, without grievous harm?"

"She is very weak as you have seen, but anything is worth trying."

"Then it will be done. My regards, doctor."

Drummond hurried into the house, to tell his sister that he was going to take her to Edinburgh tomorrow, where professors who were his friends would cure her.

The doctor's horse-and-buggy was brought round by old John Cairns whose rheumatism was worse even than the doctor's own.

Darroch helped the old man up.

"Tell me, doctor," he said, "were you one of the four doctors called in to treat Mrs Cooper?"

"Mrs Cooper?"

"The woman in Cadzow Jail who killed her own child."

"Ah yes. Interesting case, from a doctor's point of view. In my army days of course I saw many much worse wounds. We were able to sew her up well enough."

"Will she live?"

"I think so, largely because she is terrified of dying and going to hell. I shall come back tomorrow, Mr Darroch, and bring a competent woman to act as nurse for a day or two."

"Mrs Barnes is a competent woman."

"So she is, but she cannot be asked to do everything. I see it is

72

going to rain. Good-night, Mr Darroch."

He flicked the reins and the old horse, which had rheumatism too, set off stoically.

CHAPTER 15

Darroch met his brother-in-law coming out of Margaret's room, with a very glum expression.

"She wants to speak to you, George," said Drummond. He was about to say something else but decided not to. He went into the sitting-room where Agnes was waiting for him to hand out the presents.

Darroch went in. Mrs Barnes was tending Jessie.

"I've given the mistress her medicine," she said. "She should go to sleep soon. Jessie is sleeping, thank God."

"May we have a lot more to thank Him for very soon, Mrs Barnes."

"Yes, Mr Darroch."

As she went out he could not help noticing what a very fine figure she had, and how well the red dress became her.

He sat by the bedside holding his wife's hand.

"I am going to die, George," she whispered.

"Please do not say that, my dear. We shall soon have you well again."

"Robert brought wonderful news, George."

He thought her mind was wandering.

"He said that there is going to be no division in the Church. That is what they are now saying in Edinburgh."

But Robert had been saying that all along. He had always been convinced that the rebels, as he called them, faced with the loss of their livelihoods, would give in.

"But that was not all the wonderful news, George. His friend,

Sir Thomas Blaikie of Glenquicken has offered you the living at Glenquicken."

He was sure now that the medicine was affecting her mind.

At College one of his fellow students had been William Reid, son of the then incumbent of Glenquicken. He had taken Darroch to visit it. Darroch still remembered the opulence of the kirk's furnishings. Craignethan was a barn by comparison.

"The stipend is £400 per annum, George. Think of all the advantages to our family."

What a pity it was not true. Glenquicken was the kind of living he would need if he was ever to rise in the hierarchy of the kirk.

"Promise me that you will accept, George."

There was no harm in promising a sick woman to accept an offer which existed only in her confused mind.

"If it is offered I shall accept."

"You will remember to thank Robert."

"Yes, I shall remember."

She was fighting against sleep. Her eyes kept closing.

"There is something else I want to say to you, George, something more important still."

He humoured her. "What is it, my dear?"

"I want you to give me your solemn promise."

"I have already given it."

"No, this is something else."

He supposed she was going to ask him not to take part in the Disruption if Robert and his friends were proved wrong and there was one. When she was well she had supported his right to act according to his conscience. Now that she was ill, with her mind not under control, if he gave such a promise surely he did not have to feel bound by it?

"What is it I have to promise, my love?" he asked.

"You know I would never ask you to do anything that might be harmful to you."

That was true. She had always been a loyal wife.

"All our married life, George, I have denied you nothing."

He was silent. She had denied him a great deal, but it had not been her fault.

"So you will not deny me this, my dying request. Do you promise?"

"Yes, Margaret, I promise."

"As God is our witness."

"As God is our witness."

"When I am gone I want you to marry Mrs Barnes. Her name is Jessie, like our little girl's."

He was thunderstruck.

"I am thinking of all my little girls, George, and my baby. They are fond of her. She will devote her life to looking after them and she will make you a good wife. What do you say, George?"

What he thought but did not say was that Mrs Barnes' proper role was that of handmaiden, not of mistress.

"I say that you are going to be my beloved wife for many more years."

"I pray to God I may be, but if it pleases Him to take me soon you will marry Jessie Barnes. You have promised, George."

"She might not wish to marry me or anyone else. She is used to being a widow. Did she not refuse Mr Runcie?"

"She is willing to marry you, George. Why should she have all the duties and burdens of a wife without the honour?"

Even if he had given such a promise Mrs Barnes would never hold him to it. It was the nature of handmaidens not to presume.

"I am going to sleep now, George. I feel more content. In Glenquicken you will all be very happy together."

She still had this delusion about Glenquicken.

She was already asleep.

He was kissing her brow when there was a soft knock on the door and Mrs Barnes came in.

"Is she asleep?" she whispered.

"Yes."

"Thank God. She needs rest. I shall sponge Jessie again."

"You are very kind to us all, Mrs Barnes."

He put out his hand. After a moment's hesitation she took it. He raised hers to his mouth and kissed it. He could not have said why.

"God bless you," he said, and quickly left.

He had just reached his study when Robert arrived at his back, looking grim.

"I'm not going to say much, George. Mrs Barnes tells me the meal is ready."

"I shall not be present, Robert. I am too choked up with anxiety to eat."

"I think Dr Fairbairn would tell you that we must eat to keep up our strength, for prayer and other things. But please yourself. Did Meg speak to you about Sir Thomas Blaikie's offer of the living at Glenquicken?"

"She did, Robert, but I thought it was delirium caused by pain."

"It certainly is incredible good fortune, George."

"She said the stipend is £400 per annum."

"So it is, and the kirk has an organ and stained glass windows representing, I believe, Faith, Hope, and Charity. Sir Thomas does not require an answer immediately. You have till the 18th. All you have to do then in St Andrew's Church is sit still and say nothing, like hundreds of others. Better still, stay away altogether. I am not going to try and persuade you, George. If your wife, who is dangerously ill, cannot then I assume no one can. I have taken the liberty of informing your sons. You may think it is none of their business. I do not agree. Their futures, and those of their sisters, are involved. They have a right to know and to speak. I hope you will listen to them, George. That is all I intend to say on the subject."

He went off as grim as ever.

CHAPTER 16

After a subdued meal presided over by Drummond the presents were at last handed out. Drummond's having had to drink water instead of wine did nothing to lighten his gloomy mood.

Agnes did her best to bottle up her excitement but it kept bursting out. She screamed when he made to give her her present first: she wanted hers to be kept to the last. Then she took more interest in the others' presents than the recipients themselves. She snatched them from her uncle and handed them over. Jessie's doll with the china face she kissed, and then she whispered into its ear that its mother was in bed with fever and it would have to wait before it could see her. She tried on Sarah's bib with its pictures of farmyard animals before running across to where Sarah sat on the sofa beside Mary and put it on her, not too patiently. She shook loudly at first and then, remembering, softly, Baby Matthew's rattle with Edinburgh Castle painted on it. She pointed out pictures of bluebells to Mary in the latter's book of wild flowers. She informed Arthur that the building on the frontispiece of his Guide to Edinburgh was Holyrood Palace. When James's pale blue silk handkerchief was unwrapped she shrieked with envy, and then clapped her hand over her mouth. With her other hand she seized the handkerchief and pressed it against her cheek, until James took it from her and pressed it against his.

Bessie and Isa had helped Drummond to choose the presents. It had been easy in the case of the others but James had stumped them. Darroch himself had suggested a pocket Bible since

78

James was intended for the ministry, but Bessie and Isa both thought such a gift would not be gratefully received. It was Isa who had suggested the silk handkerchief. Drummond had said she was being silly. "But, Papa, he would *love* a silk hankie. He wanted me to give him mine." Drummond had been reluctant. "I know he's like a lassie in looks," he had muttered to Bessie, "but that's all the more reason why we shouldn't encourage him." She had assured him he didn't have to worry about James who might look like a lassie but was no softie. James was very good at looking after James.

When Drummond had told his nephews about Glenquicken, in the garden while waiting for the doctor's verdict, Arthur had turned away his head to hide tears and said he hoped this good luck hadn't come too late; in any case he couldn't see how his father could accept, since it would mean his having to desert the Evangelicals and join the Moderates. James had shrugged his shoulders and said he was sure his father could be persuaded. It had been obvious to Drummond that James, who would never himself make sacrifices for the sake of inconvenient principle, found it difficult to understand how anyone intelligent could.

For his sister Drummond had brought a little bottle in the shape of a lady with a crinoline, filled with expensive French perfume. Before he could stop her Agnes had it opened and was putting a dab of perfume on her nose. She cried she would keep it for her mother, but her uncle made her hand it back to him.

Given her own present at last she was overjoyed and yet at the same time querulous. It was a box of Edinburgh rock, her favourite sweet. It wasn't fair, she cried, that her present was the only one everybody would expect a share of. Who, aged eight and a bit, wanted to play with wee girls' dolls? Who wanted to look at silly books about flowers and streets? Who could share a handkerchief? Perfume could be shared but she would be told that it wasn't suitable for a girl of eight or rubbish like that.

Again she reminded Drummond of her mother at the same age. Meg too had given way to tantrums. Their father, stern-faced as Moses, had comforted her on his bony knees.

Down in the kitchen Mrs Strachan and Bella, about to leave

79

for home, heard her and agreed that she needed her wee arse skelped.

Drummond had brought his brother-in-law nothing, except of course the offer of Glenquicken living. "I'll take him at his word," he had said to Bessie. George was too fond of announcing that he found no pleasure in material possessions. Drummond himself liked very much to acquire a new book or picture or piece of furniture or even a good pair of boots. It made him happy to see people take delight in beautiful, well-made objects. George appeared to think that by denying himself material things he was demonstrating superior spirituality. It was one of the reasons why his sons did not respect him.

Was it to show that disrespect that they brought up the subject of the woman who had killed her own child? They had heard their father express concern for her. One of their school friends whose father was a police official had given them the gruesome details.

"There was blood all over the room," said James, "even on the cat."

Drummond knew he should have stopped them. He had heard High Court judges and leading ministers of the Kirk jovially discuss rape over the port, but there had been no little girls present and no very ill woman in a room across the landing.

"Did she use the bread-knife?" asked Agnes.

"It was a razor," said Arthur.

"Will she be hanged? If she is, can I go and see it? Jenny Hislop said she saw a man hanged in Cadzow when she was just three. She's twelve now. Hundreds of people were there. She said it was like a picnic."

"Why did she do it, Uncle Robert?" whispered Mary.

"I don't think she could tell you herself, Mary."

"She was drunk," said James.

"I hope Papa is praying for her," said Mary.

"Papa wouldn't pray for somebody who did a terrible thing like that, Mary Darroch," cried Agnes.

"Mr Saunders of St John's in Cadzow is the prison chaplain," said James. "It is his duty to pray for her."

"Father says he doesn't have sympathy for the prisoners," said Arthur.

"Ever since one threw the contents of a chamber-pot over him," said James.

"That's quite enough, you two," said Drummond, although in spite of his low spirits he was hard pressed not to laugh. He had met Mr Saunders, a wishy-washy auld wife and a braying Evangelical to boot.

At that point Mrs Barnes came in to say it was time for the girls to wash and go to bed.

CHAPTER 17

Though he had prayed thousands of times Darroch still did not find prayer simple: there could be so many complications. To begin with there was always the problem of whether to speak aloud or inwardly. Whether God Himself had a preference was impossible to discover but for the person praying it could matter a great deal, since there could be circumstances in which, try how he might, he would not be able to keep out of his voice a girn of complaint or whine of self-pity.

There was another danger in praying aloud. A voice raised in prayer could of its own accord become loud and domineering. Though the walls of Craignethan manse were thick he had been overheard often.

Safer therefore to pray in silence.

From childhood while praying he had given God a face, not always one that He would have been flattered to own. For years it had been that of old Mr Thorburn, a Greenock minister with a long white beard, clapped in jaws, glaring eyes, and gappy yellow teeth frequently bared as he consigned sinners to Hell. By the time he was twelve an element of wilfulness had intruded: he began to give God a face according to his own mood and the purpose of his prayer. If he was letting God know of some good deed he had done or was intending to do, he had God smiling, like a schoolmaster pleased with a bright pupil. If on the other hand he was telling of some remissness on his part he had God scowling, like the same schoolmaster confronted by a dunce. When he had become a man and it was time to put away childish things he had tried to replace faces with impersonal visions, like the sky at sunset or sun shining on water or an apple tree covered with blossom. There was of course a way of making sure that the problem did not arise: that was by praying with his eyes open. But he could never think it right, while addressing his Maker, to be staring at worn places in the carpet or the scuffed legs of chairs or mouse dirt.

That evening, with so much need for prayer, he could not pray: he was not, it seemed, in a sufficient state of grace.

There were Margaret and wee Jessie, both seriously ill. There was Mrs Cooper in jail, suffering intolerable pain of body and soul. There was Taylor the radical hunted by the police. There were the Websters desperate because their wives and children were hungry. There were ministers of the Kirk tempted by worldly inducements (such as kind but treacherous offerings of lucrative livings) to forsake their principles.

Preventing him from praying for all these were a sense of his own unworthiness and also memories of transformed Eleanor.

Letting himself dream, he saw her and not Mrs Barnes as mistress of his handsome manse at Glenquicken. She would disclaim responsibility for his children but with her money and his ample stipend they could afford enough servants.

More extravagantly still, he imagined himself going with her to Italy and taking his children with him.

Then, with a pang of apprehension, he remembered her remark, that in Italy sinners were more honest. What had she meant? There religion was more primitive and superstitious. Sinners could be absolved by priests, if some degree of repentance was promised. In rigorous Scotland such absolution was not possible Sinners therefore tried, by slippery self-justifications to convince themselves, and God too, that they were not really to blame.

Had Eleanor been accusing him of being one of those self-deceiving and self-justifying hypocrites?

Out of this turmoil of soul-searching, he thought, I shall emerge a better and braver man, and a more resourceful minister.

He was interrupted by the sudden clatter of horses and a

carriage coming up the drive fast.

Very shortly Arthur and James came knocking at the door to tell him that Sir James had sent a carriage to take him to the Big House, where old Lady Annie was dying: she wanted to see him.

Robert came downstairs to find out what was going on. He did not think George should go. "Your place is here tonight, George," he said, but he realised that George could hardly disregard an order, for such it amounted to, from Sir James who paid a good part of his stipend and on whose land his manse and kirk stood.

Drummond went outside with his brother-in-law and nephews. It was turning dark, with a threat of rain.

"How will you get home, George?" he asked, sympathetically enough.

"Sir James said Darroch could stay the night if he wanted to," said Saidler, for it was he who had brought the carriage.

"I don't think you should do that, George," said Drummond. "You may be needed here."

"I shall walk home, Robert. It is less than two miles and I know the road well."

"Would you like me to go with you, Father?" asked Arthur.

"I too," said James, who was always keen to visit Hairshaw House.

"Thank you, boys, it is very kind of you, but there is no need. In any case I may be rather late."

Darroch thanked Saidler who was holding the carriage door open.

Saidler touched his forehead, but as soon as they were out on the road he drove recklessly, so that Darroch was flung about the carriage.

Often in church from his pulpit he had watched Saidler, standing at the back, for there were no seats for menials, and thrusting his loins against the buttocks of the servant girl in front of him.

Most men like Saidler had contempt for the minister. It was unjust. He knew they drank, swore, blasphemed, gambled, and fornicated, but, as he had once told a group of them, including Saidler, he was well aware that men in their situation, uneducated, poorly paid, and overworked, could hardly be expected to behave like polished gentlemen. They had not been appreciative.

There were two entrances to Hairshaw House, one used by the carriages of the owner and his guests, and the other by servants and tradesmen. It was the latter Saidler chose, and so he deposited the minister at the back door.

No doubt he was obeying Lady Loudun's instruction. She had more than once told Darroch that clergymen in England, where she used to live when her husband was attending Parliament, were gentlemen, often the sons of noblemen, whereas so far as she could see most of the ministers of the Church of Scotland were the sons of shopkeepers.

He was greeted by Mr Simmonds, the English butler, in the vast kitchen thronged with maids washing dishes and scouring pans. It was an indication of how far religion had declined in Scotland. In former days in a household like this where the master's mother was dying every servant would have been dressed in black and there would have been frequent communal prayers. As it was these maids giggled when they saw the minister and one at least blew kisses.

The butler led the way through bare narrow corridors and then up steep stairs into the part of the house where the family lived, and where the corridors were wider and carpeted, with pictures on the walls. The staterooms were kept closed, so that Darroch would not get a chance to see himself and Eleanor in the painting on the ceiling.

"Lady Annie is at present asleep," Simmonds had said. "I have to take you to Sir James."

Sir James was alone in his smoking-room, seated in a leather arm-chair beside a huge fire, with a pipe in one hand and a glass of port in the other. A mastiff lay stretched out at his feet.

Usually Sir James had less to say than many men with estates a hundred times smaller than his. Some said this was because he was empty-headed, others that it was because he had been so often contradicted by his wife that he had long ago decided it was better to say nothing. Darroch though had always found him quite talkative.

85

He was about sixty, with a simpleton's face often twisted by grimaces of pain from gout.

"Sit down, Darroch," he said. "Thank you for coming so promptly, though it may be a while before you can see my mother. I think the doctor's given her too much laudanum. Fellow from Edinburgh. She's been having everybody up to see her, down to the newest stable-boy. My wife's not too pleased, but then my mother's always been more democratic. Here's an odd thing, Darroch. See if you can advise me. My mother says she doesn't want anybody to see her die. I've heard that elephants when they're old and know that they're going to die seek out solitude, but human beings aren't elephants, are they? They've got souls and that kind of thing. Phew, Captain, you're stinking." He kicked the big dog with his slippered foot. It opened its mouth in a yawn and went to sleep again.

"Your mother will not be alone, Sir James," said Darroch.

Sir James looked at him knowingly. "Are you saying my wife won't stay away?" he asked.

"I meant, Sir James, Our Lord will be with her at the end."

"I expect He will, Darroch, but she won't see Him so He won't count."

Darroch decided not to try and explain, to a maudlin baronet in a stuffy room with a dog exuding foul smells, how immeasurably Christ counted.

"You should have a glass of port, Darroch," said Sir James, "You look very pale. Usually you're such a pink little fellow."

"My wife and child are not well, Sir James."

"I hear she's with child again."

Darroch wondered who could have told him. It was supposed to be a family secret.

"Women get better, Darroch, or they don't. You would say it's in the hands of God. I hear that Jarvie, the fat minister, died this morning. He was a friend of yours, I believe."

"Yes, Sir James.'

"They say he had to be shoved up into his pulpit; got stuck in it once. Remarkable-looking woman, his wife. Black as a gipsy. Like Alexander up there."

Sir James pointed to the portrait above the fireplace of his

Covenanting ancestor Alexander Loudun, whose hair and moustache were black as jet and whose expression was fierce and haughty. In one hand he held a Bible, in the other a pistol. Bible and pistol now lay side by side on velvet cloth in a glass case in the great hall of the house. Sir Alexander had been killed at the Battle of Bothwell Brig, not many miles away. His Bible was stained with his blood.

"We should be glad we live in more enlightened times, Darroch," said Sir James.

"Yes, Sir James, though it is sad that religious faith is now so much weaker."

"Come now, Darroch, I just can't imagine you down on your knees praying for men that didn't agree with you to be killed. My mother may have laughed at you sometimes, Darroch, but she always liked you. It was your dimples, you know. She was greatly taken with your dimples. And why not? No point in a parson glowering like a Turk, is there? It's a pleasure in your church, Darroch, to look round at all the ladies smiling so happily. If it's your dimples that do it and not your sermons, what does that matter?"

He poured himself another glass of port and gave the dog another affectionate kick. "Just look at the history of the Kirk, Darroch. Not many smiles or dimples there. All those black-browed martyrs, Alexander among them. In the end what good did they do? Take Hackston of Rathilet. He was a guest in this house once. They say you can still hear him praying in the room he used. Look what happened to him. Tied to a horse, with his face to the tail, and led through the streets of Edinburgh by the hangman who carried Cameron's head on a pike. A boy came behind with another head in a sack. God knows whose it was. At the place of execution Hackston had both his hands chopped off, then he was hanged and beheaded and cut up into four pieces, like an animal's carcase. And all for nothing. If he and those like him had just swallowed their pride and submitted, as most sensible folk did, the times would have got better all the sooner. Times do get better, Darroch. Left to themselves people become more reasonable. Martyrs just hold things back. Today it's not so much religious martyrs that cause trouble, but political martyrs. There's a fellow been making seditious speeches to out-of-work weavers in Cadzow. I had to sign a warrant for his arrest. If he won't live in peace he has to be locked up. Better if he could be shipped off to Australia, to bother the kangaroos. If everyone acted sensible we'd all get on fine together. Isn't that so, Darroch?"

Yes, but people left to themselves could not be trusted to act sensibly. They acted selfishly, greedily, callously, and cruelly, as well as stupidly. Sir James himself would still have children of ten working in his coal mines if it had not been for philanthropic troublemakers like Lord Shaftesbury, and men and women would still be hanged for petty thefts but for reformers like Sir Samuel Romilly. It could well be that agitators like Jeremiah Taylor were needed in every generation if political freedoms were to be extended and social justice advanced.

Sir James was looking at him slyly. "They tell me, Darroch, you're a supporter of Chalmers and his crowd that want to put the Church before the State. That would be the surest way, you know, to weaken them both. That's what fellows like Taylor are waiting for. That's when he and his revolutionaries will step in and cut all our throats."

"Dr Chalmers is a very responsible citizen, Sir James. He is very much for the Establishment in all other respects. He believes that the Church must be free to conduct its own affairs."

"That's all very well, Darroch, but if everybody goes about demanding that kind of freedom there would be disorder, don't you think? I wouldn't like to see you leave Craignethan, Darroch, for I've got used to seeing you there, but if you fall in with Chalmers I'll have no option but to ask you to go. I'm a magistrate, you understand, with pledges to keep."

"I am well aware of the consequences, Sir James."

"You astonish me, Darroch. You don't look like someone who would rock the boat. Have you considered that you wouldn't just be leaving the kirk, you'd be leaving the kirkyard too? You've got children buried there. Well, what if the fellow who takes your place — you can be sure my wife's got someone

88

in mind — refused to let you put flowers on your children's grave? He'd have the right, you know."

Yes, Darroch had considered that; he had stood beside the grave, often, considering it.

Two sharp knocks were heard on the door. The mastiff shuddered: he knew whose hand made them. In came Lady Loudun, a tall thin stern-faced lady in a dark blue dress. She gave Darroch the usual frown of surprise, as if he ought not to be there but in the servants' hall.

"That dog, James," she said, with a sniff, "is disgusting."

"He's old, Grizel. Like ourselves."

"Don't dare compare me with that brute. She's gone, James. A few minutes ago, at twenty minutes to ten to be exact."

"Who's gone?"

"I thought so. You've been drinking too much. Your mother, James. She's passed on."

"Passed on?"

"Dead, James."

"In her sleep?"

"Her eyes were open but she had said nothing for the past hour. Yes, in her sleep."

"I hope she didn't see you, for I gave my word she would be alone."

"And you kept your word. I gave no such promise. I could not bear for the old lady to be alone at the end. It would not have been Christian. Would it, Mr Darroch? Now I think you should go up and see her and Mr Darroch can go home. By the way, Mr Darroch, your services will not be required at the funeral. This will take place at Cadzow Castle."

"She didn't care where she was buried," said Sir James, "but I expect they want to put her in their mausoleum. I'd prefer the kirkyard myself. I'd like a plaque in the kirk to commemorate her, Darroch. Could that be arranged?"

"Certainly it could be arranged," said his wife, "though it may not be Mr Darroch who will do it. I understand he has other plans."

She was letting Darroch know that if he and his family ended up in a cowshed she would think it was what he deserved.

He was tempted to tell her that if he wished he could have a grander church, a more comfortable manse, a more beautiful garden, and a much larger stipend. It would almost have been worth discarding his principles for the pleasure of seeing that smile of malice turn sour.

He must not be bitter or vainglorious.

"Would you like to see my mother, Darroch?" asked Sir James.

"I'm sure Mr Darroch wishes to get back home as soon as he can," said Lady Loudun. "Simmonds tells me it is raining quite hard."

"You can stay the night if you like, Darroch."

"Mr Darroch has a family waiting for him, James."

"Well, can't we send him home in a carriage?"

"It's pitch dark, James."

"You look worn out, Darroch. What you need is a good night's sleep. That should be easy for you, eh, with a conscience as clear as yours. There's your wife's illness, though. I hope she feels better soon. If it's raining really hard ask Simmonds to lend you one of the groom's capes. They're waterproof."

"Thank you, Sir James."

But when, a minute or so later, he was being let out at the great front door by Simmonds, stealthily, to save him a hundred yards walking in the rain, he did not mention the waterproof cape. He would welcome being soaked, as a symbolical washing away of all that day's sins.

CHAPTER 18

"I think I'll stay out for some fresh air," said Arthur, when the carriage was gone and Uncle Robert had returned into the house.

"In the rain?" asked James.

"It's not much."

James knew where Arthur was going. He had noticed him slipping the telescope into his pocket. Previously he had found this folly of his brother's amusing, but not tonight.

"Do you mind if I come with you?" he asked.

"I thought you hated getting wet."

"As you said it's not much."

"It could get heavier."

"In that case we'll both come home, won't we?"

"Please yourself."

Arthur led the way in the light rain through the wicket gate into the kirkyard and among the tombstones. In the distance a curlew called, and crows cawed in the nearby wood.

In the corner where they often held their discussions and where more than a hundred years ago nine Covenanters had been buried, Arthur stopped, with his back to the drystone dyke. Beyond it was Farmer Cuthbertson's field and beyond that again Arthur's Mecca, Mrs Wedderburn's house. It took an effort of will for him not to turn and gaze in that holy direction.

"Mother's going to die,' said James, quietly.

"You do not really believe that, James. If you did you would not have said it so coolly."

James then screamed, putting all his grief, rage, and frustration into it: "Mother's going to die."

Disturbed, the crows in their nests above cawed noisily.

"Have you gone mad?" asked Arthur.

"I looked in at her, Arthur. I thought she was already dead. Did you notice Mrs Barnes weeping?"

"I don't want to talk about it."

"*We're* still going to be alive. We've got to look after ourselves, and the girls."

"You don't care a button for the girls, James."

That was unfair and untrue. In his own way James loved his sisters, especially Mary.

"If Mother dies Uncle Robert will withdraw his offer of Glenquicken."

"She's not going to die."

"And if Father comes out with Dr Chalmers and has to leave Craignethan we'll have nowhere to go. Father seems to believe a miracle will happen. We've got to convince him that this offer of Glenquicken is the only miracle he can expect."

"I told you I don't want to talk about it."

James became angry. "Because you'd rather dream about Annabel's little white arse," he said.

"I should knock you down for saying that."

"Do you think I don't know where you're going, with that telescope in your pocket? I followed you once, you know."

"Liar. You're afraid of the dark, and of cows."

"I saw you climb into your tree. What would Uncle Robert say if I were to go to him and tell him that you were up a tree looking into Mrs Wedderburn's bedroom through a telescope, while Mother is dying?"

"You're a filthy-minded little sneak."

"What would he say, Arthur? What would Father say? What would Annabel herself say?"

"Do you think I care what anybody says? I love her. You don't know what love is, James."

"I know what it isn't. It isn't skulking up a tree in the dark, playing Peeping Tom and indulging in Onanistic practices."

"I should kill you for saying that."

"We should be talking about how to get Father to accept Uncle Robert's offer before it's withdrawn."

"These are trivial concerns."

"Trivial?"

"Materialistic and therefore trivial. Love transcends everything, James."

With that breath-taking absurdity, worthy of their Father himself, he climbed over the dyke and ran across the field.

James watched him till he was lost in the gloaming.

He was amazed at what had happened to his brother. Before this infatuation with Annabel Arthur had been clear-minded and witty about other people's follies, and indeed he still was; yet here he was, letting himself be foolishly and dangerously obsessed. All for nothing too. He must surely know that whoever was going to get the pleasure — if such it was — of fondling Annabel's bosom and bum it wasn't him. She might be hungry enough for such caresses, but from a man's hand, not a boy's.

If he fell out of the tree and broke his leg he could hardly plead that he had been studying birds or stars. The whole family would be involved in his disgrace.

Just as the whole family would have to share in the misery and hardships if Father lost kirk and manse, in the service of Christ, as he would claim. That seemed to James no less absurd than if Arthur were to claim that his spying on Annabel Wedderburn's nakedness was in Christ's service too.

Under his feet lay the bones of men who had been willing to kill other men and let themselves be killed, for Christ's sake. His blood turned cold as he imagined them still alive, leaning against this very dyke, groaning in pain, thinking of their families, and waiting for Claverhouse's dragoons to find them and finish them off. Had they reproached God for abandoning them to their cruel enemies? No, for being fanatics they would have had no difficulty in seeing their bloody defeat as a glorious victory. So too would Father acclaim it as a triumph if he was reduced to preaching to a handful of zealots like himself, in barns or fields.

If I had been alive then, thought James, I would not have

risked having my face slashed or my body maimed for a cause of such little moment as the preservation of the Presbyterian form of religion. On the contrary I would have been for the alliance of Church and State, although I would have stayed at home and let others shed blood for it. Father is fond of telling us that spiritual power is greater than physical power, but all history, and everyday experience, prove him wrong.

CHAPTER 19

Panting, Arthur waited in the beech wood next to Annabel's garden until it would be dark enough for him to climb over the fence and up the elm tree, without being seen. It was raining more heavily now, but it would not be the first time he had got sodden while keeping vigil: for that was how he saw it, though he knew the rest of the world would see it as James did. He had meant it when he said he loved her. If he did not why had her house become a shrine for him, and why was he able to look upon her naked body and feel only reverence?

She was only seven years older than he. If he worked very hard he could become an advocate in six years and then he could marry her. She would be thirty then, which was rather old, but she would still be beautiful and he would still love her. They would have a house in Edinburgh and entertain poets, musicians, painters, and lawyers, but not ministers. He had had a surfeit of those, Moderate and Evangelical.

Having been there so often in the dark he could have gone to the tree blindfolded, but he had to be very cautious, not because of Annabel's little Pomeranian dog, which seldom came out of doors, but because Mrs Maitland, Annabel's housekeeper, was more likely than not to be peering suspiciously out of one window or another. Children from the colliers' rows came at night to steal clothes off the line or apples off the tree.

There was no light yet in Annabel's window. He climbed up through the wet leaves to the place where he had a clear view and could sit for an hour or so before becoming too numbed and cramped. If he were to fall and break his leg, it would indeed be disastrous. Rather than be discovered lying there, and his purpose jaloused, and Annabel shamed, he would drag himself across the fields to the river and drown himself. But perhaps that would be unnecessarily drastic. It might be enough to crawl to the foot of some other tree that didn't have a view of her window.

He had come close to disaster once before, two years ago. One March morning he had not gone to church with the others because he had a sore throat. He had been left alone in the house with Mrs Meikle, then Jessie's wet-nurse, and eighteen-year-old Cissie, Bella's predecessor. He had been waiting for such an opportunity for months, though the sore throat was genuine. Plump and gallous, Cissie had often given him winks, which he had taken as allurements. Therefore that cold morning, when he heard her singing in his parents' room across the landing he had tiptoed there, clad only in his nightshirt. She was bending over the bed. As he had looked in at her he had heard, or was sure he did, psalm-singing from the church. It should have deterred him but it had the opposite effect. He rushed in and lifted up her skirts, exposing her fat white behind, for she was wearing no drawers. More startled than offended, she had turned and, paying him back, raised his nightshirt, revealing John Knox, as one of his schoolmates, also a minister's son, called it, ready to preach. Laughing, Cissie had grabbed it with her rough chilblained hand. The result was that John Knox had reached his peroration immediately, with the rest of the sermon still unsaid. More amused than angry, Cissie had wiped him with his own nightshirt, like a mother her child's nose.

A few weeks later it was discovered that Cissie was pregnant. Mother had instantly dismissed her. Arthur had been glad and yet sorry to see her go. He had offered her a little money he had saved up, partly as a bribe not to give him away and partly as a gift of gratitude for having kept John Knox out of the pulpit. She had refused it, saying his father had given her a year's wages. He had been annoyed with his father for this reckless generosity, for money was never plentiful in the manse, but he had been grudgingly proud of him too. His father did not let

96

inconvenience to other people keep him from performing Christian acts.

But it was not seemly for a knight keeping vigil on his lady to remember lustful escapades. He should be filling his mind with pure and noble thoughts. Unfortunately, those were much less easy to conjure up. Suddenly he was doing what he particularly did not want to do: he was remembering his mother. He had snarled at James for saying that she was going to die, but the rain pattering on the leaves all about him was now saying it. He felt cold, overwhelmed by sadness. In the dark wood lurked a beast called Death whom no knight could vanquish. It might at that very moment be devouring his mother, while he skulked in this tree; but even if he had been by her side, holding her hand, he could not have saved her.

Through tears he saw that the lamp in Annabel's room was now lit. Sometimes it was Mrs Maitland who lit it, and she always drew the curtains. Sometimes Annabel had little Maud with her, in which case she undressed behind a screen. Tonight she was alone. He felt very glad that she was safe from the beast.

She came over to the window and looked out. So powerful was the little telescope and so close the tree to the house, that he could see her tongue as she yawned.

There had been occasions when, having removed her dress and petticoats, she had put on her nightdress and then, under its cover, removed her bodice and drawers. There had been other occasions when, with a lack of modesty just as baffling, she had flung off every stitch of clothing and danced about the room in a frenzy almost. Once she had picked up a bolster and embraced it passionately, as if it were a lover.

Tonight with her clothes on she sat in a chair and read a book. She read it for almost an hour. Then, yawning again, she tossed the book aside and began to undress, with her back to the window. Soon he was seeing what James in his viciousness had called "her little white arse", and which indeed was little and white, but also chaste and beautiful. Within a minute she had her nightdress on and the lamp out.

Arthur then realised he was so stiff and sore, and so bedraggled, that it was going to be a labour getting back home

97

where, if James had carried out his threat to clype, Uncle Robert would be waiting to castigate him, or worse, far worse, his mother might already be dead.

CHAPTER 20

Though Darroch kept shivering and was more and more discomforted especially about the legs, he congratulated himself that this was indeed a thorough lustration. He even sang a snatch or two of grateful psalm. Nonetheless, after nearly an hour's stifflegged walking, he was very glad to reach the manse.

He did not see the person waiting at the gate in the shelter of the rowan tree, until he spoke: "Good evening, Mr Darroch. A nasty night."

It was Taylor, the radical.

He was remarkably cheerful, considering that he too was soaked and was a fugitive from the law, with nowhere to lay his head.

Darroch could not very well agree that the night was nasty, so he said, 'Good evening, Mr Taylor. I thought you would be safely back in Glasgow."

"I wanted to see you, Mr Darroch. I have a favour to ask."

"A favour?"

Darroch could not show favour to a hunted criminal. It would make him a criminal too.

"Not for myself, Mr Darroch. For Mrs Cooper."

"Mrs Cooper?"

"You may have heard of her. She's in Cadzow Jail."

"The woman who killed her own child?"

"That's the one."

There at the gate of the manse Taylor was almost his guest. He should at least be offered shelter from the rain. Darroch himself, the insides of whose thighs were becoming sorely chapped, must take care not to catch a cold, with the greatest challenge of his career to be confronted in two weeks' time. He could not invite Taylor into the manse: that would be tantamount to harbouring him; or even let him shelter in the stables, for though they were large enough for three horses and there was only one they were still part of the manse premises. There was however the kirk. Churches once had been sanctuary even for murderers. This man's crime was being too outspoken in his pity for the poor and oppressed. There could be no harm, in Christ's eyes at any rate, in allowing him to rest in the church for an hour or two till the rain lightened.

"I am very sorry, Mr Taylor, that I cannot offer you the hospitality of my house."

"I would not accept it, Mr Darroch. I don't want to get you into trouble."

"Thank you, Mr Taylor. I see no reason however why you should not take shelter in the church."

Taylor laughed. "I had the same idea myself, but the door's locked."

"The main door is, but not the small side door."

"I didn't think of trying the side door. Most churches are kept locked up like jails."

"Not Craignethan. Anyone who wishes may go in at any time to pray. What is the favour Mrs Cooper wants of me?"

"She wants you to go and help her to pray."

"I? I did not know she had ever heard of me."

"You are too modest, Mr Darroch. You have uplifted more hearts in Cadzow than you know of. Don't ask me how, but I got a message smuggled out from her. As you would expect she's greatly vexed in her mind."

"Poor woman!"

"There you are, you see, that's why she wants you. Not many ministers, especially soaked to the skin and with their teeth chittering, would have spoken of a murderess with sympathy."

"Mr Saunders of St John's is the prison chaplain. Has she not asked him to help her?"

"She's afraid of him. She's afraid of everybody and

everything. Except you, it seems. That in itself should get you into heaven, Mr Darroch."

"Was Mr Syme, landlord of the inn, speaking the truth when he said you were an atheist?"

"Let me put it this way: I've got too much respect for God to believe in Him."

"I do not understand, Mr Taylor."

"Never mind. Just my little joke."

"He also said you have children, Mr Taylor."

"Three. Two boys and a girl. The oldest fourteen and the youngest nine."

"I hope they are all well. My own little girl Jessie is ill."

"I'm very sorry to hear that, Mr Darroch. I heard Mrs Darroch is badly too. You have enough troubles of your own without taking on other peoples'."

"No, no. I shall certainly go and see poor Mrs Cooper as soon as I can. I would offer you food and drink, Mr Taylor, but I am not heroic. I have six other children besides the one who is ill. Hostages to fortune, Mr Taylor."

"You *are* heroic, Mr Darroch, and I am proud to have met you. Don't worry about me. I shall be on my way by first light."

"I should warn you that Mr Runcie, the church officer, looks in every morning on his way to Cadzow. He is also a special constable."

"At what time does he look in?"

"About half-past six, I believe. He carries a club. He is always expecting to find trespassers."

"I shall be well on my way before Mr Runcie arrives with his cudgel."

"If you come with me, Mr Taylor, I shall show you a short cut."

They went quietly through the manse garden to the wicket gate.

"Thank you again, Mr Darroch," said Taylor. "Good night."

"Good night, Mr Taylor. God bless you."

Taylor laughed, but not cynically, as he went into the kirkyard.

Darroch had no sooner stepped dripping into the manse hallway, where a lamp was burning, when Mrs Barnes appeared on the stairs, wearing a blue dressing-gown and a white nightdress. Both, he could not help noticing, were clean, as were her ankles, which were also neat.

She came down to him, smelling fragrantly.

"How are they both?" he asked hoarsely.

"Mrs Darroch is still asleep," she whispered, "and so is Jessie. The crisis that Dr Fairbairn spoke of I think is safely past. She is not so flushed and is breathing more easily.

"Thank God."

"I have been thanking Him this past hour. Come. You must take those wet clothes off or you will be the next to be ill. I have a fire burning in your room. I shall prepare some hot milk."

"Thank you, Mrs Barnes." She was indeed an estimable woman.

"Shall I go up and see Margaret?"

"She is asleep. You must take care of your own health."

"Yes. Thank you, Mrs Barnes."

The room was warm. The fire burned brightly. There was a fresh towel. He could hear Mrs Barnes in the kitchen heating up the milk.

He undressed. He was wet through to the skin. Fits of shivering made it difficult for him to dry himself. His teeth chittered. What if he were to die, with his great qualities unrealised? He felt terror.

Mrs Barnes came in, carrying a tray on which was a cup of hot milk. Putting this down she gathered up his sodden clothes and took them away. Moments later she was back. Modestly but thoroughly she began to dry him.

He had always thought of her as representing the world of coal scuttles which had to be filled, chamber-pots which had to be emptied, pulleys which had to be hoisted, pots which had to be lifted from hob to sink, and tables which had to be laid. Had he been underestimating her? There was a beauty in her humble devotion that showed that she, rather than Eleanor, might be his true Leah.

He was still shivering. It was not now entirely caused by cold.

She helped him put on his nightshirt. Stiffly he climbed into bed.

In a moment, her nightdress off, she was in beside him, enfolding him in her arms and pressing her soft warm body against his. Never had her face been more plain, indeed more ugly, because of the desperation on it. His own, no doubt showing shock, whatever else, was wet with her tears.

She tried, as Leah might have, gently and reverentially, to rouse him. Why she failed, whether it was because that part of him too was exhausted by the walk in the pouring rain or he had been emotionally drained by Eleanor that morning, he could not have said. He remained soft and lax as a child of three; more so indeed, for once in the back streets of Cadzow, he had seen a child of that age in his mother's arms, stiff as a stick.

Sobbing, she comforted him. He had had too much trouble. When they were man and wife it would be different. Then their love would be successful and joyous, as the Lord had intended it to be. Otherwise would He have given them their beautiful bodies?

She got out of bed, tidied the blankets, put on her nightdress, and handed him the cup of milk.

"Drink it and then sleep, my dearie," she murmured. "Jessie will see to everything."

She had to go to her own room to see that Baby Matthew in his cot there was safely asleep. Then she would go upstairs and keep watch on poor Margaret. Whatever happened she would cope with it on his behalf. In her own eyes she was now as good as his wife. She had Margaret's blessing and therefore the Lord's too.

CHAPTER 21

Every weekday morning on his way to his business in Cadzow, at first light, in the smart gig made by his own hands, greybearded Archie Runcie, master joiner, church officer, and special constable, stopped at the kirk and looked in to see if it had been used as a dosshouse and lavatory during the night by beggars or tinkers or worst of all by vagrant Irish Papists, who, like dogs, shat in any corner. He had spoken up strongly at kirk sessions against the side door being left unlocked, in accordance with Mr Darroch's new-fangled idea.

The minister had told him, as if it were a thing to be praised, that in Papist countries like Spain and Italy churches were always kept open, so that worshippers could go in at any time of the day or night, either to pray or just to sit in the holy silence. Archie had wanted to know if nobody there had work to go to. He had asked, too, when were those churches scrubbed out and how were they kept clean. But then if they were filthy it wouldn't matter to Papists, who, judging from the few in the district, were the poorest of the poor and the lowest of the low. In Craignethan kirk there might be no fancy altars or statues, but a body could take his meat off the floor.

Mr Darroch had other dangerous ideas: he had a hankering for organ music and coloured windows. Luckily there were still among his congregation plenty of old-fashioned Presbyterians to prevent such abominations. From the beginning, from before the beginning really because they had voted against accepting him, Archie and his friends had not been happy with the minister. Even when fresh out of College, Presbyterian ministers ought not to be sweet smilers, and when denouncing sinners they ought to make it sound that they would have relished watching them roast in Hell. Mr Darroch sounded as if he would have liked to join them in the flames so that he could hold their hands. He had always been too fond of holding hands, especially young women's. When conducting examinations in the catechism he did not, as he should, pour scorn on blunderers and tongue-tied defaulters; instead he spoke kindly to them and stroked their hands, particularly if they were blushing lassies. Archie's deceased spouse, Nellie, had once scandalised him by casting up that if he were to try to delight her soul before climbing on top of her perhaps she would conceive. Like Mr Darroch, she had brazenly added. It was above all that delighting of women's souls that made Archie distrust the minister. It was a gift more likely to come from the Devil than from the Lord.

They were saying that Darroch was on the side of Dr Chalmers in the present dispute in the Kirk, like Archie himself, but Archie doubted it. He had once let the minister know that if a new kirk and manse had to be built he would give his services free, and there were others who would do likewise, including Archie's friend, Andrew Sillars, a building contractor. Darroch had been lukewarm in his appreciation. Archie suspected that he, and Andrew, and others he could name were too fierce on sinners and backsliders for the minister's taste.

Catching sight of the manse in the distance, on top of the brae, against the pink sky, Archie's scowl changed to a smile, though, as Nellie had often said, there was little difference. There lived the woman who was to be the second Mrs Runcie: Jessie Barnes, the minister's housekeeper. She wasn't nearly as bonny as Nellie had been, but all the better for that. Nellie had thought her bonniness gave her privileges. There was no more sensible and serviceable a woman in Scotland than Jessie. As a joiner's daughter she was especially suitable. At thirty-six she was just the right age, still able to give him a son to carry on his name and inherit his business — at fifty-six he was not too old to father one — but not young enough to give him cause for jealousy. He had already asked her and she had refused, but he would ask her again soon and this time she would accept. She would be glad to leave the manse where she was overworked, having to look after the children as well as run the house. She would make an excellent mistress of Hebron Cottage, with its much admired furniture made by himself and its prolific apple trees.

Such were his thoughts that May morning as, with baton in hand, he walked cautiously up the path through the field in front of the kirk, where, when it was Craignethan's turn, the inter-parish communion gatherings were held, with hundreds attending. That morning there were only a few finches to be seen. After last night's heavy rain the path was muddy and the grass wet. The sun shone on the gravestones, among them his Nellie's. He had used to stop beside it for a minute or two, removing dead leaves and crows' droppings, but he had given this up. After a while a good Presbyterian left the dead to God.

He always went in by the front door, which was inches thick and fortified with iron bars. The kirk's windows too were so small and narrow that not even a child could squeeze through. Small wonder it had once been used as a prison. After the Battle of Bothwell Brig Bluidy Clavers and his butchers had rounded up fleeing Covenanters and imprisoned them here. Some had died and been buried in the kirkyard. There were marks on the walls inside and out where bullets had struck. Archie did not really envy those martyrs their wounds and painful deaths, but he did envy them their place in heaven high up the Lord's table.

Inside the church he walked carefully, for he was wearing his working boots with tackets in them. He was sure that one morning he would surprise a squad of skinny Irish brats camping there. He would greatly enjoy driving them out, with some good hard blows.

Baton at the ready, he walked down the aisle, looking into every pew. He always looked with greatest interest into the laird's enclosure at the front, ever since the Monday morning when he had found a guinea there which must have fallen from Sir James's pocket when the baronet pulled out his handkerchief to blow his nose.

That morning he got a greater shock than that of espying a gold guinea. A grey-haired man was asleep there, stretched out on the laird's bench and covered with the laird's wife's flannel hap.

Archie knew who he was. He had seen him in Cadzow. He was wanted by the police. A reward was offered to anyone who helped to have him arrested. Here then was not one guinea, but twenty.

Stealthily, so as not to waken this desperate but profitable rogue, Archie made his way out of the kirk, locking the front door behind him, and then rushed round to the side door to lock it with the key which he always carried just in case.

Louping over flat gravestones and some low vertical ones too he raced down the path towards his gig, and in a minute was galloping past the manse on his way to Cadzow to fetch policemen.

He did not notice Arthur Darroch come running out of the manse, waving and shouting. Nor did he see him sit down on the manse steps and cover his face with his hands.

CHAPTER 22

Shortly after five, while it was still dark, Mrs Barnes, lying beside her mistress, awoke suddenly, aware that something was wrong. She heard Jessie's breathing and her own, but no one else's. She turned her head and saw that she was now the minister's wife, though no ceremony had yet taken place: the first Mrs Darroch was dead. Mrs Barnes lifted the bedclothes to see if there had been a gush of blood, but there had been no miscarriage: the poor lady's heart must have stopped while she slept.

Mrs Barnes got up, as carefully as if the woman beside her were only asleep. She put on her robe and went over to look at Jessie. She felt the little girl's brow. It was not nearly so hot. The crisis was safely passed. Jessie was going to live. Indeed, she opened her eyes and, recognising Mrs Barnes, smiled.

The Lord had shown some mercy.

Jessie could not be left in the room with her dead mother.

Wrapping her in a blanket Mrs Barnes picked her up and carried her downstairs. She was taking her to her father.

He was still asleep. In the dim light she looked at him with new eyes, for she was now his wife. She crouched beside him. "George, my love," she whispered, laying a finger on his lips.

He awoke with a start. "What's the matter, Mrs Barnes?"

"It is Jessie, my love. Here is another Jessie, well again, thank God."

She laid the child, asleep again, beside him. He looked as wistful and perplexed as a child himself.

"Margaret is dead," she murmured. "She passed away in her sleep."

He got up, sobbing and shuddering. She helped him on with his dressing-gown and then, kneeling, with his slippers.

She held him close and said, in a voice full of love but also very determined: "After what happened last night, George, we are now husband and wife, in God's eyes. We shall wait then we shall be married. That is what Margaret wanted."

His answer was a heavy sigh. It would not do.

"Is that agreed, George?"

He sighed again and nodded.

"You must say it."

"It is agreed."

She was not satisfied. "Say that we are now husband and wife."

"We are now husband and wife."

She kissed him, glanced to see that Jessie was asleep, and then they went out together to break the news to the rest of the family.

"I shall tell the girls," she said. "You tell Arthur and James, and Mr Drummond."

They went first to see the dead woman. When he drew aside the sheet he groaned and wept.

"She was a good, faithful wife," he wailed.

Afraid that he was going to indulge himself in an extravagance of grief, not opportune then, she spoke firmly. "You must be brave, George, for the children's sakes. Agnes's especially. You know how hysterical she gets."

"I did not know she was so ill," he said, weeping more quietly.

It had been obvious to everyone else, but she said nothing. Later she would have many opportunities to cure him of his little self-deceptions.

Arthur and James slept in a room on that landing.

"They will be asleep", he said. "Should I waken them with such dreadful news?"

"We cannot sit and wait till they waken. They must be told now."

"Very well. Shall I tell the boys first?"

"Yes. They are her sons."

She left him knocking on their door, while she went upstairs. The door of Mary's room opened and Mr Drummond appeared, wearing a nightcap. He often complained the manse was draughty.

"Is there anything wrong, Mrs Barnes?" he asked.

She wept then, and there was no design or hypocrisy in her weeping. "Your sister is dead, Mr Drummond."

He closed his eyes, in prayer, she thought. She could never have guessed that he was wishing he was a soldier or a farmer, and not a clergyman. Then his grief for his sister could have been more natural, spontaneous, honest, and manly.

"Thank you, Mrs Barnes. I think I was expecting it. I shall put on some clothes and come down. Are you going to tell the girls?"

"Yes, but I think now I should wait till they waken."

"That would be best. Time enough then. How is Jessie?"

"She has recovered. She is going to be well."

"Thank God for that." Though it would mean seven motherless children, not six.

He went back into the room while she went downstairs again.

Arthur and James were in their mother's room. Very soon their uncle joined them.

Arthur was dry-eyed and sullen. Drummond understood. James was weeping. Drummond understood that too. He loved both his nephews then.

He looked down at his sister. Again he felt inhibited by his calling not from feeling, but from expressing, human grief unadulterated by professional religious consolations. He did not believe in an after-life, at any rate not in one where terrestial relationships would be resumed. He would never see Margaret again, but he must pretend he would. He had once taken part in a debate at university on the theme that tragedy and Christianity were irreconcilable. As a divinity student he had been asked to speak against the proposition and he had done so cleverly; but he had felt then, as he was doing now, that they *were* irreconcilable, and because his sister's loss to him was tragic he could not therefore be a Christian, as Dr Cook understood the term, and Dr Chalmers, and George Darroch.

He went to speak to George and found him already wearing the obligatory mask of Christian acceptance and resignation, which would in due time be replaced by that of Christian consolation, which would announce to the world how happy he was that his wife had exchanged the tribulations of human existence for the bliss of heaven.

Drummond told himself not to be so mean-spirited. Was it envy of George's simple faith?

"Well, George, I'm very sorry," he said.

"It is a great and sudden loss, Robert."

Not so sudden, thought Drummond. You should have seen it coming years ago. You helped to kill her with your blindness and lack of consideration. Aloud he said, trying to be generous, "I'll go home today, George. Bessie and I shall return for the funeral. The offer of Glenquicken still holds. I'm sure Sir Thomas will understand. Meg knew that she might not be spared to enjoy a new and happier life there, but she wanted it for her children, and so do I. I should think all of you would be glad to be quit of this place where you have had little luck and much misfortune."

"Thank God Jessie is better."

"Thank God indeed. You will require someone to help you look after your little girls, some good, kind, dependable woman. May I take the liberty of pointing out that you do not have far to look. I want to tell you, George, that I would have no objections, and neither would Sir Thomas and Lady Blaikie, if, after a proper interval, you were to marry Mrs Barnes. She may not be a lady, but she is something rather better and rarer, a woman who would devote her life to looking after another woman's children. I have seen how your girls like and trust her. She would make you an excellent wife too. It seems to me there could be no better arrangement."

"I believe Mr Runcie, the church officer, intends to marry her."

111

That was said in a peculiar small distorted voice. Perhaps grief was the cause.

"Has he asked her? And has she consented?"

"I understand there is an agreement between them."

Drummond was disappointed. "Well, if this is so it is a great pity. You will not easily find another woman willing to take care of four little girls, one an imbecile, and a babe of eleven months in addition. No servant would do it, not for ten times the wages you could pay her."

"Mr Runcie will be passing the manse at any moment on his way to Cadzow."

"What about it?"

"Nothing, Robert. I am not thinking clearly."

Drummond himself had a clear thought. "He could take me into Cadzow and let me catch the early coach to Glasgow."

"Tell Arthur. He may be in time to intercept him."

Drummond hurried off, while Darroch sat staring at his face in the mirror. He saw on it an expression of guile he had never noticed before. But then he had never been a vulnerable widower before. He had not quite lied about Mrs Barnes and Archibald Runcie, but he had not spoken the whole truth either. Runcie had asked her to marry him and she had turned him down, very definitely; but if she were compelled to leave the minister's service since many people would think it improper for her to continue as his housekeeper, being younger than himself, she might well change her mind and have Runcie who, though a bigot and something of a miser, owned a prosperous business and a fine house.

She, and Margaret too, had been at fault in trying to trap him, for that surely was their intention. Now Robert too had joined the plot. He must be free to choose for himself. Robert had been too pessimistic. Mrs Wedderburn for instance loved the girls and would take care of them, and would be honoured to be his wife. There were others too he could have named, young, pretty, and willing, and others more at Glenquicken. As minister there, with £400 per annum he could afford to employ sufficient servants.

On the other hand he must not be too hasty in rejecting Mrs

112

Barnes. Last night he had been too tired and bewildered to be fully aware of what was going on, but it had been pleasurable at the time and still was in retrospect. Moreover, if he stood by his principles and walked out of the Established Church, and of Craignethan manse, Mrs Barnes might then become indispensable. She could make a home out of a cowshed.

Away at the back of his mind flickered another thought: there was always Eleanor and Italy.

Then he heard what he had been dreading. Agnes screamed and went on screaming. She had been told her mother was dead. He heard too Mrs Barnes comforting her, in a voice gone strangely deep with love and pity.

CHAPTER 23

Runcie brought back with him in his gig the sergeant of police. Behind came a carriage drawn by two horses; in it were six stalwart policemen, armed with batons.

They stopped at the manse. The sergeant thought the minister should be told about what was happening in his kirk. There was no great hurry. Taylor wasn't going anywhere, but just in case the constables were instructed to take up positions surrounding the kirk and reminded to be respectful of the graves.

Then the sergeant and Runcie, hats in hand, knocked on the manse door.

It was Mrs Barnes who came, with the minister's baby in her arms. Already pleased with himself Runcie imagined her at his own door with his own son in her arms and was still more pleased. Her face did not light up at seeing him but then the wean was greeting.

"What is it?" she asked.

"I'd like a word wi' the minister," said the sergeant.

"He's in no state of mind to speak to anyone. His wife died during the night."

"I'm very sorry to hear that," said the sergeant, sincerely.

"That was gey sudden," mumbled Runcie, wondering if it made her more or less likely to want to marry him. More, he thought.

"We'd best not be bothering him then," said the sergeant.

"What do you want anyway?"

"Who is it, Mrs Barnes? asked a man's voice too deep to be the minister's.

"It's a police sergeant and Mr Runcie, Mr Drummond," she replied. "They want to speak to Mr Darroch."

This would be the good-brother from Edinburgh, thought Runcie, the one with the big kirk. He was Runcie's kind of minister, big, strong, heavy-faced, and glowering.

"I'll deal with them, Mrs Barnes," he said.

She took herself off with the baby, like the obedient creature she was. Nellie would have wanted to poke her nose in.

"Well, gentlemen, what is the matter?" asked Drummond. "As Mrs Barnes has told you there has been a bereavement in the house. My sister is dead."

"If we'd kent that sir, we wouldn't hae come to the door," said the sergeant.

"Well, you're here now. What is it you want?"

"I thocht I should let the minister ken we've got Jerry Taylor the radical locked up in the kirk."

"The impudent rogue was sleeping there when I looked in this morning," said Runcie. "So I locked the doors and brought the police."

"How did he get in?"

"Weel, you see, Mr Darroch won't have the side door locked. He says folk should be able to gang in ony time they feel like it to pray or just sit doon. And see whit happens!"

"I don't expect much trouble, sir," said the sergeant. "He'll come quietly when he sees there are seven o' us."

"Seven should be plenty. He's not a young man."

"Hae we your permission to proceed, sir?"

"Yes, sergeant. Do your duty. I'll let Mr Darroch know. Then I may come and see how you are getting on."

The sergeant and Runcie then went through the wicket gate into the kirkyard.

Drummond found his brother-in-law in his study reading the Bible. At any rate he had it open. He was still unshaven and red-eyed.

"Who was at the door, Robert?" he asked.

"A sergeant of police and Mr Runcie. It seems that Taylor the

115

seditionist took shelter in your kirk last night. Mr Runcie found him there this morning, still asleep, so he locked the doors and fetched the police. A resourceful and responsible citizen, Mr Runcie. Mrs Barnes will do well to have him."

The news had an odd effect on George. First he jumped to his feet with a cry of dismay, as if he were about to dash off and rescue Taylor from the clutches of the law, in melodramatic fashion. Then he sat down again as if he had thought better of it and was not going to talk nonsense about his kirk being a sanctuary.

"I think I shall go and see what happens," said Drummond. "I would like to see the look on Taylor's face."

George said nothing, but there was a queer look on his.

Drummond found his nephews outside, on their way to the kirk to watch.

The sergeant and Runcie were conferring as to the best way of going in and seizing the criminal, if he was not prepared to come out willingly. The sergeant wanted if possible to avoid a scuffle inside the church. Perhaps, he said, if Jerry was told about Mrs Darroch's death he would show respect and leave quietly. He wasn't really a bad fellow at heart. Runcie differed. He said he wouldn't be surprised if Taylor set the kirk on fire, out of atheistic spite.

The policemen stood chatting and yawning among the graves. This was an earlier start to the day's work than they were used to. They would, thought Drummond, take it out on Taylor, especially if he put up a fight. He would be lucky not to be black and blue all over by the time they got him to jail. It served him right.

Drummond and his nephews watched from behind the big yew tree.

"I hope he gets away," said Arthur. "He's like a lion cornered by jackals."

"I hope he gets twenty years in prison," said James, "or transported for life."

116

"Why, is society so perfect that no one is allowed to criticise it?"

"He wants to destroy it."

"He does not. He wants to make it more just."

"Have you heard him speaking?" asked Drummond.

"Yes, in Cadzow," replied Arthur. "What's wrong with saying every man in the country should have a vote?"

"Colliers too?" said James, with a sneer. "Who can't read or write? And those drunken creatures you can see any day in Cadzow?"

"Everybody is entitled to an education," said Arthur. "He said that too."

"What do you think, Uncle Robert?" asked James.

Arthur was generous and hopeful, as the young should be, James hard and bitter, as the young ought not to be. But Drummond agreed with James. Radicals like Taylor were dangerous. Universal franchise was an absurdity.

"Look, they're going in," said James. "By the side door."

Probably that door had been chosen because it was narrow and not so easy for Taylor to make a bolt through it. Two men were left guarding it, while the four others, the biggest plus the sergeant, cautiously entered the church.

Runcie stood a good way off.

At least, thought Drummond, as he listened to a lark, it is keeping our minds off Meg's death. Looking towards the manse he saw George come out and walk slowly towards the kirk.

It was not possible to tell if there was a struggle going on. The walls of the church were too thick. But judging by the time it was taking to bring him out Taylor must be resisting.

Darroch joined his sons and brother-in-law.

"Have they gone in to arrest him?" he asked.

"Yes, George."

"I hope they do not use violence."

"I would say that would depend on whether or not he gives them trouble."

"Perhaps I should go in and remind them that they are in God's house."

"I doubt if they need reminding, George."

117

Yet did it look like God's house? Outside and in every effort had been made to keep it from having grace and beauty. It must many times have crushed George's romantic heart. Exposed too, and surrounded by sodden, illkept fields. Poor Meg's spirit would not be happy here.

At last, feet chained together and hands manacled behind his back, Taylor was dragged out. One of the policemen from behind struck him on the leg with a baton, another punched him in the back. They were elated and vengeful. Taylor's face was bleeding. It would have been satisfactory, thought Drummond, if he had cringed and been cowed but it was not so. He kept his dignity. His persecutors had none.

Captors and captive waited among the graves, resting and recovering their breath.

Suddenly George ran towards them, stumbling over gravestones and holding up his hand in an ambiguous gesture.

He went right up to Taylor.

They stood staring at each other.

"They tell me your wife died during the night, Mr Darroch," said Taylor. "If it is true I am very sorry indeed."

"Yes, it is true. I am sorry to see you in such trouble, Mr Taylor."

"My ain fault, Mr Darroch. Nobody to blame but myself. I slept too long. It's not that the bed was all that soft, mind you."

Was there, wondered Drummond, something between them? Did they know each other better than George had let on yesterday in the inn?

"I would be much obliged, sergeant," said George, in a trembling voice, "if there was no more violence. Remember we are all Christian men."

"He's nae Christian, sir. He's a self-professed atheist."

"But *we* are Christians, commanded by Our Lord to show compassion."

"Scarcely to the likes o' him, sir. He's got freen's wad cut oor throats as soon as look at us."

Then George, the actor, seeing that the moment was right, performed his masterstroke. He stepped forward and wiped the blood off Taylor's face.

118

Robert despised him for it and yet was moved. Even the most brutal-looking policemen looked ashamed.

Then they made off with their prisoner. Taylor was no longer kicked and punched, at least not while he was in view. When they got him into the carriage they would make up for it. George, wishing to spare him, had earned him heavier blows.

"Well done, Father," said Arthur.

James did not think it well done.

Sir Thomas Blaikie would have agreed with James. He hated and feared revolutionaries and would have had them all hanged. It would be better if he never heard about this little incident.

PART TWO

CHAPTER 1

In the Presbyterian Kirk of Scotland, as Andrew Melville reminded King James VI, every man was equal in the sight of God. Therefore in Craignethan Parish Church no place was specially reserved, except of course for the chief heritor. It was only natural however that the families of substance, without whose contributions there would be no Church Sustentation Fund or Poor Law Fund, should be privileged to occupy the pews at the front. Also Farmer Cuthbertson's cowmen and pigmen knew without having to be told that it would have been insolent on their part to usurp the seats claimed every Sunday by their master and his family. It was the same with all other employers and employees. In any case the elders on duty at the door would have seen to it that no man entered ahead of his social superiors, even if the latter were late. Sometimes the whole congregation was kept waiting in the rain until Sir James and Lady Loudun arrived.

In a parish where only the laird had a title and lands extensive enough to be called an estate, the profitableness of a man's business or the smallness of his wage was the criterion by which his place in society and therefore in the kirk was decided. No arbiter was needed. It was known instinctively who should precede whom.

The pews were divided by a central aisle. Those on the right, as seen from the minister's pulpit, were the preserve of worshippers either in the direct employ of Sir James or economically dependent on him. Foremost among them was

Mr Mitchell, Sir James's chief factor, a lawyer with offices in Cadzow and a house on the estate. Next came the tenant farmers, headed by Mr Cuthbertson who managed the Home Farm; then officials of Sir James's four coal mines; then a few shopkeepers, such as Mr Pendreich, grocer and wine merchant, whose shops were in Cadzow but whose houses were in Craignethan parish; then the senior servants from the Big House; and finally a miscellany of subordinates.

Like Sir James they were all Tories in politics and Moderates in religion.

Those on the left were Whiggish and Evangelical. They were mainly merchants and tradesmen who, though far from revolutionary in their thinking, nonetheless believed that they should have more influence not only in the parish and the county but in the whole country, for its prosperity was derived more from their endeavours than from the landed gentry's. This was not to say that they had adopted the doctrine of social equality. Towards their employees they were patriarchally strict, and towards sinners, particularly adulterers and fornicators, harsh and unforgiving. Their leaders were Mr Sillars, a builder, and Mr Harkness, a coal merchant. Among them sat, never quite at ease, several men who owned small farms or holdings.

In a special pew at the front, against the wall, sat Mr Crawford, the precentor. He was also the school dominie.

The church being small there was not a seat for everyone, though everyone was obliged to attend. The lowliest farmhands and the most menial servants had to stand at the back, though services lasted at least two hours. Places empty because the usual occupants were absent could not be taken by persons of inferior grade.

On Sunday morning, 7th May, no women and children were present. The previous Sunday the minister had announced that this would not be an ordinary service but would take the form of an address by him on the subject of the great dispute then dividing the Church.

It had been taken for granted that the ladies would not be interested.

Sir James was absent, owing to his mother's death. Mr Mitchell, as his representative, sat in his enclosure.

In his dual role of chief factor for the estate and leading elder of the church Mr Mitchell, accompanied by his wife and three grown-up daughters, had paid a visit to the manse yesterday afternoon, to convey his condolences and also to find out if the minister intended to go ahead with his long-deferred statement. He had been informed that the minister, though stunned with grief, did so intend.

As was his duty Archibald Runcie conducted the minister to the foot of the pulpit steps. Some of those at the back grinned at one another. Their joke was that church officers had to do this for some ministers who were still too dizzy after last night's debauch to know where the steps were, and Runcie had to do it for Darroch who might not have the strength to climb the steps after all the houghmagandie he'd been up during the week. That his wife had died as a result of it caused some grins, Saidler's and his cronies', to be broader than usual.

Pale and calm, Darroch spoke in a clear brave voice. "Let us pray for God's guidance."

As he prayed he noticed that men were standing at the back though there were many empty places.

As soon as the prayer was finished he suggested that everyone should be seated.

Mr Harkness, white-haired coal-merchant, stood up. "First of a', Mr Darroch, on behalf of myself, and my family, and everybody in the kirk, I wad like to say hoo grieved we a' are at Mrs Darroch's daith. She was a kind, gentle lady who will be much missed." He paused, and then went on in a more business-like voice. "Some of us, on this side and I daursay on the ither side tae, think that the maist sensible thing wad be for them standing to be excused and sent hame. No' to beat aboot the bush, the maitters to be discussed don't concern them."

"Surely they concern every member of the church, Mr Harkness."

"That is true, minister, but they are no', in the full sense o' the word, members. They attend worship, as they should, but they tak nae pairt in the management o' the kirk, and they mak nae

125

payments towards its upkeep. I wad like to hear Mr Mitchell's opeenion."

Mr Mitchell stood up. He was a tall solemn man, with a gleaming brow and white beard. He never used Scotch words. "I concur with Mr Harness," he said. "I have Sir James's authority..."

He was interrupted by a voice a good deal louder than his own. Wild eyes, shaggy hair, agitated brawny fists, and a corpse-like hollowness of cheeks, went with it. This was Jonas Galloway, a tender of pigs who lived in a hovel little better than a sty. He had eight children, often sent home from school for being smelly and having lice in their hair. He was a kind of man not uncommon in Scotland but hard to find anywhere else in Christendom. In spite of his poverty and lack of education, and the din that must have gone on in his house, from pigs and children, he read the Bible more diligently than many a professor of divinity in the quiet of a university library. Unfortunately he was given to quoting it, often with daft irrelevance. As indeed he did now. "In the reign of King Jehoash, when the Lord's house was to be repaired it was proclaimed that no bowls of silver, no snufflers, no basons, nor trumpets, nor any vessels of gold or silver, were to be bought with the money given for the repair of those breaches. That money was to be given to the masons and hewers of stone and the carpenters who carried out the work of the repairs."

By no means for the first time Darroch courteously interpreted. "I suppose you mean, Mr Galloway, that every man, whatever his capacity, has a right to play his part in attempting to repair the great breach now threatened in the Kirk. That is my view too."

Alas, Galloway could not leave well alone. "Saith the Lord," he now bellowed, "whatsoever man that hath a blemish he shall not approach: a blind man or a lame or he that hath a flat nose or anything superfluous. Or a man that is broken-footed or broken-handed. Or crookbacked or a dwarf or that hath a blemish in his eye, or be scurvy or scabbed, or hath his stones broken."

Using the words of the Lord he had managed to insult almost

every man in the congregation. Some had noses that could be called flat. Some had rough complexions. Some had eyes that squinted or were so weak as to require spectacles. There were no dwarfs but some were diminutive, including Mr Sillars. Some had moles or scars: these were superfluities. Some stooped or limped, from old age or infirmity. There was even one whose stones were broken, or so it was rumoured. In his youth Mr Cuthbertson had been kicked in those parts by a horse.

Galloway was not aware of the affront he had caused. He had immediately fallen into a dwam, with his mouth opening and shutting, like a child's mechanical toy. He did this often. With luck it could last for over an hour.

Meanwhile most of those standing, led by Saidler, were making their way out, like children given an unexpected holiday. They could be heard laughing outside, until Archibald Runcie closed the door.

Darroch was able at last to begin his resumé of the history of the Great Dispute.

CHAPTER 2

"It has always been the principle of the Church of Scotland, and part of her constitution, that in every vacancy the wishes of the congregation must be effectually considered. Nine years ago therefore, in 1834, the General Assembly passed what became known as the Veto Act, giving authority to congregations to reject ministers presented to them by heritors. The highest legal authorities of the time were consulted and agreed that the Church was legally within her powers to pass that Act.

"In autumn of that same year the parish of Auchterarder became vacant and Lord Kinnoull the patron presented to the living Mr Robert Young, a preacher of the Gospel. Five-sixths of the congregation solemnly protested. The Church therefore requested the patron to make another appointment.

"Unfortunately Lord Kinnoull and his presentee thereupon took the case to the Civil Courts. There it was decreed that in the settlement of pastors the Church could have no regard to the feelings of the congregation. It was therefore ordered to proceed with the ordination of Mr Young.

"The Church then appealed to the House of Lords. There the sentence of the Scottish Courts was confirmed. According to the law of the land, it seemed, the wishes of congregations were not to be heeded.

"The case of Auchterarder was followed by those of Lethendy and Marnoch. At Lethendy the congregation had rejected Mr Clark, an unhappy man who afterwards became a drunkard. The patron and the Presbytery agreed to settle another minister, Mr Kessen, in the pastoral charge, but Mr Clark took it upon himself to drag the Presbytery into the Court of Session. There he obtained an interdict prohibiting the Presbytery from proceeding to ordain Mr Kessen. That interdict was disregarded and Mr Kessen was ordained.

"A summons was issued against the Presbytery and they were brought to the bar of the Civil Court. There they made it clear that though they were deeply impressed with the obligation of giving all honour and reverence to the judges of the land, nevertheless in matters spiritual they were bound by their ordination oaths to act in obedience to the Court of the Church. The outcome was that they were severely rebuked and given to understand that if they were guilty of another breach of interdict they would be sent to prison.

"In the meantime an action was raised by Mr Clark and the Presbytery were cast in damages to the extent of several thousands of pounds.

"Meanwhile at Marnoch in Strathbogie Mr Edwards was presented to the living. Only one man signed his call while six-sevenths of the congregation entirely opposed his settlement. He was accordingly set aside by the Church. He too appealed to the Civil Courts and a decision was given in his favour. The opinions and feelings of the parishioners were to be ignored.

"A new feature, however, came to view. The majority of the Strathbogie Presbytery agreed with the Civil Courts in wishing to retain for the patron the power of intruding presentees on to resisting congregations. So, when the Court of Session ordered the settlement of Mr Edwards to go forward, they readily lent themselves to the work. The Supreme Court of the Church was now obliged to intervene. At the Assembly of 1839 the Presbytery of Strathbogie were expressly prohibited from taking any steps towards the settlement of Mr Edwards. A majority of the Presbytery resolved to ignore this prohibition. They were thereupon suspended from their offices as ministers of the Church. Still they persisted and on 21st January resolved to meet at Marnoch to carry out the settlement of Mr Edwards.

"The snows of winter lay deep on the ground, but when the seven Strathbogie ministers met at the church two thousand people were gathered within and around it. A solemn protest was handed in. Then in a body the people rose and, gathering the Bibles, silently retired. Not one remained.

"The seven suspended ministers of Strathbogie then applied to the Court of Session for their suspension to be lifted and their sacred functions as ministers restored. This the Civil Court did by a formal decree. That was to say, civil or secular judges assumed the power of restoring sacred functions which the spiritual authorities had taken away. This too had been done at the request of some of the Church's own sons, who whether they were aware of it or not were ceding to the Civil Court the right to strip from the Church the spiritual authority it holds from Christ. Those seven ministers were put on trial by the Church. They refused to withdraw, and so at the Assembly of 1841 they were deposed from the office of the ministry.

"The question was now reduced simply to whether or not the Church should be spiritually independent of the secular power.

"At last year's Assembly a Claim of Right was drawn up by Mr Alexander Dunlop and urged on the Court by Dr Chalmers. It was passed by an overwhelming majority. It consisted of an appeal to the Queen and the Government, narrating the grievances of the Church and claiming a right to be protected from the encroachments of the Civil Courts.

"At first no notice was taken in high quarters of that appeal."

At that point, as Darroch paused to sip some water, old John Cairns stood up, in his place at the end of the minister's pew, and crept out of the church, slowly and painfully.

He was hardly noticed. Some thought that being old he could not contain his need to pass water, others that he had some household task to do. In any case none was interested. He was old and poor, and he had no relatives in the district. He would probably die in the poorhouse. But for the minister's charity he would be there already.

Only Darroch knew the old man's secret. He had come to the manse door seven years ago, asking for work. Darroch had taken him on as gardener-and-stableman, with a room above the stable for accommodation, and he had worked as hard as his frequent aches and stiffness allowed. He had little to say to anyone. Obliged to attend church, he had sat at the end of the minister's pew, never once looking at a Bible or joining in the psalm-singing. He had been excused because he was senile. Then one summer day, when he and Darroch were cutting grass in the manse garden, he had suddenly confided that as a young man he had been a friend of Thomas Muir of Huntershill, the famous champion of liberty, and had been in court the day Muir had been sentenced to transportation. He had been a fervent radical himself in those days.

Had the mention of the Courts in Darroch's address reminded him of those melancholy days? Or had he thought that the injustices heaped on the Church were as nothing compared to those his friends and comrades had had to endure? Or had the physical pain become so acute that he had to go where he would be alone?

Evangelicals and Moderates alike would have sided with the law against Muir, and today would side with it against Taylor, whose arrest and imprisonment they would approve. Mr Mitchell and Mr Harkness would shake hands on that; so too would Dr Cook and Dr Chalmers.

The Church was right in fighting for spiritual independence, but when this was won what use would be made of it? Would the new Free Church set an example to the old Church, still a servant of the State, and to the whole nation, of courage, compassion, self-sacrifice, and love, for Christ's sake? If it did not the future would deservedly belong to men like Taylor who would set up a just social order, from which God was excluded.

These thoughts passed through Darroch's mind as he watched the old man hirple to the door, open it, and go out.

Then he continued, not quite so confidently as before.

"In August of that year the House of Lords pronounced the final decision on the Auchterarder case. Mr Young was granted £10000 damages against the Church authorities.

"Meanwhile a number of ministers, calling themselves Moderates, and led by Dr Cook and Principal McFarlan, resolved to side with the deposed ministers of Strathbogie. They took their stand on the civil law. It was a direct challenge to

those of their colleagues who took their stand with the Court of
the Church.

"Last November 474 ministers, the largest assemblage of
ministers which up to that time Edinburgh had ever seen, met in
the capital. The matter was debated at that Convocation with
great solemnity. Some of the more ardent Evangelicals regarded
the issue as already settled and wanted at once to precipitate the
separation of Church from State. Others shrank from such a
course, preferring to leave to the State the grave responsibility
of breaking the tie and driving them out.

"The Convocation ended with a series of resolutions, by
which ministers pledged themselves that if the claim for redress
was refused by the Government they would tender their
resignations and give up the civil advantages which they could
no longer hold in consistency with the free and full exercise of
their spiritual functions. Those resolutions were agreed to by
480 ministers.

"That is how the position stands today. On the 18th of this
month, in St Andrew's Church in Edinburgh, the Assembly will
finally decide. Those ministers adhering to the resolutions of
last November will accordingly relinquish their churches, their
manses, and their stipends. They will thereafter attempt to form
a new Free Church, with the co-operation of those members of
their congregations who think as they do."

Darroch sat down, in silence, and took another sip of water.
He spilled some, so shaky was his hand. He had prepared the
stage and the background. Soon he would be called upon to say
what part he personally intended to play in the drama.

According to Robert Drummond of those 480 ministers
(including Darroch himself) who last November had pledged
themselves to withdraw if the Government remained obdurate
no more than thirty would do so, when faced with either the bold
act of rising up and walking out or the much less dramatic but
more prudent act of sitting still.

If Robert was right and there were only thirty faithful to their
pledges would it be noble or foolish to be one of them?

In Darroch's case there was the extra complication of the
offer of the very desirable living of Glenquicken. How galling it

would be to lose this by a premature declaration, later rescinded, to no avail. Wiser therefore to do what many others would do: that was, speak evasively in the meantime, and leave the way open either to walk out or sit still, when the time came.

CHAPTER 3

Mr Mitchell and Mr Sillars rose simultaneously. The tall man and the short one looked at each other. Mr Sillars hesitated and sat down.

Before Mr Mitchell could begin to speak, while he was smiling benignly all round, Jonas Galloway came out of his dwam with a rush of grunts which might have been copied from his pigs if they had not been so anguished. It was thought that he was still quoting Scriptures, though no one could be sure. Children were frightened of him in that phase, though no man could have been more harmless. The only thing to do was to take him by the arm and lead him out, which was what Archie Runcie did, patiently enough. His children who had brought him to church would take him home again. Dr Fairbairn had said that his brain was deranged by reading what he didn't understand. It was a lesson to be temperate in all things.

Mr Mitchell began. "We are all indebted to you, Mr Darroch, for an account which lacked nothing in lucidity but perhaps a little in impartiality. It seemed to me that throughout you assumed that the Evangelicals, or the would-be disruptionists, are in the right, and the Moderates, who wish to keep the Church intact, are in the wrong. Forgive me if I have misunderstood.

"I am on the Moderate side myself, as is our patron Sir James. There are many eminent men among us, in addition to Dr Cook and Principal McFarlan. We believe that to dissolve the connection between Church and State would be extremely dangerous, in that we would appear to be showing an example of disregard for the law, whereas we ought surely, as members of a Christian Church, to be showing an example of obedience to the law. If in order to do so we have to yield up a little of our independence does not every loyal citizen have to do likewise, so that the nation can function as a harmonious whole? This is how civilisation itself is maintained. Surely we must not as a nation put ourselves into a position where we would be giving encouragement to radicals, republicans, revolutionaries, socialists, and atheists, who increase daily and await their opportunity. We on the Moderate side do not accuse Evangelicals of lack of patriotism, but rather of lack of judgment. Fervour can stir souls but it can also cloud minds."

He paused. Some of those on the other side of the church looked worried. He had touched their rawest nerve. They feared and hated subversion as much as he did.

"That is the general view. Coming to Craignethan, our own small part of Christ's kingdom, I am empowered by Sir James, our generous patron, absent today owing to the death of his revered mother, Lady Annie, to state on his behalf that he would be disturbed and disappointed if Mr Darroch were to see fit to resign over this matter and to lead an exodus from the church. It was Sir James who, twenty years ago, presented Mr Darroch to us. Some of you may recall that there were a few voices raised in objection, but these soon changed to murmurs of approbation. Conscientious, attentive, and modest, Mr Darroch has served us well. One of his admirers was Lady Annie, so much so that in her will — I have been given permission to disclose this — she has left to this parish church the sum of £1000, to be spent as the minister and kirk session think fit. In his mother's honour Sir James has decided to donate £1000 himself. Many repairs and improvements will now be possible, both to this building and to the manse. Sir James thinks, as I do, that it would be a great pity if those benefits were not to be enjoyed by the present minister and the present congregation.

"For a long time we have been a happy, united, peaceful community here in Craignethan. It is Sir James's hope that this

135

blessed state of affairs will be allowed to continue. Should it not be the hope of us all?

"I must add a warning. Though Sir James would not wish to prevent any man from following the dictates of his conscience he would consider himself bound by his own position as chief heritor and magistrate to give his full support to the Established Church should there be a split or hiving off, and furthermore he would expect all those in any way owing allegiance to him to follow his example. The harmony of our community is in peril, gentlemen. In Sir James's name I call upon you all to join him in protecting it."

Reluctantly, for he loved the sound of his own voice, he sat down, but not before he had given his audience a smile with warning in it.

No one was deceived. Every man there who was vulnerable knew he had been shown a stick with which he would be beaten if he did not do what Sir James bade. There would be dismissals and evictions. Leases would not be renewed. Privileges would be withdrawn.

Mr Sillars rose, after a conference with Mr Harkness. "We on this side think it would be best if we heard a' the arguments of the ither side before we put forward oor ain."

He sat down again.

Up jumped Mr Dalrymple. Coarse in mind and feature, pitiless and unscrupulous, and a heavy drinker, he was a man Darroch greatly disliked. He was the manager of Sir James's largest pit. Some years ago when there had been an accident he had refused to let Darroch go down to give the comfort of Christ to some dying miners who would never be brought to the surface alive. Why endanger your life and my reputation, for animals which don't believe in God and wouldn't know what you were talking about? That had been his attitude. He still had children under twelve working underground though it was now against the law. Who is the true Christian, he had jested, you, Mr Darroch, who wishes to take the extra slice of bread out of their mouths, or I who wishes to put it in?

He came to the front to speak and turned his back on the minister.

"Gentlemen, I am going to speak to you about the colliers. Hitherto they have been willing to perform their ordained task with due submission, but recently they have begun to complain, demanding, if you please, more pay and safer conditions. They have been contaminated by the lawless and seditious elements which Mr Mitchell spoke of. One of these, as you may have heard, was arrested in this very church yesterday morning. To show his contempt he pelted with Bibles the policemen who arrested him. I do not have to tell you how necessary it is for the economy of the country that colliers keep to the work God ordained for them. As you may know, not long ago if a mine was sold the miners were in effect sold with it, like the ponies which draw the hutches. Thus a bond was established. That bond was broken, in my opinion recklessly. Here is another valuable bond, that which binds Church to State. Let it not be broken also."

He turned and gave Darroch an insolent grin.

Darroch's heart beat fast, as always when he heard abominable things said. Many times he did not have the courage to denounce them. This time he had.

"Mr Dalrymple, do you include me among the elements who have contaminated the colliers? I visit them every week in their homes, against your wish, I know. I have found many of them very decent people. I cannot listen without protest to their being likened to ponies. They are human beings, in God's image. They deserve our compassion and our gratitude. On cold winter's nights I for one think of them gratefully when I warm myself at the fire."

"Especially when your coals are supplied free, Mr Darroch."

Not all heard that remark. Of those who did some looked shocked but others, who had to pay dearly for their coal, smiled with malice.

"Please, gentlemen, no acrimony," cried Mr Mitchell. "I am surprised that Mr Darroch should introduce it."

Mr Crawford, whose temper was uncertain, lost it then. "Mr Darroch introduced charity, not acrimony. He said what as a Christian minister he was bound to say. If he had not said it I would have thought little of him."

137

They all thought that was rash of the dominie who could so easily be dismissed and who at his age would find another post hard to come by.

Darroch came down from the pulpit and sat beside his sons.

"Well done, Father," whispered Arthur.

But James turned his face away. He thought his father's selfishness had caused his mother's death and was now going to make them all paupers. He had vowed never to forgive him if he did not accept the Glenquicken living.

It was now Mr Pendreich's turn. Grocer and wine merchant, he had the dignity of a Moderator, even when dusty with flour. He weighed his words as carefully as he did his sugar.

"I have to say that a congregation should hae the richt to refuse a meenister if for its ain guid reasons it doesnae want him. But I've been telt that this richt will be granted by the Government before lang. In that case should we no' juist wait?"

"Mr Pendreich, you have put the matter in a nutshell," said Mr Mitchell. "We have the assurance of Dr Cook and other leaders of the Church that that right will be granted soon, if we have patience."

"With respect, Mr Mitchell, that is not the point," cried Mr Crawford. "The point is: what right has a Government in London to dictate to the Church of Scotland how it should manage its affairs? Are you aware, gentlemen, that some congregations gathered together to discuss this matter, as we are doing this morning, have proposed that not only should the Church secede from the State but also that Scotland should secede from the Union?"

"That is an extremist view, Mr Crawford," said Mr Mitchell, "one that I am sure Dr Chalmers himself would never countenance."

"Tamas Semple has something to say," said Farmer Cuthbertson, in the high thin voice that had given rise to the rumour he had been genitally maimed. "Tamas, come forrit and say your piece."

Semple was one of those standing at the back. He worked for Cuthbertson as a ploughman. Everyone liked him. It was said of him as a compliment that more gulls gathered round his head than that of any other ploughman. His wife had died in childbirth three weeks ago.

He shambled to the front, shyly, turning his hat in his big hands.

"Begging your pardon, Mr Darroch," he said, "but when my time comes I want to be buried beside Katie and oor two wee weans, in Craignethan kirkyaird. They tell me that if I gie up membership to join some ither kirk I'd forfeit a' my rights. I don't ken if that's true or no' but I cannae tak the risk, so I think I'll stay on here. Katie always had a guid word to say for you, Mr Darroch."

A big hulking man who could have carried Darroch under his oxter, he had tears running down his cheeks.

Darroch himself shed tears in sympathy.

"Every man here should bear in mind what Mr Semple has said," cried Mr Mitchell. "Is there anyone who does not have some loved one buried out there in our kirkyard?"

Mr Harkness stood up. "I'm no' going to mak a statement for oor side o' the argument," he said. "Andra Sillars is going to do that. I just want to say this. My faither and mither are in the kirkyaird, and two o' my brithers and one sister, as weel as my ain lassie Elspeth. Like Tamas Semple I want to lie beside my ain kind. So I've been to lawyers, and I've been informed that naebody can tak awa' my richt."

He sat down, fingering his gold watch like a man well able to afford lawyers' fees.

"It is a matter that may have to be settled in the courts," said Mr Mitchell.

"Who spoke of acrimony?" cried Mr Crawford. "Would it not be acrimonious in the highest degree to deny people the right to be buried in their own lairs, beside their own people?"

"Whatever our differences," said Darroch, "we shall all remain Christians and, I trust, treat one another accordingly."

They all remembered that he had several weans buried in the kirkyard and on Tuesday his wife was to be laid to rest beside them. It occurred to some that in a way he was lucky. If she'd died in a month's time he might have had to look elsewhere for a grave for her.

Mr Sillars now rose.

Darroch waited with foreboding to hear the reasons given by this small, hard-headed, tight-mouthed, puritanical, money-making business man for defying the Established Church. Whatever they were they would be shared by many men like him throughout the country. Their money and their enterprise would be needed if a new Free Church was to be formed, with churches, manses, and schools of its own. Yet he had never been heard to express pity without some stern qualification. He lacked imagination and magnanimity. He distrusted passion and believed that the making of love was a duty. If anyone had told him it should be a communion with God, an inspiration, a self-fulfilment, and a liberating joy he would have called that person filthy-minded, impious, and mad. In the Church of Scotland were many men like him, and so there would be in the new Free Church.

Darroch remembered the painting on the ceiling, with the goddess reaching out to her fair-haired swain, on the bank of flowers, and in the distance the shining city.

"With respect," said Mr Sillars, in his corncrake's voice, "Mr Mitchell and Mr Crawford baith hae missed the main point. We on this side agree wi' every word that Mr Mitchell said aboot radicals and revolutionaries and atheists. Like him we would shut them up for life or pack them aff among cannibals. But these are political maitters and whit we are discussing this morning is a religious maitter. I was never at college but I ken the history of the Presbyterian Kirk of Scotland. I heard it frae my faither, wha heard it frae his. In the past men gied their lives to preserve it. In this very kirk they dee'd. Whit was it they fought and dee'd for? It was because they refused to acknowledge as the heid o' their kirk ony earthly king or government. The heid of their kirk was Our Lord, Jesus Christ, and always would be. Today in oor generation we are ca'd upon to defend His supremacy, no' wi' guns or swords, but wi' oor he'rts and oor bank-books. Speaking for myself, I hae ancestors wha would come to me in the nicht and ca' me traitor if I was to betray the Kirk they bled for.

"I'm no' sure whit Mr Darroch's position is, though I ken he

140

put his name to the Claim of Right last November. This is no' the time to press him for an answer wi' his wife so recently deid, but I want to tell him that if he comes oot on the 18th of this month and joins a new Kirk whose Heid is Jesus Christ then I for one will gladly gie him a' the support I can. So will others. Mr Mitchell drapped a hint that obstacles will be placed in oor path. They will a' be swept aside."

He sat down then, in silence.

All over the church men frowned and avoided other men's eyes. It was well-known that Mr Sillars paid low wages, yet here he was grandly offering to pour out money on the building of a new kirk and manse. Was he trying, like Roman Catholics with candles and masses, to buy his place in heaven? When he was dismissing some mason for being drunk or sick or old he wasn't bothering then about Our Lord, Jesus Christ.

In his mind Darroch heard Taylor's voice, good-humoured but mocking. "Aye, Sillars and his friends will build you a handsome new kirk and manse. They can well afford to considering the big profits they make and the low wages they pay. It will be their kirk, though, not yours. Just as this kirk is Sir James's. He hired you to preach submission to the authority of rank, and so you did, for twenty years. Sillars will expect you to preach submission to the authority of money, and so you will."

I shall preach submission to the authority of Christ, thought Darroch.

"Excuse me, Mr Darroch," Taylor's voice continued in his mind, "but I don't ken what you mean by that. Do not nations that go to war and kill thousands, coal-mine owners that won't spend money on making their mines safe, coal merchants that give short measure, farmers that order their men to work in pouring rain for no extra pay, builders that use cheap materials but charge for dear, shopkeepers that put threepence on the price when a penny would give a fair return, and lawyers that batten on the misfortunes of their clients: do not all these claim to be good Christians and prove it by attending church regularly?"

Meanwhile other voices were being raised.

Mr Runcie's: "I wad like to ken if this new Kirk wad abjure sich abominations as coloured gless in the windaes and music and new-fangled hymns."

Mr Crawford's: "Are we, the countrymen of Wallace and Bruce, to yield to Englishmen the right to tell the ancient Kirk of Scotland what it can and what it cannot do? If we give way in this the time will come when there will be no need for the name Scotland on the map, for we shall all have been turned into Englishmen, of an inferior sort."

Farmer Cuthbertson's: "I don't care for new ministers ony mair than I care for new boots. It's too much trouble breaking them in. Mr Darroch suits me fine. He kens his place and he's very easy to listen to. My womenfolk are happy to come to church because of him. So I'm hoping this will a' blaw ower and the sun will come oot and we'll a' be yin again."

Mr Mitchell's again: "Mr Cuthbertson has expressed a hope which in the opinion of many knowledgeable judges, is very likely to become a reality. This threatened division may not take place at all. In the event it could well be that Mr Darroch's 480 ministers will have dwindled to a handful by the 18th. From Edinburgh the latest estimates are that as few as 20 will remain obdurate."

They then waited for the minister to speak. He did so sorrowfully, with sighs, as became a bereaved husband.

"You must forgive me, gentlemen, if I do not commit myself here and now. My heart is heavy, my mind not entirely clear. When I go to Edinburgh shortly I shall have the benefit of final discussions with colleagues and be better able to decide what course would be best for the Church and therefore for our nation. Until then, with your indulgence, I prefer to suspend decision."

On the whole he had their indulgence. His sighs had done it. They couldn't very well hustle a man whose wife lay in her coffin, on a table in his house. They had all been to see her, so they knew he wasn't this time anyway hiding behind politeness. He had good reason for a heavy heart and hazy mind.

CHAPTER 4

Annabel Wedderburn was writing her weekly letter to her older married sister in Glasgow.

"Dearest Clarabel,

This has been a very eventful week. I have the most exciting news. I keep blushing as I write and my toes curl in my slippers and there are other physical manifestations I dare not mention, not even to you.

I should be ashamed of myself. My news really is very *sad*. During Friday night poor Mrs Darroch passed away in her sleep. I was shocked when I was told but I wasn't really surprised, for I was speaking to her on Friday morning and I thought she looked as if she wouldn't last another week. The doctor came, old Fairbairn who used to be an army surgeon, and ordered her to bed but that was all he could do for her and it wasn't enough.

Her brother from Edinburgh, the Rev. Robert Drummond, arived in time to see her before she died. He was in a very dour mood and not at all pleasant to poor little George, blaming him, I suppose for her illness and then her death, with all those pregnancies.

In her coffin she looks like a virgin, and so she was in so many things, except the one most people mean when they talk about virginity. There were so many subjects she wouldn't talk about because the weren't fit for ladies, and the subjects she did talk about, like embroidery, were so boring. She was like so many 'weel brought-up' ladies of her generation, modelled, you would have thought, on Sir Walter Scott's heroines, who, if you'll pardon my saying so, had no bladders or bowels. Do you remember those giggly conversations in corners in Miss Garvie's Academy for Young Ladies? The *dirty* pictures which were handed round, of naked men (mostly Greek statues)? The torture it was to keep from laughing when old Miss Garvie, without ever saying a word that our grannies would have found objectionable, warned us against a certain practice (indulged in by every one of us, I'm pretty sure, and by the dear old maiden lady herself if, I shouldn't wonder) which would bring us out in ugly spots and prevent us from having babies? I don't think poor Mrs Darroch ever giggled like that or looked at dirty pictures or did 'yon'. She said herself quite often, that she was a very lively little girl, like her own daughter Agnes, but I found it difficult to believe. These are horrible things to say about a dead woman, and yet I'm saying them because I feel so sorry for her, dead at forty-four, without in so many respects having lived at all.

I have Agnes living with me in the meantime. She and Maud are great friends though they spend most of the time squabbling. Poor Agnes ran out of the manse and wouldn't go back in. She clung to an apple-tree and screamed that she was going to be the next to die. I couldn't very well reassure her by saying that it was more likely Mary who was going to be next, although that's really what I think. You would never take them for sisters. Agnes as fair as ripe corn, refusing to go near her mother's coffin, and Mary, black as coal, having to be kept away from it. By the way, wee Jessie was quite ill for a few days, with congestion of the lungs, according to the doctor, and we were all afraid she wasn't going to get better, but she's now recovered and is going to be all right. I wept when she smiled at me. Three days before she didn't even recognise me. She's going to be the best-looking of that very good-looking family, with big blue eyes and lovely soft fair hair. Like her father. They need their good looks to make up for their bad luck.

Poor Sarah doesn't seem to know her mother's dead. I doubt if she will ever know. Imagine having a child like that, Clarabel!

The loss has brought Arthur closer to his father, but has had

144

the opposite effect on James. I've told you how they give me the impression of being contemptuous of their father and I haven't altogether blamed them. Well, Arthur no longer is but James is more so. In appearance they're so unalike and in nature too. I much prefer Arthur in spite of his arboreal habit. He was up the tree again, on Friday night, in pouring rain, and as a consequence has a sore throat. He quite often has, a great inconvenience I would think in an advocate. He's seen all of me, down to the mole on my bottom, but he looks at me as a Catholic priest would at the Madonna. I try not to tease him, though I did ask him once to let me look through his telescope. James wouldn't climb a tree in the dark and the rain to look into the Sultan of Arabia's harem. (Just as well, for if he were caught, what terrible things would be done to him.) I believe I could take off all my clothes and dance in front of him with a rose in each hand and he would not lift his head from the book he was reading. Hume's "Treatise of Human Nature", more than likely. Either he's a saint or a philosopher or there's something missing. I suspect the latter.

Can you tell that I'm having great difficulty in restraining myself from blurting out the exciting news I spoke of at the beginning of this letter?

What of little George himself, now a widower? Even with his wife lying dead I can't take him seriously. He took me to look at her. He held my hand; more than that he pressed it. There were tears in his eyes. I distinctly got the feeling, there beside his wife's coffin, that he was considering me as a possible successor. How blind conceit makes men. I would as soon marry a Turk. I would hate to be daintily nibbled. I want to be devoured. Did I speak disparagingly of a Turk? There are times when I would give my best red silk drawers to have one in bed with me, turban, stink of garlic, and all. I would not want little George lying beside me, squeezing more sweetness into his smile than it can hold, like a jug of cream overflowing. You should see the ladies of his congregation lapping it up. But the black crow now sees her chance and is about to gobble up the sweet titbit. I refer to Mrs Barnes. As I've said before no woman in the world would look after a man's house and children (one eleven months old and another without a mind) just for a servant's wage. She's seen from the beginning that poor Margaret wouldn't last long, so she's waited, not sparing herself I admit, and now her chance has come. She'll have him because she thinks she deserves him, and so do I. She'll dole him out his connubial joys as if they were sweets, as a reward for his good behaviour. The cream will soon turn sour. Why do I not like her? I can't say. She's very polite to me, and everybody else has a high opinion of her, including Mr Drummond, who's not easily hoodwinked.

What other news before I uncover the tureen and reveal the piece de resistance? Mr Jarvie, the fat minister, died in Cadzow during Thursday night, in his sleep too I believe. His wife's the woman I told you about, if she washed oftener and wore good stays and spent more time and money on clothes she could be very handsome indeed, the kind I would have fancied myself if I'd been born a man. But just wait for a minute!

There was a meeting yesterday about this big disagreement in the Church. Women were excluded, thank goodness. I don't know what was said and I don't care.

I was at the manse this morning helping to receive those calling to express their sympathy and have a peep at Mrs Darroch. Who should arrive but Mrs Jarvie. But, my goodness, what a transformation! She had taken my advice, Clarabel, though I never had the temerity to give it to her. She had evidently scrubbed herself from top to toe, and then applied some very exotic and very expensive perfume. She was dressed all in black, hat, veil, costume, gloves, and shoes, everything of the best quality, like a queen mourning a king. She had on a good pair of stays so that her bosom — so much more womanly than my own meagre one — was high and prominent. The last time I had seen her, in Cadzow main street, she was shuffling along in a slow slovenly way, as if she didn't care what anybody thought of her. Today what a difference! She was still slow because she's a tall heavy woman but stately and dignified. You should have seen old Mr Saunders, another Cadzow minister, making up to her, though previously he's been known to say harsh things about her shortcomings as a minister's wife. He snuffles and girns and whines, like far too many ministers if the

146

truth be told, and he still did as he made a fuss of her. He could hardly keep his hands off her. It was disgusting but it was to his credit too. He's ugly and over sixty and is never happier than when condemning sinners, especially fornicators, but he just could not help having his thin blood warmed and his old (choose your own word for it!) uplifted by this magnificent woman. Yes, she *is* magnificent.

Well, if she was having this effect on Mr Saunders and all the other men there, what effect did she have on little George, who is so susceptible to female charms? I would need the skill of Jane Austen to describe the meeting of the newly-made widow and the newly-made widower. He held her hand and shed tears. Whether she shed any I couldn't see for the veil, but I doubt it. I think the death of her husband is a great weight off her mind, if you'll pardon the heartless pun. She's never had any children of her own and she seemed greatly taken with Mary Darroch. They looked like mother and daughter. But her visit and her transformation are not my exciting news.

By the way the funerals are tomorrow, Mrs Darroch's here in the morning, and Mr Jarvie's in Cadzow in the afternoon. Many people will want to attend both.

About four o'clock a carriage was heard coming up the manse drive. I thought it must be Mr and Mrs Drummond come for the funeral, for they were expected, so upstairs in the parlour I pulled aside the curtain and looked down and saw — sound the trumpets! — a splendid carriage, sparkling new, black, red, and gold, a fiacre I think it's called, the kind favoured by wealthy men who like to do their own driving. It was drawn by two fine horses, black as Pluto's stallions. I was sure it must be some dashing young lord from the Big House.

Jumping down from the driver's seat with an athletic bound was a powerfully built man of above average height, in a uniform that didn't look like a coachman's, nor was it worn with a coachman's servility. He had a short black beard and his face looked so dark that I thought my Turk had arrived! I could see the drawn curtains were puzzling him. It was then that I jaloused who he must be: Captain Henry Darroch, sea-captain, paying his second visit to Craignethan manse in ten years.

I raced downstairs. He was in the hall speaking to Mrs Barnes. His voice was deep, friendly, concerned, commanding, and with an undercurrent of cheerfulness. He had, no has, the brightest most humorous blue eyes I have ever seen, and on his cheek under his right eye the most thrilling scar. (A sword slash by a pirate, I learned later!)

I was mortified that he was seeing me in mourning. I wanted to be as bright as a parrot.

I blurted out that my name was Annabel Wedderburn and I was a neighbour of the Darrochs. Somebody once told me that when I blushed black suited me. I hoped it was true because I did a lot of blushing. I knew, you see, that either I was going to marry this man or else I was going to live a disconsolate widow for the rest of my days.

He held out his hand which was as bronzed as his face and called me Miss Wedderburn. I had to put him right and tell him I was a widow. He looked solicitous and *interested*. Mrs. Barnes, he said, had just told him that Mrs Darroch was dead. I burst into tears then but it wasn't just because of poor Margaret, it was also because I realised then as never before what a great deal of happiness there could be in the world for a man and woman who loved each other.

I asked Mrs Barnes to let Mr Darroch know that his brother had arrived and then, as if I was the mistress of the house, invited Captain Darroch upstairs. It's an unusual arrangement in Craignethan manse that the parlour or family room is upstairs.

He said that the last time he had been in the manse was ten years ago.

He had therefore never seen Agnes, Sarah, and Jessie, and Mary must have been a baby when he was last here.

I must be depraved, Clarabel. There we were, strangers to each other, in a house of death, and what was I thinking? I was thinking how hard as teak his body looked, and how wonderful it would be to be embraced by him. I thought of beautiful, dark-skinned, naked, native women he must have made love to, in places with romantic names.

Alas, I had to remember that I was not one of the family and also that I had to get back to my own house where Maud and Agnes would be driving Mrs Maitland mad. Captain Darroch saw me to the door and said he very much hoped we would see each other again. We certainly will.

The Drummonds arrived from Edinburgh just as I was leaving. They had travelled by carriage all the way. Mrs Drummond, it seems, does not trust trains. (A lot of work for poor old John Cairns.) They did not bring their daughter. I suspect they're afraid to bring her to a house which has known so many deaths. She is their only child, as Maud is mine, but then I hope to have two or three more.

I look out of my window. The tree is empty. I do not think that bird will ever nest there again. I cannot see the lights of the manse, for too many trees intervene. There is still a faint red light in the western sky. I think of sunsets over the South China Sea, where pirates still abound, of orang-outangs in Borneo, of pagodas in Japan, of silken dancers in Siam, and of Captain Henry Darroch."

CHAPTER 5

When the rest of the house had gone to bed the two brothers talked in George's study, among the many theological books, which, George had modestly said, would soon be increased in number, for his dear friend John Jarvie had bequeathed to him the pick of his large library.

Henry was smoking a pipe. He shook his head, still amazed at having a brother who was a minister and read those driech tomes.

"Do you remember Sugary Wull, George ?" he asked.

George had in his hands the Bible given him as an ordination present twenty years ago, but he was thinking about Eleanor Jarvie, whose beauty had been revealed and who had invited him to St Margaret's manse tomorrow after the funeral, to decide which books of John's he wanted.

At first he did not understand his brother's question.

"Sugary Wull, George. We all called him that because we never knew his other name, if he had one. Heaven knows what age he was. It could have been sixteen, it could have been sixty. He was dwarfish because there was something wrong with his legs. His face was shrivelled and he always had blobs of spittle at his mouth. He was an imbecile." Too late Henry remembered about Sarah, but his policy was to sail on, past blunders and reefs. "He was fond of sugary things; that's how he got his name. He used to sit with his tinny, begging, down by the harbour."

"Yes, I remember the unfortunate man," said George. "But why speak of him now?"

"Most of us children were scared of him. Some threw stones. The most vicious rushed forward and kicked his tinny."

"Children can be very cruel."

"But you, George, would sit beside him on the ground. You said you understood his gibberish. You once wiped his mouth. I told mother and she burned your handkerchief, but she gave you a poke of sugary baps to take to him."

They were silent, remembering their small, dainty, yellow-haired, kind mother.

"Your wee girl Jessie's very like her, George."

George's eyes filled with tears. "We thought God was going to take Jessie too, but in His infinite mercy He gave her back to us."

Henry's view of religion was straightforward. If God gave the illness, why thank Him for taking it away? If He caused a hurricane why praise Him for letting the ship come through it, battered but safe. He had got his religion from their father, George from their mother.

"I envy you your family, George." He had seen them all except Agnes.

"Yes, Henry, the Lord has indeed blessed me."

He has also given you many a sore heart. Henry did not say it. "You're going to find it hard to look after them on your own," he said.

"Mrs Barnes is very capable."

"She certainly seems to be, but she's just a servant, after all. I'm thinking of getting married myself, you know. Yes, I'm on the look-out for a wife. As Beatrice says, it's high time if I don't want to be left alone in my old age."

Beatrice was their brother Andrew's wife.

Eleanor is now free to marry, thought George, and so am I.

"I wouldn't be surprised if I've already found her," said Henry.

"Some Greenock lady?" asked George absently.

"No. Your red-haired neighbour, Mrs Wedderburn. I liked her style. She'd much rather laugh than cry."

151

George was now paying keen attention. Annabel, after all, was one of his own eligibles.

"As I told you, George, my ship's under repair at Govan. I expect to sail for India in about six weeks. She struck me as the kind of woman who'd enjoy a voyage like that."

"She has an adventurous disposition," said George, cautiously.

"I could see that. What happened to her husband? What did he do? How long were they married?"

"William Wedderburn was a lawyer in Glasgow. He was always in poor health, I believe. He died about five years ago. They were married less than three years. She has a little girl aged six."

"All the better. I'd like a little girl of six as my daughter."

"Are you serious, Henry? You do not know each other."

"Love at first sight, George. Anyway, marriages in the East are between persons who don't meet till the wedding day, and they're as successful as most Christian marriages. Don't royal personages marry strangers? But I intend to get to know her first."

"In a way she is my protégée, Henry."

"Good. We'll be sure of your blessing then."

"I would have to be very sure that it was really what she wanted."

"I'm not going to abduct her, George. But, to change the subject, for I see it's taken the wind out of your sails somewhat, how is this trouble in the Church going to affect you here in Craignethan? Andrew was telling me about it. His minister, Mr McFarlan of the West Kirk, is on the side that's threatening to pull out of the Established Church. At a big sacrifice, Andrew assured me: the biggest sacrifice in the country, because he has the biggest stipend."

"It is not a matter of money, Henry. It is a matter of devotion to Our Lord Jesus Christ."

It seemed to Henry that piety made his brother sound and look shifty, but that was its effect on most people. "I'm inclined to agree with Beatrice that it's much ado about little. That's how Mr Drummond regards it. He was telling me that in Edinburgh

152

they're convinced it's a storm which will blow itself out without much damage being done."

"What does Edinburgh know about the consciences of simple country ministers? This is not much ado about little, Henry. It is the most important issue to confront the Church of Scotland since the Reformation itself."

"Well, George, good luck whatever you decide. I think I'll go out for a breath of air before I turn in."

He would much rather look up at the stars and think about Annabel Wedderburn than talk about church politics.

CHAPTER 6

When his brother was gone Darroch held a Bible to his heart. Before going to look possibly for the last time on his wife's face he had to prepare himself, by asking God to fill him with humility. Then, humbly he hoped, he went out of his study. He heard Baby Matthew crying in Mrs Barnes' room and Mrs Barnes soothing him back to sleep. She had Jessie in her room too, so that she could look after her. She had undertaken many other tasks, including baking for the funeral tomorrow. Too much was being heaped upon her. Yet she went on smiling and never complained.

Were these exceptional endeavours in continuation of the plot that she and Margaret had entered into to ensnare him?

That was not a humble or a just thought.

A lamp burned in the room. Byt its light he saw Mary kneeling by the coffin, in her nightdress.

A great fear struck him. Was Mary to be the next of those he loved to die? From infancy she had had an obsession with death. He had heard Mrs Barnes trying to reason her out of it. He had tried himself, less confidently. It had not been easy for him as a Christian minister to explain to a little child why, if heaven was so much more desirable than earth, no one wanted to die and go there.

"Mary, my pet," he whispered, "you must go back up to bed. How long have you been there?" He felt her feet. They were cold. "You will catch a chill."

"Mama looks so lonely."

"She is in heaven, Mary."

Did he really believe that? He knew ministers who had doubts, among them Robert Drummond. He had none. He could not believe in a God incapable of impossibilities.

"Sarah needs you, Mary. She may waken and be afraid."

"She's never afraid."

You had to have intelligence to be afraid. He shuddered.

"She will miss you. She loves you, Mary."

Thank God you did not have to have intelligence to feel and show love.

Mary stood up. Only for Sarah's sake would she have deserted her vigil.

"Can I see Mama again before they put her in the ground?"

"Yes, of course." His eyes were wet with tears.

Like a ghost she left the room.

He was alone with Margaret. That dear face which he had always been able to read with ease, for her love for him had made it guileless, now kept its secrets.

How much of God's omniscience the dead were allowed to share was one of the great mysteries. In life she had never been able to understand that the pleasure he had found in young comely women and the pleasure that they had found in him had meant no diminution or disparagement of his love for her. Did she know it now, among the angels?

She had always had a distrust of passion. Any time he had tried to explain to her why, say, he felt nearer to God in a collier's hovel than in Hairshaw House she had begged him not to be so vehement and to say no more for it would only distress her. She had wanted him to be like her father the Moderator and her brother who had won prizes at College and was now minister of one of the most fashionable churches in Edinburgh. She had once burst into tears when, early in their marriage, he had declared, too vehemently perhaps, that ministers like her father and her brother with their safe and orthodox views were more to be pitied than envied, for, though they might be immune from black depressions of doubt they never on the other hand experienced the supremely joyous surprise of finding themselves in God's presence, so that the hairs on their

155

heads tingled and in their hearts their love of their fellowmen increased a hundredfold.

Though she had never said it he had seen in her eyes that she blamed him for Sarah's imbecility. His noblest enthusiasms she had suspected were the consequences of some congenital weak-mindedness. She would have been horrified by his sheltering Taylor in the church and by his intention to visit Mrs Cooper in prison.

Those too were not humble thoughts.

Could it be that she was right and he was mad? Here he stood, in tears beside his wife's corpse, intending, after her burial tomorrow, and after the burial of his friend, to go by stealth to his friend's house, ostensibly to look at books but really to be alone with his friend's widow. Most people would call him wicked at least. Yet what he was seeking was how to come closer to God. Mystics did it by profound and sustained meditation. He lacked the depth and complexity of mind. All he had was a beautiful and sensitive body.

CHAPTER 7

Bessie was full of complaints. Though it was the best in the house she did not like lying in the bed in which her sister-in-law had died only two nights before. She had always said Craignethan manse was too small. She was worried about Isa left in the care of the servants. She felt guilty about their coachman, Henderson, having to share a bed with the old crippled man Cairns, above the stables. She couldn't see how Mrs Barnes, even with the help of those two trollops Bella and Mrs Strachan, could feed all the people expected at the funeral. She ached all over from the journey.

She blamed George for everything. If he had had more ambition he could have had a bigger and better living years ago, and his wife might still be alive.

Robert did not want to talk. He was thinking of his dead sister and her children.

"Is that not so, Robert?"

"He has tried, Bessie."

"And nobody wanted him. I'm not surprised. I thought, though I did not say anything, that it was a mistake on your part to persuade Sir Thomas to offer him Glenquicken. He would not do well there and you would get the blame."

"He has not accepted yet."

"Oh, he will, He is pretending that there is a great struggle going on in his conscience. They all are. I've quite lost patience with them."

He supposed she meant the 480 ministers who had put their

names to the Claim of Right.

"I think also you are wrong in supposing he will marry Mrs Barnes."

"I said perhaps he should."

"And I say he should not. She's much too common. Lady Blaikie would never approve of her. Good heavens, she's the daughter of a joiner."

"George is the son of a shopkeeper."

"Please do not remind me. I have always thought he brought the family down. But at least he is educated. She is not."

Yes, but what George needed was someone to look after his children, not someone who could lisp a few phrases of French.

"Well, is she, Robert?"

"No."

"How could she converse with Lady Blaikie?"

Very easily, he thought, for Lady Blaikie was no blue-stocking and had more interest in domestic matters than in books.

"Then there is Sarah. I feel ill every time I think of that poor child."

"Don't think of her then."

"That is more easily said than done. Do you think I *want* to think about her? I most certainly do not. What is to become of her?"

"She will be looked after."

"By whom? Tell me that."

"By those who love her."

"And who are they, pray?"

"Mary."

"A little girl of ten. Who else?"

"George."

"He puts on a show of loving her, but his face falls when he looks at her."

"And Mrs Barnes."

"She has a motive. She must have a motive. Otherwise how could she possibly love another woman's child who cannot speak and does not seem able to distinguish one person from another."

"She knows Mary, George, and Mrs Barnes."

"I saw no sign of it."

"You do not know them well enough."

"Do you, Robert?"

"No, I do not."

"And you blame yourself for it. That is foolish. I thought that brother of George's, Captain Darroch as he calls himself, was much too cheerful."

"I rather liked him for his cheerfulness. I felt grateful for it."

"Do you believe he got that horrible mark on his face in a fight with pirates?"

"Why should he lie about it?"

"Because he wanted to show off. Sailors tell tall tales, don't they? I would not be surprised if he got it in a brawl in a tavern. Did you see him eyeing Mrs Wedderburn?"

"I saw him looking with interest at her, and she at him."

"Yes. It was disgraceful."

"I thought it heart-warming."

"Heart-warming? In heaven's name, Robert, how could you possibly find it heart-warming to watch a man of forty and a widow with a child making sheeps' eyes at each other?"

"That's one way of putting it. Another way would be to say they were falling in love."

"I don't understand this mood you're in, Robert, and I don't like it. You seem to wish to contradict me at every turn. I should not have come. I should have stayed at home with Isa."

What he wanted was to be loved, not respected or admired or appreciated or even honoured, but simply loved. Was it because poor Meg was in the coffin, cold as ice? Yes, but it was also because Captain Darroch and Mrs Wedderburn were falling in love. He liked Darroch and she struck him as a merry good-natured young woman who deserved happiness. They had his blessing. Mrs. Barnes's devotion to George was also an advertisement for love.

Whatever the reason he felt he needed as never before the warmth of love, and the only person he could legitimately ask it from was lying beside him, chilly with reproofs. Not only his mind, heart, and soul, but his body too wanted it.

He turned towards her and lay against her.

"What are you doing, Mr Drummond?" she whispered, in astonishment. "Remember where we are, please."

"I want to hold you close, Bessie. I want you to hold me close."

"Holding close is one thing, Mr Drummond, what you appear to have in mind is another. Did I not say I was sore all over?"

"Just let me hold you close."

He pressed her close to him. She kept her arms by her sides. She would submit but she would not assist.

"This is not right, Mr Drummond."

There was only one way he could get as close as he needed and desired.

She had been warned many years ago by her mother that submission was a wifely duty, but nothing had ever been said about her having to co-operate and enjoy it, and she never did, though there had been moments when she had felt a sensation that she took to be pain though it had seemed more like pleasure.

Was it something he had eaten that day, she wondered. The mutton at the inn where they had lunched had been rather spicy. Or was there something in the air of Craignethan that had this effect on men?

She became aware when his face happened to touch hers that he was in tears. It was all very well for him to grieve for his sister, but was not this an unseemly way of doing it?

He would not get it over with but lay on top of her for quite some time.

She heard an owl and was reminded of the funeral tomorrow. She would have to make sure that she, and not Mrs Barnes or Mrs Wedderburn was regarded by all who came as the mistress of the house for the time being.

She had learned that by certain movements she could make him finish when he was being too dilatory. It was degrading, but she could not have him suffocating her much longer; so she moved.

It was successful. He finished, with sighs that were almost groans. Why he should want to do what so often was a disappointment was a mystery to her. There was a great deal she could have said but she contented herself with saying, fondly enough, "You would have done better to wait till we got home, Mr Drummond."

CHAPTER 8

Attendance at the minister's wife's funeral was obligatory for all male heads of households in the parish, but most wished to attend out of respect and many enjoyed the hour's break from dull, hard, lonely work. Servants had to ask formally for permission, which was granted in every case except one. Mr Roxburgh, who employed Jonas Galloway to look after his pigs, could not give him leave, for Susannah, a valuable sow, was due to farrow that morning, and Mrs Galloway, who normally deputised for her husband, had not sufficient skill as a midwife for pigs, though herself a mother eight times. Therefore among the farm workers walking towards the manse before ten o'clock, along by-roads or across fields, Jonas and his Biblical bellowings were missing, to no-one's disappointment.

Servants walked. Masters came in gigs, traps, or carriages, and in a few cases on horseback. By ten o'clock the road for a quarter of a mile outside the manse and kirk was lined with vehicles and horses.

Ladies also attended, despite discouragement. They were not allowed into the kirkyard to take part in the service round the grave. Custom, derived it could well be from Leviticus, prohibited it. They gathered in the manse to gossip, drink tea, and nibble Mrs Barnes's home-baked baps, and wait for their husbands to drive them home again: it was an enjoyable outing. Some younger women, wishing to see how Mr Darroch conducted himself as a sorrowing husband, watched discreetly from the manse garden, far enough away not to appear to be intruding and taking care not to join in the psalm-singing. They whispered about this and that but mostly about young unmarried men, among whom the minister could now be included. It was assumed that he would marry again as soon as was proper, but they couldn't make up their minds whether his new wife's good fortune, in acquiring such a bonny wee husband, with so sweet a mouth and such soft fair hair, would compensate for her bad, in acquiring also a baby and four little girls, one a daftie.

Ten ministers in all were present, including Mr Darroch and Mr Drummond. The oldest, Mr Saunders, over 60, was to officiate, being the then Moderator of Cadzow Presbytery. Robert Drummond was displeased, thinking him a girning old wife. In the event Mr Saunders performed competently enough, in spite of missing teeth and moments of forgetfulness. As he said himself proudly this was his 1,345th burial service. Robert Drummond had never heard the beautiful words snuffled and gnashed more abominably, but not even the Archangel Gabriel's trumpeting of them would have pleased him.

The eight cord-holders, entrusted with the sad task of lowering the coffin into the damp stony ground, under the supervision of Mr Jackson the undertaker from Cadzow, were Darroch himself, his two sons, Robert Drummond, Captain Darroch, Mr Mitchell as Sir James's representative, Mr Sillars representing the elders, and, to the surprise of many, old John Cairns, the manse servant.

Mrs Wedderburn, watching, with Mrs Drummond, from the window of Arthur and James's room which afforded the best view of the kirkyard, was not surprised. Mr Darroch often did little acts of kindness like this, which would have occurred to no one else. She thought again that perhaps she undervalued him.

Mrs Drummond was not surprised either, but for a different reason. She saw it as another instance of George's peculiar foolishness.

Mrs Barnes had come to the window too, but Mrs Drummond, after suffering her presence for a few minutes had ordered her back to the kitchen, not because there was work for her to do there but because she was a servant and the kitchen was where servants belonged. She had gone without protest, smiling patiently.

Mrs Wedderburn might have protested on her behalf if she had not been so interested in studying Captain Darroch's every move and expression. She saw him clearly and closely, for she was using Arthur's telescope.

Agnes and Maud were over in Mrs Wedderburn's house, playing with dolls.

Mary was up in her room looking after Sarah, or so she was supposed to be, but Mrs Wedderburn, taking the telescope off Captain Darroch for a moment, caught sight of her peeping over the drystone dyke into the kirkyard. She was not weeping, though many of the men were, including Robert Drummond and James Darroch. Captain Darroch did not weep. Mrs Wedderburn was not disappointed in him. He would weep if someone he loved was dead. Mrs Wedderburn was crying herself, to Mrs Drummond's annoyance, for *she*, a relative, was dry-eyed.

Afterwards every man as he left the graveside shook hands with the bereaved husband. One was the sergeant of police who had arrested Taylor. His presence was unexpected. He did not live in the parish.

"My sincerest sympathies, Mr Darroch," he said. "I hope you don't mind me coming."

"I am honoured, sergeant."

"Jerry said, if I saw you again, to tell you he bears nae grudge."

"Thank you, sergeant."

The farm workers made off again, back to their byres, sties, and fields.

Their masters lingered a while in the manse with their womenfolk, talking about turnips, oats, and the minister's motherless bairns, and partaking of the refreshments served up by Mrs Barnes and Bella.

Mr Mitchell and Mr Sillars left early, pleading pressure of business. The former took with him his wife and three grown-up unmarried daughters, the eldest of whom, aged 28, had hopes of becoming the second Mrs Daroch.

Captain Darroch escorted Mrs Wedderburn to her house, taking the long way through the wood. He was eager to meet her daughter Maud and his own niece Agnes, but saw no reason to hurry. They dallied, delighting in each other's company and in the singing of birds.

Mary Darroch climbed over the wall and knelt by her mother's grave.

Arthur slipped into the church where he shouted to God that he did not believe in Him.

James lay on his bed, thinking how he could persuade or coax or blackmail his father into accepting the call to Glenquicken.

The ministers forgathered in Darroch's study. The younger ones had to stand. In subdued voices they talked about the Ten Years' Conflict, soon to be resolved. Most were not prepared to commit themselves and were scolded for their timidity by Mr Saunders, who proceeded with senile peevishness to give his reasons for being firmly on Dr Welsh and Dr Chalmers' side in the argument. The Church of Scotland had grown too lax. It no longer publicly castigated fornicators. It had begun to tolerate innovations, like music. Its leaders looked on themselves as gentlemen. They drank port after dinner. They hankered after bishops.

The youngest minister, Mr Melville, not long married, deferentially asked Mr Robert Drummond, of Edinburgh, what his opinion was.

Mr Drummond was rather surly. "With respect to Mr Saunders," he replied, "I see no contradiction in being both a gentlemen and a minister of the Church. As for bishops, institutions must have leaders, for whom one name is as good as another."

Mr Saunders put his finger in his mouth and sulked.

"I really meant, Mr Drummond," said Mr Melville, "what is your opinion as regards the dispute itself."

"For me, Mr Melville, what matters is the unity of the Church. If it is broken into parts its authority will be irretrievably weakened."

165

"You are yourself determined to stay in?"

"Yes, Mr Melville, and what is more I am convinced that ninety-five per cent of the ministers of Scotland will stay in, as you put it."

"But what of the Claim of Right, Mr Drummond?" asked Mr Ramage, a widower. "Many ministers pledged themselves to withdraw if it was denied. I myself was one. Are you implying that all of us will go back on our word? Or do you think that the Claim will be granted?"

"It is one thing, Mr Ramage, to support a theoretical proposition, which involves signing one's name to a piece of paper; it is another thing altogether to put it into practice, which would entail the loss of manse, kirk, stipend, and status, and also the break-up of the ancient Church of Scotland."

"You appear to be imputing to the ministers of the Church lack of courage and conviction, Mr Drummond."

"I am crediting them with good sense."

As a grieving husband Darroch kept silent. Nor did he speak when the conversation turned briefly on their deceased colleague John Jarvie and his wife. It appeared that Mrs Jarvie had summoned the leading elders of St Margaret's and informed them imperiously that she wished her husband's coffin, necessarily of a gigantic size, removed from the manse and placed in the church. They had been dumbfounded because hitherto she had scarcely spoken to them and had taken no interest in church affairs. There had been a strong smell of wine off her breath.

As he was seeing Mr Saunders to his carriage Darroch asked him about Mrs Cooper. He had to remind the old man who she was.

"Do not concern yourself with her, Mr Darroch. Harlot and murderess, she knows she is destined for Hell and that no one can save her."

"Have you prayed with her?"

"How can you pray with a creature who will not speak?"

"Perhaps she cannot, owing to the wound in her throat."

"If she is already suffering the torments of Hell here on earth, Mr Darroch, it is only what she deserves."

Thus spoke one who might well become Darroch's comrade in the new Free Church. Alas, there would be more like him.

CHAPTER 9

Mr Brodie, the schoolmaster, and Mr Beaton, a lawyer, leading elders of St Margaret's, met Darroch at the church door.

"Good afternoon," Mr Darroch, said Brodie, with customary pompousness. "May I say how very sorry Mrs Brodie and I were to hear of your dear wife's untimely decease."

More briskly the lawyer added his consolences. "Mrs Jarvie wishes you to take a short service," he said. "I pointed out that with very good reason you might not feel up to it. However, she insisted."

"I would consider it an honour and privilege," murmured Darroch. "As you know, John Jarvie was not only my esteemed colleague, he was also my friend."

"There are people in the church this afternoon who are not members," said Brodie, indignantly. "They have come, we fear, for improper reasons."

He meant because of the minister's famous fatness. The size of the coffin was a joke among irreverent people.

"Will Mrs Jarvie herself be present?" asked Darroch.

"She is already in the church. Most dignified. Most impressive. To be truthful, Mr Darroch, it is something of a surprise to us all. Does it not show how the Lord can melt the most obdurate of hearts?"

"I don't think I'd call it melting," said the lawyer. "She's still petty cool, if you ask me. All the same she is a very handsome woman. I had not realised that."

"None of us did, Charles," said Brodie, with a leer. His own wife was small and timid.

Darroch kept aloof from this untimely praise of the widow's beauty, but in such a way as not to offend the two elders. They were men of influence.

Brodie poked him in the stomach. "We have a fine church here, do you not think, Mr Darroch?"

"As fine as any in the country, Mr Brodie."

"For reasons not necessary to mention among friends, we would wish our new minister to grace the pulpit not only with the soundness of his doctrine but also with the elegance of his person." He leered again.

It was a not very subtle reference to John Jarvie's grotesque grossness.

"Such a minister as yourself perhaps, Mr Darroch?"

Beaton was more direct. "You have many well-wishers here, Mr Darroch, particularly among the ladies."

The Lord is looking after me, thought Darroch. St Margaret's might not be as desirable as Glenquicken but it would be a great improvement on Craignethan.

Thanking them and then excusing himself respectfully he went into the church. It was large, three times the size of Craignethan, with a lofty ceiling and a gallery.

Hat in hand, he walked down the aisle, bowing to colleagues and acquaintances.

Dressed in black, with a black veil, Eleanor sat by herself in the front pew. The huge coffin was only a few feet away, on a table covered with black cloth.

He sat beside her. People behind murmured their sympathy for the new widower and the new widow. He bent his head in prayer. Her musky perfume overpowered all the usual church smells and also that of the polished coffin.

She murmured: "You look sweet enough to eat, George."

Somewhat taken aback, he replied: "I feel consoled, by the knowledge that my poor Margaret is now with Christ."

"In which case why call her poor?"

"Even in heaven she will miss her children." Tears that had not been ordered, as it were, filled his eyes.

169

"*They* will miss her."

"It would break your heart to see them."

There was a pause.

"This evening I leave Cadzow for ever," she said.

"So soon?"

"I shall stay with my sister in Edinburgh for a few days and then I shall set off for Italy."

"I shall be in Edinburgh myself, for the Assembly."

"I thought you would forgo it, George, after what has happened."

"Margaret would have wanted me to do my duty."

"I doubt if we shall meet. I intend to keep well away from gentlemen in black."

"Shall I come to the manse after the funeral? To look at the books?"

"If that is what you want, George."

"I shall enter by the back lane."

"Take care. There's a pack of stray dogs running wild. People have been bitten."

Never before in or out of a pulpit had he spoken so movingly and so mellifluously as he did a few minutes later. Even those who had come to scoff, men and women alike, were in tears as he praised his friend and commended his soul to Christ. He was even able, in his exalted mood, to risk a reference to the affliction of obesity. Well aware that the general opinion in Cadzow was that Eleanor had contributed to her husband's condition by perniciously feeding him sweetmeats against the doctor's advice he had to be circumspect when speaking of her but managed it so well that afterwards they queued up to shake her hand as well as his.

Arrangements had been made for food and drink to be dispensed to mourners at the Coach Inn. Since there was a large concourse heading for those free refreshments after the funeral it was easy for Darroch to slip off to the manse unnoticed. His only scare was when four stray curs came barking and snarling at him.

The back door was unlocked. He entered, panting with excitement. He called Eleanor's name.

She appeared, still wearing her mourning clothes. In her hand was a glass of wine.

"Lovely little crafty George," she said, putting an arm round his neck. Her speech was slurred. "Have you come to ravish me?"

It was not the welcome he had expected.

"I think I'm drunk, George," she said, and kissed him on the mouth.

Some wine spilt on to his clothes.

Fearful of a dislocated neck he withdrew courteously from her embrace.

He noticed then that all the furniture was gone.

"To save the trouble of selling it, George, I sent it all to the mission. Even the bath. Six cart loads."

In the parlour there was nowhere to sit. Adultery, or rather fornication, might be prevented not so much by Christian scruples as by lack of bed or couch.

Her wine bottles were on the mantelpiece.

"How odd, George, if you were to be the next occupant of this gloomy house."

"That is not likely."

"On the contrary it is very likely. Mr Brodie and Mr Beaton are agreed that you would make an admirable replacement for Jarvie."

He told her then about Glenquicken.

She was interested. "I know Glenquicken. We used to drive out there for picnics when I was a child. It is a delightful little village. You would do very well there, George."

"We would both do very well there, Eleanor."

"What are you saying, George?"

He fell on his knees. "Let us get married, Eleanor, as soon as propriety allows, and live in Glenquicken."

"Good heavens, George, are you asking me to be mother to — how many is it? — six children?"

"Seven."

"I always leave out the little daft one."

"She is the dearest of them all."

"Please get up, George, You look ridiculous."

He was glad to get up. The uncarpeted floor was sore on his knees.

"Jarvie used to say, George, that God would forgive you all your silly little self-deceptions because of your love for that little girl. You are a good man, George, though you would like to be a little satyr. No, George, I am going to Italy." She spoke some Italian.

"What did that mean?"

"Never mind. Do you know what I think you should do, George? First of all you should let them know you would like to be minister here. Their wives would see to it that you were chosen. Secondly, George, you should marry that sensible housekeeper of yours, Mrs Barnes. I saw how she looks after your little girls. You are blushing, George. Are you in a sense as good as married to her already? You would not be the first minister of the Church of Scotland with an ailing wife to find comfort in his house-keeper's bed."

"Please, Eleanor."

"She may not have a bonny face, George, but her body makes up for it, does it not? She would probably give you another half dozen bambinos but there would be room for them all in Glenquicken."

"Unfortunately," he said, rather peevishly, "to obtain Glenquicken I would have to go back on my sacred word, pledged last November when I signed the Claim of Right. Sir Thomas Blaikie, the landowner, is staunchly on the Moderate side."

"Where is the difficulty, George? Go back on your word. It should be easy to find a hundred good reasons for doing so. Let me suggest just one. Say it was God's will. Say it as if you believed it."

This was drunkenness speaking, and Catholic casuistry.

"Excuse me, George, I have to withdraw for a short while. I have drunk rather a lot of wine. Look at the books again. Take as many as you wish. I have promised the rest to Mr Brodie's school."

CHAPTER 10

Dressed in the black coats and hats that had been made for John's funeral less than a year ago, Mary, Agnes, and Sarah sat on a raised flat tombstone, looking at their mother's grave, where the bluebells placed there that morning by Mary were already wilted.

Agnes held tightly on to Mary's hand. She was terrified. Yet she had asked Mary to bring her here. Instinct warned her that the great fear she had of death must be faced and overcome.

Sarah happily watched two white butterflies twinkling together in the sunshine.

Agnes shuddered as she gazed at all the gravestones, many of them with skulls and crossbones carved on them.

A girl at school had told her that sometimes at night when there was no moon people rose up out of their graves and sat on their gravestones. It seemed to her there was room for birds on those stones that were standing upright, but not for people. But perhaps dead people didn't have bottoms like living people.

Mary had said that Mama was in heaven, so no one should weep for her. But no account of heaven that Agnes had ever been given had made it appear as happy and safe a place as home. Mama would be very sad there, separated from her children.

Death was a horible thing, whatever Mary said.

Agnes stared at the family tombstone. It was taller than Agnes herself. Mary had said they were made like that so that lots of names could be put on them. On the Darrochs'

173

Malcolm's name was at the top: he had been only a year old when he died. Then came Margaret, aged 3, Andrew aged 2, and John aged 7. Agnes had never known Malcolm and Margaret. Mary had said that Mama's name would be cut on it next, which would leave room for two more, though old Mr Stevenson the monumental mason would have to lie on his stomach to carve them. Agnes was still afraid that one of those spaces would be for her. She imagined her name there: Agnes aged 8.

Mary always knew when Sarah needed to pee, so Agnes wasn't surprised when she took Sarah by the hand and led her quickly to behind the big yew tree, from where in a few seconds came the noise of piddle on withered leaves. Agnes looked about her anxiously. Among the many things not allowed in the kirkyard peeing was sure to be one, even if it was done by a wee daft girl who didn't know how to wait. Crows in the tops of trees suddenly began to squawk, as if they had seen Sarah and were threatening to clype, like children in the playground. Children clyped to the teacher. Did crows clype to God?

They had once clyped on her when she had lifted her skirts and shown her drawers. Boys had been teasing her.

Mary came back with Sarah. Sarah was so happy she was dancing.

"Will she need to have somebody to take her to pee when she's grown-up?" asked Agnes.

"Dr Fairbairn says she will, but Papa thinks she might be better then."

Agnes agreed with Dr Fairbairn. Papa *wanted* things to be better, so he said they would be. They often weren't.

"Do you know what I heard Mrs Harkness say to Mrs Barnes when John died? She said it would have been better for everybody if it had been Sarah."

They looked at Sarah playing with the bluebells on their mother's grave.

"Well, it's true," said Agnes. "Isn't it? John was clever."

Mary didn't answer.

"Would you like me to tell you something?" said Agnes.

"If you like."

"I think Uncle Henry and Mrs Wedderburn are going to get

married. Bella said they'll have to the way they're carrying on. He put his arm round her waist. She just laughed. She likes him. If they get married he would be Maud's Papa, wouldn't he?"

"Her step-papa."

"He would bring her presents, and not us."

Uncle Henry's presents were still in his big black box with the brass locks. Mrs Barnes had said they should not be given out until some days after Mama's funeral.

"He would still be our uncle," said Mary.

"Maud doesn't want her Mama to marry him. Do you know why? Because she wouldn't ever get sleeping with her mama again."

Agnes wasn't quite so afraid now. Speaking about people she knew, who were still alive, gave her courage.

"He asked her if she would like to go on a voyage to India."

Still Mary would not show interest. She was often like that. People who had been told that one of the Darroch girls was a daftie sometimes thought it was Mary, because she was often silent for hours at a time. Sarah was always making happy noises.

"Bella said that Mrs Barnes wants Papa to marry her. I said he couldn't, for Mama wouldn't let him. I forgot Mama was dead." She was always forgetting that.

She herself needed to pee. Sitting on the tombstone was giving her a chill in the bladder, as Mrs Barnes had warned it would. *She* couldn't do it behind the yew tree. The dead people might not mind if a wee daftie like Sarah pee'd on them but they would if someone like Agnes did, for she knew how to wait.

"Bella said we'll all have to leave the manse and live in a tent like tinkers," she said. She thought it would be fun living in a tent as long as the sun shone and at night they could sleep in the manse.

"She said it's Papa's fault. She said we'd be poorer than colliers. She said we'd have to beg. I told her I'd go and live with Uncle Robert and Aunt Bessie in Edinburgh. She said they mightn't want me." Agnes was indignant. There was no one in the world who wouldn't want her. Everybody liked her, even Mr

175

Crawford, though he sometimes shouted at her for not paying attention.

"If Uncle Henry and Mrs Wedderburn got married I could go and live with them," she said. "I could be Maud's sister."

"You're Sarah's sister," said Mary.

"I know *that*." She went over and kissed Sarah on the cheek. It was really her way of saying that though she loved Sarah she wasn't quite responsible for her. "It wasn't fair, not letting me go with them."

She meant Uncle Henry, Mrs Wedderburn, Maud, and Mrs Maitland who had all gone for a drive in Uncle Henry's splendid new carriage. Mrs Barnes had said it would not be right for Agnes to accompany them. Uncle Robert and Aunt Bessie had gone off home to Edinburgh, and Papa was in Cadzow at Mr Jarvie's funeral, so Mrs Barnes was in charge. Agnes had often been able to wheedle her Mama into letting her have her way. It wasn't so easy to wheedle Mrs Barnes.

"I need to pee," she said. "It's the cold stone. It gives me a chill in the bladder. Can you die from a chill in the bladder?"

"You can die from a skelf in the finger," said Mary.

"Anyway, there are ants. They're biting my bum." Though she felt like crying she couldn't help laughing.

"Don't be vulgar," said Mary.

But Agnes, thinking of her mother under the ground, felt a need to be as vulgar as she could. So as she made for the yew tree she pulled faces, spat, whispered bad words, snatched off her hat and kicked it, and lifted her black skirts to show her white drawers; but when she crouched down to pee behind the yew tree she was weeping.

CHAPTER 11

In John Jarvie's library George Darroch reached a turning-point in his life. His witnesses were Plato, Herodotus, Marcus Aurelius, Thomas Aquinas, Dante, Shakespeare, Gibbon, and others equally illustrious. They saw him go down on his knees, they heard him declaring that if every book that was ever written was searched from cover to cover there would not be found an account of a man guilty of more flagitious sins than his.

Temptation to put the blame on Eleanor pestered him, like the bluebottle buzzing about his head, but he resolutely drove it away.

Often in his pulpit he had proclaimed with fervour, to many sceptical faces in front of him, that there was no sinner so abandoned that Christ's compassion could not embrace him. Now he had discovered such a one: himself. With his wife newly laid in the ground he had come to this house intending, or at least hoping, to have carnal relations of some kind with his friend's widow. Only the lack of a bed or couch had prevented him from making the abominable attempt.

So slippery and persistent was sin that, in the midst of this turmoil of self-accusation, into his mind, like sheep through holes in hedges, flocked memories of Eleanor's naked body. These visions came unbidden and he drove them out, as a farmer might trespassing sheep, but they kept returning.

Once in Christian countries thieves' hands had been cut off, on the principle that a man without hands would not steal again. It was still practised in heathen lands. If the part with which lustful deeds were done was cut off such deeds would no longer be possible. That would be a punishment fit for the Old Testament, gory and terrible. He could imagine someone like Archibald Runcie, perhaps with a longer beard, wielding the knife.

So vivid his imagination he felt in that part unparalleled pain.

But Christ was merciful. If penance was done and shame sincerely felt forgiveness was obtainable. What penance in his case would be fitting? He could keep his promise to Margaret, unfairly elicited though it had been, and marry Mrs Barnes, in a year's time, say, after a proper period of mourning. Look what he would be giving up. It could well be that at Glenquicken there was a pretty young lady, biddable and virginal, with a substantial dowry. Married to her he could have risen in the councils of the Kirk. Dr Cook and his colleagues on the one hand, and Dr Chalmers and his on the other, were more influenced than they would admit by their wives. Those ladies, at table and in bed, would speak favourably of Mr Darroch if Mr Darroch had gone out of his way to charm them, and Mr Darroch would have gone out of his way. Mr Darroch had a beauty of face, an elegance of manner, and a sweetness of voice, gifts that out of diffidence and humility he had not hitherto exploited as he could have.

It was then that he heard clearly for the first time the still small voice in the depths of his mind. It was not the voice of conscience warning him against self-deception. It was the voice of God, with a message.

It told him that he had been picked to turn the Kirk of Scotland away from arid theology towards compassionate and responsible involvement with those many members of society, men, women, and children, degraded by poverty and hitherto ignored by the Kirk.

It was no surprise that he had been picked. There had been his boyhood befriending of outcasts like Sugary Wull. There were his charitable visits to the colliers' houses. There was his attachment to the Cadzow mission. There was, above all, his recognising in Jeremiah Taylor a crusader for justice and not, as so many believed, a dangerous nihilist.

Like so many others engaged in Christ's business he would meet outraged and relentless opposition. Therefore it would be better if his transgressions with Eleanor were never divulged. For that reason had the Lord put it into her head to go to far-off Italy.

He heard her coming. Quickly he got up and dusted his knees. When she came in he was looking intently at a book taken at random from the shelf and opened at random too. It was, he noticed, Milton's *Paradise Lost*.

She had on outdoor clothes.

"I think Jarvie must have read every single one of them," she said. "You prefer dreaming to reading, don't you, George? But take whatever you want. I've been told some of them are worth a good deal of money."

"The value of books cannot be counted in money."

She frowned, not sure whether he was being a simpleton or a hypocrite.

Others were going to be similarly perplexed. He had always had a talent for beating the hypocritical world at its own game, but he had seldom used it. From now on he would. His purpose was honourable. He had tried for many years to serve Christ meekly and honestly and had thereby acquired a reputation for sanctimonious ineffectuality. He was not as simple or shallow as many believed. He would no longer wear his soul on his sleeve. He would take old Lady Annie's advice and think for himself. Already he felt an influx of confidence.

Eleanor was staring at him. "You really are a crafty little rogue, George," she said. "Either you will rise to be Moderator or end up in jail."

He saw his face reflected in the glass of a bookcase. He did not look discomfited. He did not feel discomfited. He would never be discomfited again.

CHAPTER 12

Hitherto, frequently in a confusion of morality, with one scruple scurrying at the heels of another, Darroch was now enjoying this ordered calm in his mind. He had discovered the secret of mastery over others: it was to have so strong a faith in his own rectitude that they became inevitably unsure of theirs. It must not be done by boasting. On the contrary he would be more modest than before, letting righteousness shine out of his eyes but keeping it out of his voice. He must not however make the mistake of being modest to the point of being underestimated or disregarded. His modesty must be able to assert itself.

He soon had a chance to demonstrate how it should be done, in the main street, outside Mr Pendreich's shop, with the big round white cheeses in the window. He met Mrs Mitchell and her unmarried daughter Catherine, a not-so-young woman of at least thirty, made to look permanently sullen by a bad cast in her left eye. Previously he would have raised his hat, bowed, blushed, stammered a word or two, listened obsequiously, cringed a little, and then hurried away, stumbling in his nervousness, for Mrs Mitchell, a colonel's daughter, was an intimidating woman. That afternoon he stopped, calmly, doffed his hat more like a gentleman than a minister, turned his face so that its handsomest angle was presented to them, smiled sadly (no harm in reminding them of his bereavement, bravely borne) and enquired after their health. Mrs Mitchell was charmed, detecting in his manner the merest trace of deference, which was all she looked for. Besides, she was in the market to dispose of her daughter, and he, in a year's time, could be a likely buyer. Poor Miss Mitchell had acquired a habit of closing the lid of her bad eye, giving the appearance of a coquettish wink.

Some out-of-work weavers passed, shouting. Was it not absurd, asked Mrs Mitchell, that they were complaining of their wives and children being hungry yet they themselves had money to waste on gin? They were to be pitied, he replied, in that they were under the delusion that in strong drink they would find courage to face their ills, whereas he knew, and Mrs Mitchell and Miss Mitchell knew, that only in the love of Christ could such courage be found. He was then able to take a graceful leave while Mrs Mitchell gaped and Miss Mitchell winked. Mrs Mitchell called after him that she and her daughter would call at the manse to see his little girls. He called back that they would be most welcome.

For a few minutes he considered Miss Mitchell as a possible wife. She would bring a generous dowry. She had very good connections. She would be grateful and therefore pliant. But for her squint she was quite personable. Relieved at having escaped lifelong virginity, she would be a willing bedmate, in the early days at any rate. Yes, she deserved a place on his list.

In the east end of the town he was delicately stepping among the filth on the street and judiciously pretending not to hear the obscenities shrieked by girls as well as boys, when it occurred to him that there could be no better test of his new self-confidence than to keep his promise to Taylor and visit Mrs Cooper in prison. He had been reminded of her in the cemetery when he had seen among the mourners, Mr Cunninghame, the prison superintendent, a stout red-faced jovial man noted in the district for his prize pigeons.

Cadzow Jail, a fortress-like edifice, had been built in the seventeenth century when it was taken for granted that the only way to discourage criminals was by making their lot as miserable as possible. If it proved fatal, so much the better. Therefore, though the administrative part was almost palatial with marble floors and chandeliers and coloured glass in the windows, the prison proper consisted of a number of small cells with thick walls, brick floors, iron doors, little light, foetid air, and a wooden bench that served as seat and bed. As a result, since the food provided was always unappetising and lacking in nutrition, many prisoners who went in strong and well came out sickly and wasted, and a good number never came out alive. These consequences were on the whole considered satisfactory, in that enfeebled men (and women) were less likely to resume careers of crime, and the dead could be counted on as certain not to.

In the more enlightened nineteenth century there were some people, among them George Darroch himself, or at any rate the George Darroch of yesterday, who wondered if a little kindness might not prove more redemptive. He had noticed, when he had been shown round the prison by Mr Saunders some years ago, that the turnkeys, especially the women, had not only looked brutal but had prided themselves on their brutality, since it was the only language that prisoners heeded. Mr Saunders had condoned it as being an unfortunate but necessary part of the process of atonement, and Darroch's murmur of dissent had been cravenly inaudible. The George Darroch of today would have said frankly that while violent and dangerous prisoners might have to be forcibly restrained there must be others, harmless and remorseful, who should be spared beatings.

The safest way to gain a reputation for courage and charity was by saying boldly what few people would find objectionable: the new George Darroch was going to be adept at this. On the other hand the surest way to become unpopular and distrusted was by speaking the truth, in the face of universal opposition. The old George Darroch had occasionally made this mistake, such as when in a sermon he had denounced wars as unchristian, without taking care to except those waged and won by Britain.

The jail doorkeeper was an old man with a sore, runny nose which he wiped every few seconds with his rough sleeve. He recognised Darroch and said Mr Cunninghame's permission was needed before anyone was allowed to see Bella Cooper.

"Please take me to Mr Cunninghame, then."

"Alang the corridor, sir. His name's on the door. If you see

182

Bella will you tell her auld Jock Armstrong was asking for her?"

Doubtless the concern was senile but it moved Darroch nonetheless.

"Yes, Mr Armstrong, I will. God bless you."

Too late it occurred to him that perhaps the lewd-looking old man had been one of Mrs Cooper's customers. However, a blessing once given could hardly be taken back.

Mr Cunninghame's office was large and well-furnished, with a fire burning in the grate. Its windows were of red, blue, and yellow panes of glass, and had bars across them. On the walls were hung paintings of grim old men who looked like judges. Three stuffed pigeons adorned the desk at which Mr Cunninghame sat, still dressed in mourning clothes. He looked merry and reeked of wine. He had had a very good dinner in the Coach Inn, he said, at Mrs Jarvie's expense.

Rather primly Darroch stated his business.

"Yes, I heard she had asked to see you, Mr Darroch, but to tell you the truth I thought you shouldn't be troubled at such a time. May I say how very sorry I was to hear of your dear wife's untimely decease? It is one thing, knowing that she has gone to a happier place; it is another thing altogether learning to live without her. You may remember my own dear wife departed this life two years ago."

Darroch had forgotten. It was a blunder. Not remembering such a thing not only gave the impression of fallibility, it also gave the feeling of fallibility.

"God's will be done," he murmured, a safe thing to say in all circumstances.

"Aye, and now John Jarvie has left us too. A great loss, Mr Darroch. Did I hear a rumour that you might be taking his place?"

Darroch smiled ambiguously. "It has been suggested."

"You could do worse. It's a fine big kirk, with a bien congregation. It's where I worship myself, you know. From what I hear the manse would have to be scrubbed from attic to cellar. Mrs Jarvie was not what you would call a zealous housewife. But a remarkable woman, just the same."

For a moment he forgot he was speaking to a minister of the

Gospel. Desire turned his eyes moist, and the tip of his tongue protruded.

Thus Darroch learned that he was not the only man who had lusted after Eleanor. Probably there had been many. Had not Mr Brodie let slip his wonder at her beauty? It was possible some had been her lovers. Darroch felt no jealousy. She had been given to him by the Lord for a purpose which had been fulfilled.

"I hear she is going to Italy," said Mr Cunninghame, with a sigh that he hastily turned into a cough.

"Yes, I have heard that too. Tell me, Mr Cunninghame, how is Mrs Cooper?"

"She'll live to be hanged. Dr Fairbairn sewed up her throat expertly."

"Is she able to speak?"

"According to Mrs Frew, who looks after her, she can if she wishes to, in a very small voice certainly; but most of the time she does not wish."

"Will she be tried here in Cadzow?"

"At the next assizes, in six weeks' time. Lord Carmunnock presiding."

"You think she will be hanged?"

"Murder is murder, Mr Darroch. Mind you, the hanging of a woman is a distressing business. I've seen four hanged and I still get bad dreams. Lord Carmunnock will tell you that executions have to be terrifying spectacles if they are to have a salutary effect, but I must say people do not appear to be terrified by them. They bring their children as if to a circus. Have you ever witnessed a hanging, Mr Darroch?"

"No."

"She may ask you to witness hers."

The old icy feeling of helplessness in the face of the world's evil was creeping down from Darroch's heart into his very testicles. He was in danger of lapsing back into his former timorous self. Closing his eyes, he imagined himself on the scaffold, Bible in hand, Christ's representative. The frolicking spectators fell silent and prayed.

"If she wishes me to be present," he said, "if she thinks I can be of any comfort to her, I shall be there."

The crisis was safely passed.

"Mr Saunders always takes a dram before it and after it too. So do I. Were you aware, Mr Darroch, that people being hanged mess their breeks?"

Mr Cunningham laughed, when surely he should have wept.

Had the sordidness of his profession deranged him? But then every citizen of substance, whose taxes paid the salaries of judges and hangmen, were also involved. It could well be that all society was mad, in an insidious, unconscious way, because of the abominable things done in its name.

Suppose, at the General Assembly on the 18th, *that* was the question put to the massed ministers of the Kirk? "Were you aware, gentlemen, that people being hanged mess their breeks?"

I can indulge in such an ironical fantasy, and smile at it, thought Darroch, because I know now the world I live in and can cope with it.

"Do you still wish to see her, Mr Darroch?"

"If you please, Mr Cunninghame."

The superintendent rang a bell. An orderly came in who was instructed to take Mr Darroch to Mrs Frew.

He found her drinking ale and enjoying lewd jests with two other wardresses as burly as she. In the distance some poor creature screamed intermittently. They paid no heed. They were intent on eyeing him lasciviously. No longer ignorant as to the sexual appetites of women, he knew what was going on in their bodies and minds. The old George Darroch would have blushed and cringed. The new George Darroch gave them smiles that inflamed their lust still more. Desire that could not be satisfied was its own punishment, as he well knew.

Mrs Frew took him to a gloomy cul-de-sac that had only three cells. Two were empty. Mrs Cooper was the only murderess in residence.

Mrs Frew opened the heavy iron door. There was a stink of excrement and vomit. It came from a chamber-pot in a corner.

"Bella, here's Mr Darroch the minister frae Craignethan to see you," said Mrs Frew, to the woman huddled on the bench, her face to the wall.

"Must her conditions be so lacking in comfort?" whispered Darroch.

"She's no' used to luxury."

"But she is ill."

"Wha's fault's that? Come on, Bella." She shook the prisoner. "Don't let on you're sleeping, for I ken you never sleep. You'll find her awake, sir, at three in the morning."

"Perhaps if you leave us alone, Mrs Frew, she will speak to me."

"I'll leave the door open. Keep in mind whit she's here for."

Mrs Frew made to leave. He asked her to remove the source of the smell which was making him sick. She was reluctant: it wasn't her job to empty "chanties"; she'd send one of her assistants. He pleaded. She patted his cheek, and then took the chamber-pot away, covered by her apron. He heard her laughing.

By this time his eyes were used to the poor light, so that when Mrs Cooper turned her head to look at him he was able to see that she was younger than he had supposed, and smaller. She had, too, fair hair, like himself and his three little girls. There was a bandage round her neck. He had seen many corpses with faces less hideously discoloured.

It was neither the old nor the new George Darroch that put his hand on her head. It was a George Darroch long since left behind, the one who at the age of ten had sat on the ground beside Sugary Wull.

She whispered: "I'm sorry, Mr Darroch, to be a trouble to you, when you've got sich sair trouble o' your ain."

With tears in his eyes he murmured how sorry he was to find her in such unhappy circumstances, and if he could comfort her in any way he would be very glad to do so.

"You ken whit I did?"

"It was not you who did it, Mrs Cooper. You were not yourself."

"I deserve to be hanged. I deserve to gang to hell."

So did he. But then he was exempt.

"Don't mak excuses for me, Mr Darroch."

"But you must have loved your daughter."

186

"So I did, but she was bad."

"Bad? In what way, bad?"

She had her eyes closed. "They'll hae telt you I was a whure. So I was. I did it for money so that I could live. She did it because she liked it."

"But she was only twelve."

"No' yet twelve. She did things I cannae mention."

Thanks to Eleanor, he had an idea what those unmentionable things might have been.

"Will you show me how to pray, Mr Darroch?"

Yes, but after thousands of prayers he was not sure himself how it should best be done. But that had been the old George Darroch, too timid to claim the privileges due to the Elect.

"Do you believe in God, Mrs Cooper?" he asked.

"I'm no' sure."

"But you cannot pray if you do not believe in Him."

"I think I believe in Him but I don't think He believes in me."

"I assure you, Mrs Cooper, He believes in you."

"I must be the worst sinner in the haill world."

He knew one at least as bad. She would rot in jail and then be hanged. He would go to Edinburgh and perhaps win fame.

"I've tried to pray, but naebody listens."

"God does not shout from the sky, Mrs Cooper, but He is listening nonetheless. He hears our every heartbeat. We must trust Him. If our repentance is sincere He will forgive us."

It would have been difficult even for the new George Darroch to answer her if she had asked why, if God had forgiven her, her fellow men would still hang her. Mercifully she did not ask.

"Will you pray for me, Mr Darroch?"

"Most willingly."

He was about to go down on his knees on the hard rough floor when she stopped him and gave him her blanket to kneel on. "Thank you," he said. Then, hands clasped, and eyes shut, he prayed. "Almighty Father, have mercy on this poor woman and bring peace to her soul. Her sin was dreadful, as she has acknowledged, but so also is her suffering dreadful, which she bears without complaint. I do not think she knows herself what evil impulse possessed her, but to You all things are clear. In

Your bounteous compassion let her be reunited and reconciled with her child in heaven."

She was weeping. She put out her hand and he took it in his. He believed that for those two long minutes his hand was God's. He wept too, and his tears were God's.

On his way out he paid a brief visit to the superintendent's office. This time he did not sit down.

"She is far from well, Mr Cunninghame."

"You can't cut your throat and expect to be in the best of health, Mr Darroch. Besides, she's diseased. So was her girl."

"Diseased?"

"They were both prostitutes, Mr Darroch."

"Whatever she may have been she is now a very unhappy woman."

"Many people would say she deserves to be. She says it herself."

"God help us all, Mr Cunninghame, if we got only what we deserve."

"What do you suggest could be done for her?"

"She could be housed in less dismal quarters."

"She is housed where the regulations require her to be housed."

"If it was possible I would take her home with me and see that she was properly cared for."

"To what end, sir? So that she would be fit for her hanging?"

"To this end. So that we ourselves do not become too hard of heart."

Mr Cunninghame was impressed. "Aye, there's that. I'll see what can be done to make her a bit more comfortable."

"Thank you, Mr Cunninghame. You will be rewarded. By the way, is Jeremiah Taylor still here?"

"Jerry was taken to Glasgow on Friday. He'll be tried there, and get ten years, I wouldn't be surprised. I understand he was caught hiding in your kirk at Craignethan, the impudent rogue. You should claim share of the reward, Mr Darroch."

The new George Darroch hesitated. His former self had felt

188

sympathy for Taylor and had been imprudent enough to show it. It should have been easy now to say, piously, that a long spell in jail was what was needed to cure the radical's contumacy. Mr Cunninghame would be pleased and might mention it to others, men influential in the community, like Sir James Loudun and Lord Carmunnock. But he could not say it, so soon after holding Mrs Cooper's hand. The Lord stilled his tongue.

CHAPTER 13

Annabel Wedderburn was again writing to her sister.

"Dearest Clarabel,

I expect you are as bursting to hear my news as I am to give it to you. Sit tight, and have the sal volatile handy. Captain Darroch and I are going to be married! He hasn't actually asked me yet and being a lady I can't ask him, though I'm sure my eyes have spoken volumes. He will, though, and I've got my answer ready. I see you chewing your hankie in agitation at the antics of your shameless younger sister, but I invite you to go to the sideboard and pour yourself a glass of William's Madeira and drink a toast to me and my slayer of pirates. Speaking temperately for a moment, I'm sure I'm in love with him and he's attracted to me. He's so quick to see the funny side of things. What a contrast to his brother, about whom I shall tell you astonishing things in a moment! Mind you, Henry can be very brusque when he likes. He thought it would be a good idea if he took me and Maud and Agnes and Mrs Maitland (as a chaperone) for a drive in his carriage, on the same day as Mrs Darroch's funeral. We could all do with some cheering up, he said. But Mrs Barnes objected to his taking Agnes. Mr Darroch, you see, was in Cadzow attending Mr Jarvie's funeral and she had appointed herself Agnes's guardian in his absence. Henry was quite brusque with her, but my goodness nothing like as brusque as he was with Mr Runcie whose gig we met on the road. Runcie, if you please, stopped and dared to reprimand us. Henry very sharply indeed told him to mind his own business. What impudence really, the

190

man's just the kirk beadle. You'd have thought he was a Moderator at least. It seems he wants to marry Mrs Barnes. They'd make a good match.

"Henry wants me, Maud, and Mrs Maitland, to go with him to Govan to visit his ship which is being refitted there. You should have heard him boasting about the commodious quarters he has as captain. I said, slyly, that a merchantman wouldn't be a very comfortable ship for women and children to make a long voyage in. He was quite indignant and said his ship was a good deal more comfortable than many that carry passengers. So you see, Clarabel, we do a *pas de deux* round the main question, or should I say the main mast? but we'll direct ourselves to it very soon. Don't be surprised if our trip to Glasgow turns out to be an elopement. One doesn't have to go all the way to Gretna Green to be married by declaration. Maud and I would stay with you, if you and William have no objections, and Henry and Mrs Maitland at a hotel. Mrs Maitland, by the way, thoroughly approves of him. It will be an opportunity for you to meet him and judge for yourself. He is having a house built in Greenock, overlooking the Firth of Clyde, with the hills of Argyll on the other side.

"Poor Arthur Darroch! After his mother's death he told me bitterly that he's sure now he does not believe in God. After watching Henry and me enjoying each other's company so much he doesn't believe in me either. He says he has nothing left to live for. Henry's amused but sympathetic. I told him about Arthur in the elm tree and he just laughed.

"Goodness, what prudes little girls are! We were out walking, Henry and I, with Maud and Agnes trailing behind. Well, when we came to a muddy part of the path he helped me across by putting his arm round my waist. I turned and you should have seen those two, blushing aghast. Maud asked me that night if I was going to marry Captain Darroch. I said it was possible. She then asked — imagine my blushes! — if he would sleep in my bed. I replied demurely that husbands and wives usually slept in the same bed. She wanted to know why. What would you have told her, Clarabel? I just said it was the custom. She then asked if she could sleep with me when he was in his ship at sea. I said of course she could, for I couldn't bring myself to tell her I would be in his ship with him at sea. So I would too. In six weeks he'll be sailing to India with a cargo of 'cannons and cannonballs, wines and cheeses'. The company he works for has a contract to supply the Army there. That would be our honeymoon. Could anything be more marvellous? Except that I might have to leave Maud behind. He's hinted that children thrive on board ship. He has a friend who takes his whole family on voyages.

"I said I had something astonishing to tell you about Mr Darroch. Well, he came home from Mr Jarvie's funeral in a very peculiar state of mind. It must have been a terrible day for him, first his wife's funeral and then his friend's, and in addition what did he do, before leaving Cadzow, but go to the prison there and pray with the woman, a prostitute, who cut her daughter's throat and then her own. Henry says George has always been too eager to rush to the help of people in distress. I said surely that was to his credit. Yes, he replied, but George often wants to help people who can't be helped or don't want to be. Anyway, George came back quite excessive with morality, chiding all and sundry for not being Christian enough. To show what I mean, Henry brought presents for the whole family, including Mrs Darroch. (Lovely silk cloth from Siam. Guess who has it now?) Well, Mr Darroch, to Agnes's indignation, proposed that they should be given instead to sick children in the parish. Agnes's own present was the most beautiful little doll from Japan, dressed in Japanese costume. Agnes thought her father was mad to suggest she should let someone else have it. Of course, from the *Christian* point of view, he was right. Nobler to give than to receive, etc. But to expect a little girl of eight to act up to standards that greybearded leaders of the Church fall short of was most unfair, and I was proud of Henry for telling his brother so. Henry said he'd brought the presents for his nieces and nephews and they were going to get them.

"Then little George got his revenge or tried to get it by rebuking Henry for taking us for that drive through the countryside. He made it sound as if we had done something that the inhabitants of Sodom and Gomorrah would have been ashamed of. He smiled so sweetly when he said it. Then he went on to reprove Henry, in my presence, if you please, for taking advantage of my youth (and me nearly twenty-five!) and innocence. I could have kicked him. Henry was more patient and tolerant. He remembered his brother was under a severe strain. So he just said he did not see how giving people a little happiness was showing disrespect to the dead, and as for himself and Mrs Wedderburn it was their business and he would be obliged if George kept his parsonical nose out of it. He said it pleasantly enough, but I could see if George persisted he was ready to tell him to go to H - - -. George did not persist. He contented himself with giving me a long sad look, as if I were already a fallen woman.

"But George's most astonishing act of piety so far has been his dismissal of Mrs Barnes. Yes, he has told her she must go. Apparently he said it would not do for her to continue as his housekeeper now that he was a widower. It was a position for an older woman. He was very sorry because she had given good service and his little girls were fond of her, but he was a minister of the Gospel, with a duty to set a high standard of morality for his congregation. He would be obliged however if she would remain until he returned from the Assembly. Thereafter he would do what he could to find her suitable employment, though it might be in her best interests to accept Mr Runcie's offer of marriage.

"You may well wonder how I know all this. The reason is simple. Mrs Barnes herself told me. She asked me to come to her room and poured it all out. She was in tears. You know I don't care for her much and to tell the truth I saw the force of little George's argument, but I felt sorry for her. She seemed to have difficulty in comprehending. She thought Mrs Drummond must have turned Mr Darroch against her. I pointed out, as tactfully as I could, that ministers had to be more careful than other men, and she was after all some years younger than Mr Darroch. What seemed to hurt her most was his suggestion that she should marry Runcie. I hadn't myself known that Runcie was interested in her. Yes, she said, he had asked her to marry him. She had refused, because she had thought her first duty was to Mrs Darroch and the little girls. For a woman normally reticent she said a great deal. I couldn't help feeling that she was carrying on a bit too much for a housekeeper who, whether or not unfairly, had been dismissed. She seemed to think she had a claim on Mr Darroch. She must really have believed that she would become the second Mrs Darroch. Perhaps that was the real reason for her dismissal. Little George was not going to be swallowed up by the Dragon.

"Little Jessie continues to improve. She's the most beautiful child I have ever seen and the sweetest-natured, We all love her. Henry says she reminds him of his mother.

"Mrs Mitchell, wife of Sir James's factor, paid a surprise visit to the manse, bringing with her her thirty-year-old skelly-eyed daughter Catherine. The second Mrs Darroch? I think not, for she doesn't seem to like children. Perhaps she resents not having any of her own at her age.

"As usual I have written so much about myself that I have left no room to enquire about you, William, and the children. But when we meet soon we shall blether for hours."

PART THREE

CHAPTER 1

In the train carrying him and his sons at alarming speed and with distracting din from Glasgow to Edinburgh George Darroch looked as soulfully contemplative as a minister ought on his way to attend the most momentous General Assembly of his Church in over two hundred years. What he was really brooding over was Mrs Barnes' disclosure yesterday that she might be with child: her monthly period, regular for years, was eight days late. She had agreed that there could be other reasons, such as emotional stress, and God knew they had all suffered a great deal of that recently.

He suspected another ruse. She had been married to Barnes for six years, when she was younger and more fertile, and yet she had never conceived. Was it likely that what had happened between her and Darroch, when he was feeble with cold and exhaustion, had succeeded, if such an outcome could be called success? Still, he knew, from experience, that from unsatisfactory and incomplete coition conception could result.

Nonetheless, it looked as if she was persevering with the scheme to blackmail him into marriage, with Margaret's posthumous collusion.

He was amazed as well as indignant at her unscrupulous persistence. As a handmaiden should, she had always known her place and kept to it.

He could not help remembering Leah creeping into the dark tent and deceiving Jacob: with the Lord's connivance too.

By spreading her lies or even by telling the truth, that she had

197

been in bed with him, she could ruin him. That he had been innocent and had been taken advantage of would not matter. If his crusade to bring warmth of heart into the Kirk was to have any hope of success no taint of any sort must be seen in him. Ministers and elders like Mr Saunders and Archibald Runcie would seize any opportunity to revile him, while others, more woundingly still, would laugh. Not only Eleanor would call him a crafty little rogue. She had said it in fun, others would say it with hatred or derision.

He would need the Lord's counsel and guidance.

He came out of this disquieting reverie to find James eyeing him appreciatively.

Two days ago James had come to his study and pleaded with him to accept the Glenquicken living. He had replied that he had not yet decided. When he was in Edinburgh he would attend meetings of both Evangelical and Moderate ministers and listen to what they had to say. He was also awaiting a Sign.

Thereupon James, with deliberate irrelevance, had accused his brother of climbing a tree in Mrs Wedderburn's garden at night many times and looking into her bedroom window through a telescope, while she undressed.

The old George Darroch would have been dismayed to learn that one of his sons was a Peeping Tom and the other a mischievous clype.

The new George Darroch, after a pause, had pitied Arthur for being in the grip of illicit passions he was as yet unable to subdue, and praised James for being compelled, through love of virtue, to expose his brother's prurient inclinations, in order of course that he might be helped to overcome them.

It had been a noble little speech, movingly spoken, and it had reassured James. He had gone away satisfied that his father not only had learned the value of hypocrisy but also had become adept at practising it.

In the train the brothers at first conversed amicably. Arthur talked about James Boswell, the Scotch biographer of the famous Samuel Johnson, who when he was leaving Edinburgh to seek his fortune in London had bowed three times to Arthur's Seat and three times to Holyrood Palace.

Darroch would have preferred his son to be inspired by someone worthier than the foolish and sottish lawyer from Auchinleck.

James said that the two places he was eager to visit were David Hume's grave and Burke's house in Tanner's close.

For years James had had this obsession with human turpitude. He kept a notebook into which he copied accounts from newspapers of violent and sordid crimes. Remonstrated with, he had pointed out with his usual precocious pertinence that just as no one should become a doctor who found the effects of diseases too loathsome to look upon, so no one should become a minister who shrank from the study of sins and malefactions, however atrocious.

"Do you know what I think?" he now asked, imitating Agnes.

Darroch smiled. It was a family joke, that preamble of Agnes's.

Arthur smiled too.

"I think that Uncle Henry and Mrs Wedderburn planned to get married when they were in Glasgow."

Henry, Mrs Wedderburn, Maud, and Mrs Maitland a few days ago had set off to visit Henry's ship at Govan. Agnes had wept to be allowed to go with them. Darroch had reluctantly yielded. He had wanted her to stay and help Mary look after Sarah and Jessie. Since her mother's death she had slept more often at Mrs Wedderburn's house than at the manse. He was afraid of losing her. Robert and Bessie had once offered to adopt Mary. Henry and Annabel if they got married might offer to adopt Agnes, as a companion for Maud. They would get the same answer. Only the Lord could take his children from him.

"If they have offspring," said James, "they would be our cousins." Though he again spoke in imitation of Agnes he knew he was pouring salt into his brother's wound.

Arthur gave him a look of hate.

"They'll have lots," added James, in his own voice. "Uncle Henry will want to make up for lost time. They say sailors are like that, don't they?"

Apparently guileless, he nevertheless conjured up a picture of

199

Henry and Annabel heaving in the throes of impatient love.

It was evidently torture for poor Arthur.

With grief Darroch realised that his sons, for years close friends and faithful allies, now distrusted and disliked each other.

CHAPTER 2

With a hissing of steam, a belching of smoke, and a screeching of iron wheels the train arrived in Edinburgh, less than two hours after leaving Glasgow. The passengers alighted shakily. Their faces were streaked with soot. They congratulated one another on a swift but nerve-wracking journey.

Many were ministers, arriving for the Assembly. Other ministers were in the station to meet them. All were dressed in black; all wore solemn expressions. Whatever the outcome of the Great Debate they would uphold the dignity of the Kirk and of God. Not only the citizens of Edinburgh but also visitors from other parts of Scotland, not to mention some from across the border and beyond the sea, would be watching them during the next four days. What they decided on the 18th would have repercussions throughout Christendom. Few nations cherished religion more dearly than the Scots, and the rest of the world honoured them for it.

Darroch felt privileged and proud to be one of them.

His sons were not so thrilled.

"Are they all in black," asked Arthur, "and are they looking so pleased with themselves, because they have banished joy from Scotland?"

"People in Edinburgh say the brothels do their best business during Assembly Week," said James.

Their father pretended not to hear. He would have had to admit that their gibes were partly justified. Too many of his colleagues condemned joy as a dangerous frivolity. As for those

201

few who sneaked off to brothels he would have had more sympathy with them if they had gone blithely.

The new George Darroch had inherited from the old his love of colour, splendour, and gaiety, and also, in a modified form, his belief that physical love could illumine the soul.

He caught sight of old Dr McFarlan, minister of the West Kirk, Greenock, whose stipend was the largest in the land. He was having a mote removed from his eye by a colleague.

Because his eyes were watering he was slow to recognise Darroch.

"George Darroch, sir, born and bred in Greenock. My brother Andrew worships under you. I myself am minister of Craignethan, in the Presbytery of Cadzow."

"Of course, of course, Mr Darroch. I was speaking to your brother on Sunday last at the kirk door. He told me of your sad bereavement. Please accept my profoundest sympathy."

"Thank you, sir."

"Are these fine-looking young men your sons?"

And in truth they were fine-looking, in their dark grey jackets and brown trousers, and with their air of intelligence and respectfulness.

"How do you think it will go on the 18th, sir?" asked Darroch.

"Dr Chalmers remains most sanguine. He is veritably a tower of strength. By the way, Mr Darroch, some of us are forgathering in Mr Haddow's manse this evening, from four o'clock to eight, for consultation and prayer. Perhaps you would like to join us?"

"I would very much."

"Excellent. And if you have any friends finding it difficult to keep to their resolve please bring them with you."

"I shall do so, sir."

"Dr Chalmers has promised to look in at some time during the evening."

They watched the old man being escorted out of the station by three younger ministers, like a general tended by his aides-de-camp.

"It is easy for him," said Arthur. "Uncle Henry says his

congregation has a house ready for him if he has to quit his manse."

"You are being unfair, Arthur," said his father. "Dr McFarlan will be giving up more than most. His stipend is the largest in the country."

"If it was the smallest, Father, that might be something to boast about."

"I wonder who has the smallest?" said James. "Could it be you, Father?"

Daroch laughed, a little uneasily.

"I think it is, Father," said James. "Other ministers demand increases from time to time. You have never done so."

The old George Darroch had not, but the new one would. The Glenquicken stipend was £400. He would ask for £450.

"If Dr Chalmers is so sanguine," said Arthur, "why are they so anxious to round up all those finding it difficult to keep to their resolve?"

Among the ministers waiting outside the station for a cab Darroch saw Peter Fotheringham, who had been close friends with him and John Jarvie at College. Poor Peter was the kind of switherer Dr McFarlan had meant. Even now he could not make up his mind whether to wait or to walk. He was a tall man but everything about him sagged, his mouth, eyes, voice, shoulders, arms, and trousers. It was as if not one but a mass of indecisions weighed him down. Last November when he had put his name to the Claim of Right he had confessed that all he wanted was to be left in peace to read, fish for trout, cherish his wife and children, of whom he had six with a seventh expected, and tend his small flock. If he came out he did not expect many of his congregation to follow him. He and his family would become penurious and homeless.

Many country ministers were in a similar plight. Lacking the imagination to grasp the greater issues involved, they might well decide at the last minute to remain in the safety of the fold.

Darroch ran up to him. "Peter, my dear friend!" he cried.

"George Darroch!"

They shook hands. Fotheringham's grip was limp, Darroch's firm.

203

Fotheringham noticed the Darrochs' black arm-bands. Timidly, he enquired.

"My dear wife, Peter. She departed this life two weeks ago."

Fotheringham's sympathy was so heartfelt as to be almost inarticulate. Tears were in his eyes. Finally he managed to say that in Darroch's place he would not have had the courage to come to Edinburgh: he would have stayed at home with his children.

"I hope Mrs Fotheringham had a safe delivery, Peter."

"Yes, thank God. Another little girl."

"Both well, I trust?"

"Both very well, thank you, George."

Then Robert Drummond's carriage came in sight, sent to take them to the manse. Henderson caught sight of them and raised his hat.

"This is our carriage, Peter," said Darroch. "Let us take you to your lodgings."

"That is very kind of you, George, but I am afraid they are well out of your way. They are in Cambus Street, in the Old Town."

"No matter. Henderson will take you there."

Henderson did not look pleased. It meant a long detour through many narrow streets. Cambus Street was the address of one of Edinburgh's most celebrated brothels.

Probably Mr Fotheringham did not know that. Arthur Darroch did.

His friend, Ronald Ramage had told him. Maggie Phelps, the madam, had once been the mistress of a royal personage. Though now nearly forty, she was still a gorgeous dame who reserved herself for a few special customers, who included a High Court judge. It was not cheap at Maggie's, a guinea a go, but the setting was opulent and the girls beautiful, and a glass of wine was thrown in. There was little chance of catching a dose of pox, for only gentlemen were permitted. It was said that Edinburgh mothers sent their sons to Maggie's to be initiated. Therefore, if Arthur went he would not be turned away on account of his age.

Meanwhile Arthur's father and Mr Fotheringham had passed from the melancholy subject of their late friend Mr Jarvie to the equally melancholy subject of their friend Mr Somerville, who was dying of consumption.

"He wished very much to come," said Fotheringham, "but I doubt if he will be able. The latest news I had of him was that he was coughing up blood."

Again with tears in his eyes Fotheringham looked out at the bustle of life on the street. "I would have thought," he murmured, "that it would be a small matter, to a man about to die, leaving behind him a wife and four small children, whether or not presentees should be objected to or not."

"In itself that is a small matter, Peter," said Darroch, "but surely it points to a matter that is very great: the need for the Kirk to be truly free. That is a matter worth dying for."

But Donald Somerville was not dying for that cause: he was dying because his lungs were diseased. Fotheringham would have dared to say that only to his wife: no one else knew him well enough not to misunderstand. Besides, there was something about George that put him off. Last November George had been as apprehensive as any. Today he seemed quite fearless. Had the death of his wife given him a brief false bravado, which would soon be replaced by despair? Or had his influential brother-in-law, Mr Drummond, whose luxurious carriage they were travelling in, promised him assistance? Mr Fotheringham had often wished *he* had relatives with influence. As for George's talk about the Kirk being truly free it sounded grand, but Fotheringham wasn't sure what it meant. He himself would preach the same sermons as a member of the Free Kirk as he had done while a member of the Established Kirk. He would have a smaller congregation, a smaller stipend, and an unhappier family: that was about all the difference it would make.

"I have been invited, Peter," George was now saying, with that dubious zeal, " to attend Mr Haddow's manse this evening for prayer and consultation. Dr Chalmers will be present."

Fotheringham never felt comfortable at such gatherings. Though he read as many books as he could afford to buy or was able to borrow he never seemed to have anything to contribute to theological and eschatological discussions. As he had said

205

whimsically to his wife, if they talked about fishing or brambling or flying kites he could speak with authority.

"Dr McFarlan of the West Kirk, Greenock, who invited me," said Darroch, "suggested that I should bring with me any friend who might be finding it difficult to keep to his resolve."

"Do I give the impression I come into that category, George?"

"Do not most of us come into it, Peter?"

Fotheringham nodded. He could think of only one exception: Donald Somerville; and his certitude was being paid for with his life's blood.

The carriage stopped at the entrance to Cambus Street.

They watched Fotheringham walking awkwardly over the steep, slippery cobbles, carrying his bag which like the rest of him was scuffed and shabby.

"*He* must have the smallest stipend in the country," said James.

It was intended as sarcasm but, thought Arthur, it was really praise. In spite of his down-at-heel shoes and his sad voice Mr Fotheringham was heroic. He was evidently vague about the cause he was fighting for, like most soldiers in most wars, and he was by no means confident that victory would bring him benefit, but he had given his pledge and he had come to Edinburgh to keep it. If there was no battle, if instead a peace treaty were signed, he would go home rejoicing.

By comparing his father with Mr Fotheringham, who was as transparent as the stream he caught trout in, Arthur realised how unfathomable his father was, or rather had become.

CHAPTER 3

The Darrochs had not been in St Magnus's manse half an hour before twelve-year-old Isa crept up to her mother in the drawing-room and whispered into her ear that Uncle George was different.

Mrs Drummond was cross because she had been left to receive the Darrochs on her own. Robert was at a meeting and had not kept his promise to be home before they arrived. She was playing the piano therefore, rather loudly, as she often did when her temper was ruffled.

She stopped. "What are you saying, Isa?"

"I said Uncle George is different."

"Different? What do you mean, different? I saw no difference." What she meant was she had seen no improvement. George had seemed to her the same sweet-smiling little humbug. When she had handed him the letter which had been waiting for him, delivered a few days ago by a cadger or messenger, he had not had the good manners to open it there and then and tell her whom it was from. He had taken it up to his room to read. It was scented, but Bessie did not really believe it was from a woman, arranging and assignation: George might not be too moral for that, but he was certainly too craven.

Isa was thinking hard how to put it. "Well, he's not so — ." But she could not think of a suitable word. "I thought he would be sadder because of Aunt Margaret."

"He seemed to me quite sad enough." Those tears in George's eyes at the time of Margaret's death had struck Bessie as being almost as gruesome as the snot at Sarah's nose. Poor Sarah could not help it. George could. She was sure his tears were artful in some way she could not fathom.

Suddenly she realised what it was Isa had noticed. George was no longer meek. His meekness had often exasperated her; his lack of it was going to exasperate her even more, especially if its cause was that he had decided to accept the Glenquicken living, which in her view should never have been offered him. If not thoroughly snubbed at the outset he would go all the way from being tiresomely humble to unbearably conceited. He was really a very odious little man.

"Arthur's different too," said Isa. "He never used to be so grumpy."

"You forget he misses his mother. Arthur is a good-hearted lad. He loved his mother."

"James is a cruel beast. He stepped on Dandy's paw. He said it was an accident but it wasn't."

Bessie felt that it was only fair to assume that James too missed his mother. "Was Dandy growling at him?"

"Yes, but he wouldn't have bitten him. It would just have been a nip anyway. I wish they had brought Mary instead of him."

"Mary it seems has to look after Sarah."

"I'm glad they didn't bring her. That would have been awful."

So it would have been, but as a Christian mother teaching her daughter to be kind to those less fortunate Bessie had to reprove her. "That is unkind, Isa. Sarah is a contented little girl."

"But she smells, and her nose is always needing to be wiped."

"Don't let your father hear you say such things. He seems to be fond of Sarah."

Isa could not see how anyone could be fond of a daft wee girl who scarcely knew her own name. "At least they could have brought Agnes. She's not good at playing for she goes into sulks but she would be better than nobody."

"Why not ask James to play with you?"

"James!"

"He's not much older than you, and it would do him good to be a child for a change."

"What would we play at? Dressing up my dolls?"

"He might like that." Bessie smiled.

"He'd break them just for spite."

"Then play with a ball."

Isa whispered. "But we're in mourning, Mama."

Bessie ought not to have been playing the piano. "We are not sour-faced Evangelicals," she said. "Play quietly, on the back lawn."

"All right. I'll ask him. But he's sure to be a butter-fingers."

"Ask him politely. Remember he too must miss his mother, in his own way."

"He's too selfish to miss anybody."

Isa, however, murmured that when she was out of her mother's hearing.

To her surprise James consented. He was courteous. He apologised for stepping on Dandy's paw. He even patted Dandy.

She did not know that he was desperate to enlist everyone's help, even hers, to persuade or coerce his father into taking the Glenquicken living. He was afraid that his father, who for years had been dreaming of the grand sacrifical gesture of walking out of manse and kirk, might not have the strength of will to forgo it.

It was difficult for him to keep up the appearance of enjoying himself, for he kept dropping the ball, to Isa's indignation, and the dog kept jumping up on him, to her amusement; but he had to try, for Aunt Bessie was spying on him from a window.

After five minutes he had had enough. As well as exhausted and disgusted, he was also sweaty, a condition he abhorred. He went and sat on a bench in the shade of an elm tree, wiping his face with his blue silk handkerchief.

"You're not tired already!" screamed Isa.

"I'm having a rest. It's too warm."

"But we've hardly started!"

209

He wondered where she, so fat, found the energy. Malice must be its source.

Suddenly he was trembling. Since his mother's death, this often happened, and not only when he was consciously remembering her. He felt that not only his own existence but all humanity's was futile.

Isa ran over and with a shriek of laughter bounced the ball on his head.

It was coated with slavers and probably was daubed with dog shit for the little drooling beast was allowed to defecate all over the garden.

She expected him to protest and was puzzled when he didn't.

"What's the matter with you?" she asked.

She was not aware of the magnitude of her question. It would have taken him hours of anguished introspection to answer it.

"You're not natural, James Darroch."

On her plump pink glistening face there was no shrewd or subtle insinuation. She was just a peevish girl who still believed babies were left by angels under bushes.

"You're not like other boys."

That was so. Most other boys did not have a mother recently dead, a sister permanently imbecilic, and a father dangerously deluded.

"You don't like things boys are supposed to like.'

It was strange how dry his mouth was, though his body was soaked with sweat. "What kind of things?" he asked.

"Well, football and golf."

"I would have thought those were very unnatural activities."

"Don't be smart," she said. But she felt relieved. This was more like the James she could safely tease. "And you don't like girls."

Again her face was merely crass and childish. For her not liking girls was the same as not liking football.

"Everybody thinks you're so good-looking, with your blue eyes and fair hair. You think it yourself. Well, I don't. Boys should have boils sometimes."

She had not mentioned boils as a general idea. She was evidently thinking of them on some particular boy's neck. Fat

Isa was in love.

"Do you know some boy who has boils?" he asked. "Beautiful boils?"

She blushed. "No, I don't. And I didn't say boils were beautiful." She was in a hurry though to change the subject. She sat down beside him. "Tell me about your Uncle Henry. Has he got a scar on his face?"

"Yes."

"Did a pirate do it with a sword?"

"A parang, a kind of sword, I believe."

"Mama thinks it could have been done in a brawl in a tavern."

"So it could."

"Do you like him?"

For the first time James examined his feelings towards his uncle. He supposed that he should have found most unlikeable a man with a hideous scar, a swaggering walk, and a hearty voice, but he did not. Uncle Henry had taken Sarah on his knees and made a fuss of her. Mary had approved. Anyone that Mary approved of James could not dislike.

"Yes, I like him," he replied.

"Because he's got lots of money?"

That was another aspect of his uncle that James had not considered. He hoped it was true. Uncle Henry if he was well-off would not let his nieces suffer. Even if he married Mrs Wedderburn it would still be all right, for she was generous too.

Unaccountably tears came into James's eyes. It was not the first time he had shed tears, but it was the first time he had let anyone see them. He was too proud to cover his face with his hands; besides, these were dirty from contact with the ball and the dog.

Astonished and fascinated, Isa stretched her neck to look.

"You're crying," she said. "Why?"

The dog too asked him, barking.

He got up and walked to where he was hidden among rose bushes.

Isa listened hard. She heard birds singing, but not James sobbing. When she wept she sobbed. He must have been

211

pretending.

She had promised her two best friends at school that they could come to the manse and meet her cousins. They were especially interested in James because of his blue eyes and fair hair.

She thought of Harry Walkinshaw, the boy whose boils were precious to her. He was a pupil at the High School and already had a deep voice. He played football on the Meadows and golf at St Andrews. He could knock James Darroch down with one blow. He was going to be a lawyer, like his father. She understood him. He wasn't a conundrum like James Darroch.

CHAPTER 4

Bessie had some words in private with her husband before the evening meal at six o'clock. Something would have to be done about George, if he was to be introduced to Dr Cook and Principal Mcfarlan, not to mention Sir Thomas. It would have to be made clear to him, sternly if necessary, that even if he were to become parish minister of Glenquicken with stained glass windows and £400 per year he must not put on airs in the presence of his superiors. No, that was not right. He did not put on airs: he was much too sleekit for that. If he had he could have been properly rebuked, for surely of all the qualities required in ministers of the Gospel, particularly those of inferior station, the foremost was modesty. As it was, snubs which previously would have had him cringing with self-effacement were no longer effective. It was not as if, being stupid, he did not notice them. He seemed to see them before they were uttered and either ignored them or worse still took them as compliments.

"What are you trying to say, Bessie?" asked Robert.

"I am trying to say, Mr Drummond, that George has come out of his shell with a vengeance and must be made to withdraw back into it at once."

"He is a little more confident perhaps, and has a little more faith in himself. Please remember he has suffered many disappointments. Some good fortune has come to him at last."

"Why should his having more faith in himself result in his showing less respect for those who have contributed to his good fortune?"

"In what way has he shown you less respect, my dear?"

"It is not a laughing matter, Mr Drummond. When I informed him as I had every right to do, that if his brother and Mrs Wedderburn were married by declaration, without a minister being present, as apparently was their intention, I could never receive them in my house, he proceeded to read me a lecture, if you please, on Christian charity. He did not actually use those words, he was much too sly for that, but that was what he meant. Sly, Mr Drummond. Your brother-in-law, your protégé, the next incumbent at Glenquicken, thanks to you, has become a little monster of slyness."

Drummond himself had thought of George as a chess-player who had been taking lessons and now made his moves more artfully.

"We must not forget, my dear, that his wife is newly dead."

"It is he who forgets that. Otherwise would he be so confident, as you have said?"

"Also he now finds himself under compulsion to depart from a course of action which for some time he has believed was his moral duty."

"This is a change of tune on your part, Robert. Moral duty indeed. I have heard you describe it as obtuse obduracy."

As one whose side had won or rather was about to win Drummond could afford to be magnanimous.

"I was not being quite fair."

"I do not agree. They could not see the truth, therefore they were obtuse. They refused to be enlightened, therefore they were obdurate."

"As you know, Bessie, we have had a survey of the whole country carried out, with a report on every individual minister. Do you know what the report on George said? That he was not known as a zealot, that he was timorous in expressing his views, that he was at heart a conformist, and that, being very fond of his children, he would shrink from exposing them to hardships for the sake of dubious principles. You and I, my dear, know him well enough not to quarrel with that estimate."

"Yes, but he has changed. Even Isa noticed it. You have admitted it yourself. And I am by no means convinced that he is

214

fonder of his children than of his dubious principles. I am glad however that you agree they are indeed dubious."

"I should prefer to call them mistaken."

"Let him be as sly as he wishes, so long as it is not at our expense or at the expense of our friends. If you will not warn him I shall do so myself."

"I shall remind him of the need for discretion."

"Tell him to hold his tongue. That is all that is needed. And to stop smiling as if he was forgiving us all."

At table, where the second-best delf was used and none of the best silverware, Bessie did not take her own advice and hold her tongue. She had an urge to speak, belligerently. She paid no heed to her husband's admonitory frowns.

She asked George point-blank who his letter was from. She did not expect to uncover some guilty secret. She would have been appalled if she had. She simply wanted to wipe off his face that angelic smile.

"That is George's business, my dear," said Robert, curtly.

"Good gracious, Mr Drummond, am I not to ask a civil question in my own house? It is not a state secret, I suppose."

George replied, with a sweetness which annoyed her but which would have annoyed her a great deal more if she had known that it was sugar disguising a bitter lie.

"I did not wish to speak about it, Bessie, because, you see — " here he paused for a long sad sigh — "it is from my friend and colleague, Donald Somerville, of Glasgow, who is dying of consumption."

She was taken aback. She hated fatal illnesses to be discussed, especially at meal times. She did not know Somerville and it did not matter to her whether he died tomorrow or next year, but what was killing him could kill her too and her husband and daughter. This was another instance of George's slyness.

"If he is so ill,' she said, "I wonder that he has come to Edinburgh."

"He is very fervent. He wishes to see for himself the outcome."

"He should have stayed at home and lived longer. Does he always perfume his missives?"

"I think, because of the nature of his illness, he is more sensitive to the ordinary malodours of life than we who are blessed with good health."

If his intention was to shut her up he succeeded, at any rate as far as that subject was concerned. It took her only a minute or two to find another.

"If your brother and Mrs Wedderburn are not married in a church, by a properly qualified minister, their offspring, should they have any, will not be able to be christened. Was that not pointed out to them?"

Unfortunately that subject, with its potential for discomfiting George, could not be pursued, because of Isa's presence. Isa was at the stage when she was beginning to doubt the fairy-tale accounts of how babies were conceived and born. Friends at school had ferreted out the truth and were poisoning her mind with it. Bessie wanted badly to tell George that his brother's children would be bastards, in the Church's eyes, but she could not. Aggravating her still more was his expression. He should have been looking downcast. On the contrary he looked exalted, a condition ridiculous in a man with dimples, particularly while he was chewing beef carefully, because of sore teeth.

He waited till he had swallowed that mouthful and wiped his mouth with his napkin. "Who would deny little children God's grace because of fault in their parents?" he asked.

Bessie could not very well reply that *she* would: though there were passages in Scriptures to support her. The Evangelicals had been impudently putting it about that they, and not the Moderates, spoke for Christ. What George had just said was typical evangelical claptrap, painful to listen to, but hard to contradict. Her husband, too, seemed determined to offer her no help.

There was a long pause.

James, as sleekit as his father, perhaps in league with him, addressed his uncle. "If it is a good day tomorrow, Uncle Robert, could we go and have a look at Glenquicken?"

216

"There wouldn't be room for us all in the carriage," said Isa.

"I think James meant himself, his father, and Arthur," said her father. "They are the ones who are going to live there. We have seen Glenquicken many times. I think it is an excellent idea. What do you say, George?"

"I hope you are not proposing that they call on Sir Thomas, without an invitation," said Bessie.

"There would be no need for them to call on Sir Thomas. All they want is to have a look at their future home."

"Are you not being premature, Mr Drummond?" She smiled. She too could be sly.

"I'd like to see Glenquicken," muttered Arthur.

His surliness, in his aunt's view, was to his credit. He seemed to her the only Darroch genuinely stricken by his mother's death.

"Well, George?" asked Robert. "Shall I tell Henderson to take you there tomorrow morning? In the evening I am having some friends here whom I would like you to meet, but you would be back well before then."

"Thank you, Robert. As you may know, like many of my colleagues at this difficult time, I await a sign. It could well be waiting for me in Glenquicken kirk, or among the massed roses in the manse garden."

It was Bessie herself who had foolishly told him about those hundreds of roses, white, yellow, and red. Just like sly George to throw them in her face, thorns and all.

Still, there was the satisfaction of seeing her husband wince at this latest and most outrageous display of George's cunning. She was enjoying it when the housekeeper, Miss Blakeston, came and announced in a voice too joyous for her mistress's liking at the time and even less so later, that Mr Darroch's brother, Captain Henry Darroch, and Mrs Darroch had just arrived. Like most old maids Miss Blakeston was too romantic for her own good.

CHAPTER 5

That evening Annabel Darroch added some paragraphs to the long letter she was writing to her sister.

"I did not want to visit the Drummonds. I was afraid *she* would slam the door in our faces. I suppose, heaven help me, I was anxious to protect Henry, him who has faced typhoons and hurricanes. He just laughed and said he liked Robert Drummond and in any case felt obliged to call on his brother and nephews to see how they were bearing up and also to report that Agnes had been sent back to Craignethan, along with my Maud, in the custody of Mrs Maitland.

"I have discovered that my husband is an optimist, while I myself am a pessimist, as regards expecting people to behave in a decent, reasonable way. I must say they usually do, towards him at any rate. Perhaps this is because he can be very formidable when he likes, but I think it's because he's so obviously frank and generous. He likes people and is prepared to trust them; which amazes me, considering that he has seen murder done, and pillage, and rape, and has had to kill other men to keep them from killing him. He is certainly the most cheerful as well as the sanest person I have ever known. Yet I do not think he believes in God. He never mentions religion. He is just the kind of person Edinburgh needs at this Assembly time, with its streets full of gloomy-faced, self-important, black-coated ministers, and it would do any manse good at any time of the year to have a visit from him, even though he is liable to use language too salty and honest for bigots.

"I must not make him out to be perfect. He spoils me too much for that. I have a hundred faults but he sees none. As you well know all my life I have been vain as regards dress. So I said, with customary pertness, that if I was to call on St Magnus's manse and be looked upon by Mrs Drummond as more or less a harlot, then I must do it with magnificence, that was to say, wearing the grandest clothes the Edinburgh shops could provide. Henry instantly was in enthusiastic agreement whereas of course like a good Scotch husband he should have severely scolded me. We scoured the shops and bought, for thirty-six guineas (enough to keep George Darroch's Cadzow mission in bread and soup for months) the most gorgeous dress, of green taffeta, with hat, shoes, gloves, and parasol to match. We chose green to go with my red hair. I was trying them all on later in our hotel room and feeling very pleased with myself when I remembered poor Margaret Darroch. I felt ashamed and wanted to wear something not quite so grand. Henry would not hear of it. He said that in my splendid green outfit I would give people pleasure just to look at me and I would do Margaret in her grave no harm. That is where he thinks she still is, and always will be, in the earth, rotting. Surely he is right. Heaven is believed in only by heart-broken women and women-pleasers like George Darroch. I am sure Robert Drummond, Minister though he is, does not believe in it.

"So it was a very happy handsome couple, she in green and he in dark-blue and gold, who stood on the doorstep of St Magnus's manse this evening in the sunshine. Manse and kirk are neighbours, both built of the same dignified grey stone. The latter is large and has one of the tallest steeples in the city, the former has one of the largest gardens. We were impressed. Mr Drummond must indeed be an ecclesiastical potentate. Even a blackbird we heard singing in a lilac bush seemed more melodious than those of Craignethan, as if it fed on fatter worms. I don't think I had realised till then how unsuccessful poor George has been, stuck for twenty years in a bleak little parish like Craignethan. I remembered Mrs Drummond telling me that *they* had titled personages in their congregation. I had replied so had *we*, in the shape of the Louduns, but she had sniffed and said heritors did not count: they were bound to be there.

"The Drummonds' housekeeper opened the door, a pleasant-faced old lady of about sixty, in a black dress and white bonnet. No doubt from overhearing her master and mistress talking, she deduced we were the newly married pair and, being romantic, was delighted to see us. She asked us to wait in the drawing-room while she informed Mr and Mrs Drummond of our arrival.

"We were astonished by the drawing-room. I had gathered from a remark dropped once by Mr Drummond that he was fond of paintings. Here was much evidence of it. Every wall was covered with paintings, and they were not all of bearded gentlemen and solemn ladies. There were even one or two of completely naked ladies. There were also busts and statues, in bronze and marble. One statue, quite life-sized, in a corner, shielded by plants, was of the goddess Diana, I think, because she had a quiver of arrows on her back — her only covering! She was not of slender proportions, and reminded me of Mrs Jarvie of Cadzow. There was a piano, a fine piece of furniture in itself, but I could tell it was not just an ornament, because of the sheets of music. There were several other handsome pieces, especially a small walnut table inlaid with mother-of-pearl, French I was sure.

"I could not help comparing this drawing-room with that in the manse at Craignethan, where there were only two paintings, of gloomy mountain scenes, and no statues at all. George has never had money to spend on works of art, but if he had had he would have given it to the poor. Robert Drummond has preferred to encourage artists. I have always suspected that George, for all his daintiness, was a Calvinist at heart. He once told me that as a young man he had written poetry, but so I'm sure did Calvin. George has always seen himself as a favourite of God, in spite of his many disappointments.

"I should have mentioned that there was the most lovely carpet, white and adorned with Chinese scenes. Henry remarked that he had two like it stored away, along with other treasures from the East. They were for our house in Greenock

220

when it was built. He also remarked that of all the beautiful things in view I was by far the most beautiful. He has a habit of saying casual things like that. Do you wonder I went over and kissed him?

"Just in time I got back to my chair. Robert Drummond came in. I do not know him very well and to tell the truth have always been a wee bit intimidated by him, but he could not have been more congratulatory if we had been married in Glasgow Cathedral and not a lawyer's office smelling of old paper. It occurred to me that if the Church of Scotland was dominated by men like him it would be a more successful institution, and the whole country would be more civilised.

"I thought he looked apprehensive, and soon discovered why.

"Mrs Drummond came in. Trying to speak calmly, she said she was sorry but she must ask us to leave her house at once. I have never seen a woman so unhappy.

"I knew why. Not yet forty, she was too young to be affected by what is called the change of life, which causes many women to be peevish and capricious. What caused her to resent my happiness so bitterly was because she knew its cause. Never once had she allowed herself the supreme joy of being possessed, body and soul, by the man she loved. She had convinced herself that any woman who did was sinful, profligate, abandoned, etc. Married over fifteen years, she had never seen her husband's body, nor wished to. During the connubial act, as she would call it, it could have been the handle of a brush penetrating her for all she knew or cared. She saw how different it was with me. It was not moral outrage she felt, but envy.

"She left the room as soon as she had spoken.

"George, Arthur, James, the fat girl Isa, and the little dog Dandy were now in the drawing-room. They all looked embarrassed, especially the dog.

"Mr Drummond was at a loss. If he had remonstrated with his wife he would have made her worse. If he apologised on her behalf it would be a kind of disloyalty.

"Henry patted the dog.

"His brother George, I could see, longed to act as peacemaker but had the sense, newly acquired it seemed to me, to realise that he would only make matters worse. So he held his tongue. From now on he was going to look after himself.

"James frowned, as I had often seen him do, at what he considered the pettiness of human behaviour.

"Isa smiled at me, uncertainly. I smiled back. She blushed, and smiled more happily. She and I were friends.

"Arthur had caught sight of Diana in the corner. He could not, after that, look at me but kept his eyes on some blue birds in the carpet.

Curiously, I was not angry. I had half-expected it, after all; so in a way I was partly to blame. I thought it was a pity, as I would have if the goddess had been knocked over and broken. Henry and I would lose no sleep over the incident, which would bring us still closer. Robert and Bessie would, and they would be further apart.

"I took Henry's hand and led him out. The housekeeper opened the outside door for us. She was woebegone. No doubt she would be reprimanded for having let us in, but her tears were also for an occasion ruined that should have been joyous for everyone. I kissed her cheek.

"We were in the carriage about to drive off when Henry remembered that we had not told George about Agnes having gone home to Craignethan.

James came out. "Father wants to know where you are staying in Edinburgh," he said. "He would like to call on you this evening."

"Henry told him the Connaught Hotel.

"We then departed, chased all the way to the gate by the little dog, barking in friendliness."

CHAPTER 6

When Bessie had ordered Annabel and Henry out of her house because they had been married by declaration and not according to Christian rites, scarcely the most heinous of sins, George Darroch, outwardly composed, had wondered what she, and all Christendom with her, would say if it was ever discovered that he had looked on Eleanor Jarvie's naked body.

No one would believe, Bessie least of all, that it had been part of his preparation for the sacred task laid upon him by the Lord. Indeed it was all so strange that he sometimes found it hard to believe himself. Yet it was true. Had not the Lord been with him and Mrs Cooper in the prison cell? (Tears came into his eyes as he remembered that sad yet inspiring scene.) And had not the Lord arranged to send Eleanor far away?

These were his reflections, during that contretemps in the drawing room. Annabel's smile of pity therefore was misconceived.

He was just as composed later that evening when, as he was walking with Peter Fotheringham to Mr Haddow's manse, through air polluted by smells from the city's thousands of privies, his stooped and shabby friend suddenly remarked that he had just learned that George had been offered the living at Glenquicken. Could it be possibly true?

It was supposed to be a secret. Who had blabbed? It could have been Bessie, but none of her acquaintances was likely to know any of Peter's. It could hardly have been Robert. It had not been Darroch himself. The most probable culprit was Sir Thomas. Benefactors did not have to be discreet.

Divinely prompted, Darroch remained cool, in contrast to his friend who was quite agitated.

"From whom did you learn this, Peter?" he asked.

"From John Forrester, of Meiklewade Parish, which is also in Midlothian, like Glenquicken. He heard it from a Glenquicken elder, Mr Osgoode, who I believe had it from the chief heritor himself, Sir Thomas Blaikie. According to John, Glenquicken is one of the most coveted livings in the country. He could not understand how it could be offered to you. I suggested that it could have been through the influence of Mr Drummond, your brother-in-law."

"May I ask, Peter, where and when this colloquy with Mr Forrester took place?"

"In a teashop this afternoon. I went out for a walk and met him. We repaired to the teashop. There he informed me. Is it true then?"

Darroch could easily imagine them, self-piteously and, alas, enviously sipping their tea. Meiklewade Parish, like Peter's own, was not lucrative.

"I realised then, George, why you were so unaccountably cheerful at the station."

"My dear Peter, how could I be cheerful, with my dear wife, the mother of my seven children, dead only two weeks?"

"I beg your pardon, George. I put it clumsily. More cheerful, I should have said, than one would have expected."

"Do not discount the cheerful comfort of the Lord, Peter."

"That is so. I apologise again. Still, you were quite surprisingly buoyant. If I may say so you still are."

"The Lord's influence is most benign, Peter."

"Yes, indeed. According to John, Glenquicken carries a stipend of at least £400 per annum."

"Among Christians, Peter, money should be the last consideration."

"So it should be, George. But, in spite of the Lord's cheerful comfort, and though money must not be of prime importance, there are times when Christians feel downcast. My own stipend is £120 per annum. As you see, my clothes are shabby, my shoes are down at heel, and I can no longer afford to buy books. Worst of all, my children often have to go without. John was not sure whether or not you had accepted. He thought you could not possibly refuse. I reminded him that you were one of us and had signed the Claim of Right. By accepting therefore you would be breaking that solemn undertaking."

"The offer was made to me the day before my wife died."

"There had been no mention of it beforehand?"

"None. It came out of the blue, as Christ's mercies often do. My dear wife, anxious for her children, begged me on her death-bed to accept."

"Did you promise her you would?"

"What husband, who loved his wife, what father who loved his children, would not? At that time too my little girl, Jessie, was seriously ill."

At that moment they were passing the house where John Knox had once lived.

"I am not a clever enough casuist, George, to be able to advise you which promise should take precedence, that given to your dying wife, or that given to your colleagues."

"What, Peter, of my promise to Christ? Does not that take precedence over all other promises?"

Fotheringham was in a trap. It showed in his lugubrious eyes which resembled those of a rabbit being choked in a snare. He was not sure what George meant by his promise to Christ. He should have known for he had been a minister of the Gospel as long as George.

"I have not accepted, Peter."

Fotheringham was glad. The snare had broken: the rabbit bounded off to the safety of its burrow.

"Thank God, George," he said.

He stopped and insisted on shaking George's hand.

"I have not refused either. I am to give my answer after the 18th."

The rabbit had bolted straight into another noose. The gladness fled from Fotheringham's eyes. He walked on, more stooped than ever: it was as if he had severe pain in his heart.

"None of us, Peter, at this moment knows what will happen on the 18th, in St Andrew's Church."

"If we are faithful to our pledges we shall all walk out."

"How many sincere changes of mind have taken place? According to Robert Drummond, a great many. The Moderates, it appears, have had a survey carried out, during the past two or three weeks. They have gathered reports on every minister, including ourselves."

"Reports compiled by people antipathetic to our cause."

"No doubt, but surely they have tried to be truthful and objective. At any rate the Moderates are now very sanguine. There will be no disruption, they say. They are convinced that on Thursday fewer than thirty will remain obdurate or as you would say, staunch."

"Do they think we are all turncoats and cowards?"

"Sheep returned to the fold, is how they would express it, I think. They are not our enemies, Peter. Whatever happens they will remain our brethren in Christ."

They were then on the doorstep of Mr Haddow's manse, which was a dour grey building next to a dour grey church. It was, though, a famous church. Men later to be tortured and killed for their Presbyterian faith had preached there. One of them was Alexander Loudun. Their names and dates were inscribed on plaques on the walls, with quotations from their sermons or speeches. Those cries from beyond the grave were not meek or modest. Those martyrs would have been scornful of their present-day successors who were fighting, genteelly at that, for so small a cause as the right of congregations to reject unsuitable presentees. Their own ambitions had been fiercer and nobler.

So now were George Darroch's.

CHAPTER 7

At least thirty ministers were present. In one large room and two smaller ones they prayed, meditated, and conversed in small groups, as often as not on their knees. Among them were old Mr Robertson of Strathbogie, who had had many in tears last November as he had told how with a family of twelve to provide for he was nevertheless ready to give up everything at the call of duty; Dr Lorimer of Haddington who in November had proposed the motion to make the state of the Kirk subject of a special prayer, to be offered up in all manses at six o'clock every Saturday evening: Dr Landsborough of Saltcoats who had been foremost in the revival of religion during the past thirty years; Dr McFarlan of Greenock; and others equally venerable and godly. Phrases like "the temple will be purified", "the Captain of our salvation", and "the interests of vital godliness" dropped from their bearded lips and were heard with reverence by all the ministers there, with one exception. It seemed to George Darroch that such language was stilted, antiquated, and lifeless: it had become an end in itelf. What was needed, if the weavers of Cadzow and the colliers of Craignethan and their like throughout the whole country were to be won for Christ, was language that they could understand and respond to, simple, fresh, and intimate like that used by Jeremiah Taylor.

Suddenly a tall stern-faced minister rose to his feet and announced: "The Lord has vouchsafed me a vision."

He was pretending to be inspired, but his inspiration was not so urgent as to keep him from waiting for the whole company to come and listen.

"In my vision I saw us as the new children of Israel, held in bondage by those who would have us worship false gods. Among the descendants of Abraham also were doubters who cried that the whips and staves of the Egyptians were preferable to the hunger and thirst of the desert and the claws and fangs of wild beasts. If these had been heeded there would have been no triumphant Exodus, no meeting of the True God face to face, no handing down from on high of the divine commandments, and no temple built to the glory of the one God. Do not let us in our generation be turned aside from our sacred purpose by those of faint heart. Let us rather go forth boldly and endure what must be endured, so that the temple may be cleansed and the Word made pure."

He sat down, apparently exhausted in spirit after saying what had already been said, and yawned at, a thousand times before.

They were all too polite or stupefied to point out to him that he would not have to endure much. His parish was in a well-to-do section of Glasgow. His congregation would strew his martyr's path with flowers and gifts.

Up jumped another greybeard who proceeded sonorously to give his version of the Word made pure. Even for those accustomed to evangelical jargon it was not easy to make out his meaning. The gist of it appeared to be that in the new dispensation joy would be frowned on more relentlessly than it was now; sinners, particularly fornicators and adulterers, would once again be publicly condemned, and all attempts to make churches and church services more beautiful would be anathema. He would have warmed Archibald Runcie's heart: he chilled George Darroch's.

Others gave similar testimony. It was as if they were playing a game, to see who could speak with most solemnity and least substance.

They would have addressed Mrs Cooper in her cell in this manner, not because they were callous but because it had become a habit.

Darroch rose to his feet. Because he was small, and with his fair hair and dimples did not look august enough to have anything valuable to say, little heed was paid to him at first. There was even a pretence that he had risen to stretch his legs, not to speak.

When he began to speak they listened. They had no choice. The Lord spoke through him. His voice was loud, clear, and authoritative.

"George Darroch, gentlemen, of Craignethan Parish, in the Presbytery of Cadzow. In my parish there are colliers, who do not come to church, though frequently I go to them. In Cadzow nearby there are weavers, most of them at present out of work, who do not attend any Cadzow church. These men, and their families, live in conditions of degrading poverty.

"A few days ago a man called Taylor, a radical and revolutionary, came to our district to spread his doctrine. To those unfortunates he painted a picture of a future where they would all have regular employment, just conditions, fair wages, good houses, and schools for their children. Who will be amazed to learn that they listened to him, as to a prophet?

"The authorities soon decided that he was dangerous. A warrant was issued for his arrest. He had to flee. He was apprehended while sheltering in my church, where the side door is never locked. He was dragged off to Cadzow Jail and thence transferred to Glasgow where he will be tried and no doubt sent to prison. Others who think like him will take his place. His is a message that will spread throughout the land."

Darroch paused. They could not have gazed at him with greater horror if he had been describing to them fornication with Eleanor.

"Taylor, gentlemen, is a self-confessed atheist. He has said that he has too much respect for God to believe in Him. He was referring, I think, to the many shameful things done or tolerated by those who do profess belief. Who will say that it is not a just accusation?

"A struggle has begun in our country, nay, throughout all Christendom, between Taylor and his kind on the one hand, and ministers of the Gospel, such as ourselves, on the other, for the minds and souls, not only of the poverty-stricken and degraded masses, but also of those intelligent and educated members of society who consider it unjust and unchristian that some men should have much more than they need while others have much less. We Christians must gain the victory, for if we do not, social justice may well be achieved but God will have been denied. We shall not prevail if we go on as we have been doing in the past, concentrating too much on the Word and losing sight of the Substance."

As he sat down, no one applauded or wished to shake his hand or look him in the eye. They did not have a response ready. During the Ten Years' Conflict they had heard hundreds of discourses but never one like this. Without discussing it, simply by an interchange of scandalised glances, they came to a collective opinion that he was at best monstrously deluded or at worst dangerously heretical.

About ten minutes later, during which time he was left on his own, Dr McFarlan came to him, out of kindness, to reveal to him the calamitous error into which he had fallen, no doubt inadvertently.

"I understand, Mr Darroch," he whispered, "that you have recently suffered a sad bereavement."

"My wife died."

"Please accept my deepest condolences."

"Thank you, sir." They had already been given at the station.

Others watched and listened, pretending not to.

"Would it not be the ruination of the Church, Mr Darroch," said the old man, "if it were to concern itself with secular politics?"

"No doubt it would, Doctor, if by that you mean engaging in party politics. If on the other hand you mean that the Church should not concern itself with social justice I do not agree that such concern would harm it. On the contrary, it would give it strength and show, to many of our countrymen indifferent or even hostile, that it has in mind the precepts of its Lord and King."

He was astonished by his own assurance. The Lord was speaking through him. He felt humble and privileged. It was so peculiar a state of mind that he could not help chuckling.

The good doctor sniffed, ever so tactfully, as if seeking a possible, though reprehensible, explanation.

"Did not our Lord say that we would have the poor with us always?" he asked.

"Yes, Doctor, but I have always believed that He intended an ironic reproach. Is it not sacrilegious to think that He, who loved little children, was content to see many thousands of them die in pain, from hunger, disease, and squalid living conditions, during the whole history of the human race?"

"But, Mr Darroch, life here on earth is but a preparation. Those who suffer unjustly will be compensated in heaven."

"Heaven is God's business, Dr McFarlan. Its existence does not exempt us from our responsibilities here on earth."

"Do you have children, Mr Darroch?"

"Seven, sir."

"This must be a most distressful time for you."

"It would be unbearable, were it not for my faith in Christ's love. Yet there have been compensations. Grief has enlarged my sympathies."

"So it should do, Mr Darroch. Tell me, these opinions you hold and express with such confidence, are they shared by your congregation at Craignethan?"

He was asking if Craignethan was a hotbed of revolution.

"No, sir, they are not."

Dr McFarlan then smelled conspiracy. "Do you have colleagues with similar opinions?" he asked.

"I hope so, sir, though I know of none."

"Upon my word, Mr Darroch, you really are a remarkable man."

I am now the man I should have been long ago, thought Darroch, and the man I intend to be till I die.

"The service of Christ, sir, should be an adventure," he said.

"The eternal verities cannot change, Mr Darroch."

"No, but we can change in our attitude towards them."

That riposte bothered the doctor. He did not know what do make of it. What had been good enough for Moses was good enough for him; it had been good enough for John Knox; it should have been good enough for the parish minister of Craignethan, with a stipend of less than £200 per annum. He excused himself and went off, not to sip some fortifying brandy, for he was a man of temperance, but to report to his closest confidants that in his judgement Mr Darroch was still deranged by the death of his wife.

When Dr Chalmers arrived a few minutes later he was greeted as a deliverer.

With his large dingy countenance, whitish eye, grey whiskers, and awkward manners, the leader of the Evangelicals had often been described by his opponents as ugly. Bessie Drummond had done so, emphatically. Nor had his rough voice and strong Scotch accent pleased her. He did not shine in drawing-rooms with ladies present, for he had little ready small talk. His place was the pulpit where, it was said, he "buried his foes under fragments of burning mountains."

That evening he was tired and hoarse. This was the sixth gathering he had attended that day. Nevertheless he spoke with passion and conviction, prophesying that on Thursday if they stood firm they would astonish not only Scotland but the whole Christian world.

Anxious questions were put to him. Was it true that Dr Cook was saying fewer than thirty would follow him out on Thursday? Was it true also that of the sixty-three newspapers published in Scotland only eight were on their side? Would the people support them? What of ministers like Mr Robertson, who with his large family would not find alternative accommodation easy to obtain?

Going forward and taking the old man's hand Chalmers assured him that he had no need to worry. Funds would come pouring in, from the widow her mite and from the rich man his many guineas. Better manses and larger kirks would soon be built. As for Dr Cook and his contemptuous forecast of thirty, were there not more than that number present in this one house? By themselves they could confute him. In regard to the newspapers, surely it meant that eight were right and fifty-seven were wrong.

It seemed to Darroch sitting in the background that

Chalmers, like the commander-in-chief of any army outnumbered and stationed on disadvantageous ground, with a decisive battle soon to be fought, was obliged to show more confidence than he really felt. One or two of his senior officers, like Dr Candlish, looked pensive and now and then indulged in quick little prayers, as if, being closer to the troops in the field, they knew better than their chief how alarmed and apprehensive these were.

Before leaving he went round the company, shaking hands.

He must have been advised not only about Darroch's recent bereavement but also about his brainstorm.

"It is very brave of you to come and give us your support, Mr Darroch," he said, and then added, with lowered voice. "After victory has been achieved, I would be pleased if we could meet for a longer and more private talk."

He meant, so that he could exorcise those wild and foolish ideas. Dr Chalmers had gone out of his way to assure the established authorities that only in regard to the freedom and independence of the Kirk was he revolutionary. In all secular matters he was loyal and conservative.

"I would appreciate that, sir," replied Darroch, by no means fawning like many of the others.

He saw no reason why, with the Lord's help, he himself should not become as dominant as Dr Chalmers or Dr Cook in the councils of the Church, with a bolder message to proclaim.

As soon as Chalmers and his entourage were gone one of the fawners, Peter Fotheringham, who hitherto had kept out of Darroch's way, as if fearing contagion, now sought him out.

"What did Dr Chalmers have to say to you, George?" he asked.

"That he and I should meet later for a longer and more private talk."

"You have made your mark, George."

"I was under the impression that I had made myself an object of suspicion to some and of pity to others: the latter think I am distracted."

"Yes, but they have all been talking about you." He whispered, so that he could scarcely be heard in the hubbub of talk all round them. "Many of us share the opinions you expressed, though perhaps not in such an extreme form. You have become ambitious, George."

"Not for myself, Peter. For the new Church, if there is to be one."

"But if you are to be minister of Glenquicken you will continue to belong to the old Church. There are no colliers or weavers living in poverty in Glenquicken. It is a prosperous area."

"Do you see this hand, Peter?" He held it out. It was smaller and more delicate than Fotheringham's own. "It became God's hand eight days ago, for as long as two minutes."

"What do you mean, George?" Fotheringham sounded as if he had joined those who thought Darroch crazy.

"I visited the most unhappy woman in Scotland. She is in Cadzow Jail. She killed her own child and tried to kill herself. Both she and the girl were prostitutes. Human degradation could not reach lower. Yet when I took her hand, and wept with her, my hand was God's and my tears were His too. Who could deny it? Let the Church take the hands of all those in despair like her and the Church's hand will have become God's."

Fotheringham could hardly bear to look at his friend's hand or his eyes. "What has come over you, George?" he asked.

He remembered that George had a little girl who had been born feeble-minded. Could it be hereditary? George had never been brilliant but he had always seemed sensible enough. Perhaps the disease, latent in him for so long, had become active. Yes, but if it took the form of his imagining that his hand and tears were God's, and if he was able to say so with this uncanny assurance, it might well serve him better as a crusading minister than sound intelligence would.

CHAPTER 8

Another excerpt from Annabel's letter, which was growing into a journal:

"On our way back to the hotel Henry said he wished George had not become a minister. He had tried to stop him, and so had Andrew their older brother, whom I have not yet met. Andrew though it seems has long since changed his mind, having discovered that it is good for business: people take it for granted that you will not give short measure or charge unfair prices if you have a minister in the family. I replied that I thought that George was as well-suited to be a minister as any I had met. Henry would not have it. George had made a mess of his life by becoming a minister. I asked what else could he have become. He was not robust enough to have become a sea-captain. According to his own account he was not bookish or scholarly, which would have prevented him from becoming a lawyer. If he had become a schoolmaster the children would have teased him without mercy, and in any case it was usually failed ministers who became schoolmasters. He was much too squeamish to be a doctor. He could never have been a coachman, for he was the worst driver of a trap in the country. Perhaps he could have been a shopkeeper, selling ladies' hats and ribbons. Henry was quite indignant at that suggestion, though of course I had meant it in fun, or half in fun. What I was really thinking but dared not say was that George would have done very well as some rich lady's pampered pet. He would not have disappointed her either when it came to conjugal services. But I did not really want to

235

talk about George. I would far rather have talked about Henry himself. I have to drag out of him accounts of his adventures. Sometimes I suspect that he is afraid to let slip misdemeanours with mahogany-coloured damsels. As if I cared! As if I did not!

"Talking about rich ladies, whom should we meet in the foyer of our hotel — the most expensive one in Edinburgh, which is why it is not crowded out with ministers — but Mrs Jarvie, late of Cadzow, whose fat husband recently died and who immediately afterwards bloomed from slut to duchess. At first I could not believe it was her, she was dressed so magnificently in lustrous red and she should have been in mourning, and also she had her hand on the arm of a swarthy gentleman with a black moustache and pointed beard, whose coat was lilac in colour and whose yellow breeches were so tight that the bulge in front, which we ladies are not supposed to notice, was most pronounced, not just because of the tightness of his breeches either, but because what was contained within them was large and roused. How Miss Fanny Hill would have approved! He had the air of a bull in a field with forty cows all of which he felt capable of serving. Eleanor — that being her name, I think — looked as contented as all those cows together, after they had been served. I wonder where she found him. Henry thinks in a ladies' hairdressing salon because he smells, most fragrantly. They are registered here in the hotel as Signor and Signora Antonelli. I cannot wait to tell George Darroch who has always spoken of her with pity as a woman who had let life, not to mention having an elephant for a husband, defeat her.

"She made no effort to avoid us or to pretend that she was other than who she was. I have to admit she was quite grand in her brazenness, like a duchess indeed. She said that she and Signor Antonelli were sailing for Italy on the 19th: their ship was lying at Leith. She asked us if we saw Mr Darroch (meaning George) to give him her best wishes. She hoped he would soon find another living, for he was wasted at Craignethan. She had proposed to the kirk session of her husband's church, that when looking for a replacement they could do no better than Mr Darroch. She confessed that she herself had never taken to Cadzow nor had Cadzow taken to her, but Mr Darroch was well spoken of there, because of his work with the mission. Did Captain Darroch know that his brother was one of the kindest and most mannerly of men, with qualities too that he was too modest to show to the world? Henry beamed with pleasure at hearing his brother praised. She was amazingly talkative. Henry said she'd been drinking, and there certainly was an aroma of wine off her breath, and gusts of it off Signor Antonelli's, but it was mainly happiness that was making her blether so freely, and I thought her respect and liking for George were genuine. I may say that every man who passed us turned to have a second look at her. No wonder Signor Antonelli swished his tail proudly. As for Henry, he said she reminded him of a man-of-war in full sail. I felt jealous.

"That night, after nine o'clock, someone came knocking on our hotel room door, at a most inconvenient time, for we had just finished making love on the floor: my idea, I said we were to think of it as the deck of a ship, in spite of the carpet having a flowery pattern. We had to scramble into nightshirt and nightdress respectively and into dressing-gowns and I had to flee into the bedroom to push up my hair under a cap.

"Our visitor was George, much transformed from the sad little soul in Bessie's drawing-room. I had never seen him looking so pleased with himself. He reminded me of Signor Antonelli, though in appearance they are so dissimilar. I was sure it was because he had decided to take the living at Glenquicken. He apologised for disturbing us at such a late hour but he had promised to call on us. He explained that he had been detained longer than he had expected at a meeting of Evangelical ministers. Henry and I had to be careful not to catch each other's eye, for if we had we might have burst out laughing, at the very idea of a meeting of Evangelical ministers, surely the dreariest of occasions. Yet here was George, a sorrowing husband too, rejoicing as if he had come from a visit to a seraglio and was going back tomorrow.

"I could not help, out of mischief, telling him about Mrs Jarvie and her Italian beau. If I had told him that another of his children was dead he could hardly have looked more stricken, except that there was something comic about the degree of his

shock, which of course there wouldn't have been if Mary or
Agnes or Sarah had died. In a minute or two, after he had
recovered, he looked more wistful than anything else. I suppose
he was thinking of his deceased friend, her late husband, whose
memory she is treating so lightly. She really is brazen, flaunting
her Italian bull in a city full of ministers many of whom must
have known her husband; but just the same I would hate to see
those Calvinist dogs get their teeth into her. She should be safe
in Italy.

"Before we went to sleep Henry and I made love again.
Afterwards I thought of George. Would he wait a year before he
remarried? He would have a good excuse for shortening the
usual period of mourning, with three little girls and a baby to be
looked after; but it will not be only for their sakes that he will be
in a hurry to find a new bedmate. He has always struck me as an
amorous little man, like a finch in spring-time. He just had to
hold my hand once for me to tell. Will it be skelly-eyed Miss
Mitchell? Or some bonnier woman in Glenquicken? It will not
be Mrs Barnes, who used to dream that the little pink and
golden cockerel would tread the drab brown hen. Am I not
shameless?

"I forgot to say that George had come to invite us to join him
and his sons on an expedition tomorrow to Glenquicken. I
wonder if it means he has made up his mind to accept the living.
I said I would like to go, and Henry, though he has little interest
in churches, fell in with my wish. We arranged to go in our
carriage, which has plenty of room for five ...

"Well, we have been to Glenquicken, and admired the marble
fireplaces in the manse, the stained glass windows in the church,
the roses in the manse garden, the stream with its weeping
willows, the very pretty village with its large public green and
many trees and gardens, the houses covered with russet ivy (the
colour of my hair, said Henry, inaccurately), the shops with the
bubbles in the glass of their windows, and the quaint little inn
with its cooing white doves, where we ate mutton pies and drank
ale. I have to confess I was entranced. I whispered to Henry that
if he were a minister — God forbid, he muttered — he would
have to accept this living or I wouldn't let him make love to me,

238

for at least three days! Seriously, the place would be like heaven for George's children. Arthur and James, who seemed very cool towards each other, were united in their enthusiasm, though they showed it very differently. Arthur generously praised everything, and in the garden plucked a rose, scarcely redder than his cheeks, and gave it to me, as a peace-offering, I believe. James, as is his way, praised nothing, not in my hearing anyway, but I saw him several times, in the manse and the garden and the church, whispering earnestly to his father, no doubt pointing out the advantages of living in such idyllic place.

"I keep remembering that if, or rather when, Henry and I have children of our own they will be blood kin to Arthur and James, and of course to the little girls and poor wee Matthew who seems always to be forgotten.

"George said very little, but I came upon him in the rose garden whistling happily to himself. He plucked a rose for me: a white one, this time. I could not resist saying that Margaret would have loved this garden and the house too, for she had often talked to me about the large rooms in her parents' house: the rooms in Craignethan manse are small. Tears came into his eyes. Why, with a blackbird singing, and the stream gurgling over mossy stones, and Henry laughing somewhere, all genuine sounds, and with the rose in my hand and all the other roses about us with bees buzzing among them and the blue sky above, all genuine sights, did I find something false in his tears and in his voice too as, clutching my other hand, he murmured that it was when he was in the presence of beauty that he missed her most? I was sure he was not thinking of Margaret at all or of me for that matter, but of what heaven alone knew. I remembered Mrs Jarvie's saying he had qualities none of us knew about, and I realised then that she was right. I don't think that they are all admirable qualities though. He is deeper and slyer and more ambitious than I ever thought.

"He had asked us to keep secret the fact that he was the prospective minister, but the old man, Mr Muir, the caretaker, from whom we borrowed the keys, when George mentioned his name, as he was bound in politeness to do, at once greeted him as the incoming minister. George did not deny it, though he did not confirm it either. Mrs Muir, a pleasant old lady in a white mutch, who offered us tea, was charmed by him. So many women, including old Lady Annie who was a Tartar, have found him charming. So he is, I suppose, but I have always had reservations, because of his treatment of Margaret. To be frank, I have always thought of him as in some ways a little mountebank: there again, a resemblance to Signor Antonelli, who is undoubtedly a big mountebank.

"However, if I can wish Mrs Jarvie well I must wish George well too, for the sake of his children. I asked him outright, in the church, if this was where he was going to spend the rest of his life. He replied, as if the words were strawberries, to be savoured slowly, that he would like that very much, but it was possible that the Lord had a greater task for him to do. Even in that sacred place I found it hard not to laugh. I felt like asking did he think that he might be sent as a missionary among the cannibals of Africa? What a tasty meal he would make, I thought."

CHAPTER 9

Robert had evidently instructed Bessie and Isa not to pester the Darrochs with questions about Glenquicken. He himself merely asked if they had enjoyed their little expedition, and Darroch, equally reserved, replied that they had, especially as the sun had shone all the time.

Arthur said he thought his sisters would love the garden.

James, however, with uncharacteristic enthusiasm, praised Glenquicken. They would all be much healthier there, for it was not bleak and exposed like Craignethan. There would be fewer fevers, sore throats, aches, and coughs. He spoke as if their removal there was settled. Though his remarks were addressed to his uncle and aunt they were really aimed at his father. Bessie was put into a quandary. She wished to agree with James as a way of siding with him against his father, but she did not want to say anything that would help to install the Darrochs at Glenquicken where she was sure they would disgrace her and her husband. Therefore she contented herself with saying, twice, that much higher standards of decorum would be necessary at Glenquicken.

Darroch saw into all their minds with inspired insight.

Never had his own mind been in such good order. On one side were arrayed, fairly, all the arguments in favour of standing by the Evangelical cause, and on the other side all the arguments against. This was for the convenience of the Lord, to whom was left the final decision. Let Robert and his clever friends deride that as a simpleton's hope. He knew better.

In the evening Dr Cook came separately by himself. He could not stay long, as he had been invited to address in private a group of ministers who, though they had subscribed to the Claim of Right, were worried as to the legality of their act according to the laws of the Church, a subject on which the Doctor was an acknowledged expert.

The leader of the Moderates, who was then over seventy, looked tired and strained, but as always was calm and precise. His opponents accused him of lacking imagination and passion, but even they conceded that in debate he was formidable, because of his vast knowledge of the Church, having written a history of it, in three volumes.

"It is a matter of law, Mr Darroch," he said. "If a law has to be changed then let this be done according to the proper procedures and with the proper safeguards. If it is simply set aside as being no longer convenient there is a danger of anarchy ensuing. Laws are a bulwark painstakingly built up by our predecessors. They are our protection. Without them we are a ship without a rudder, being blown upon rocks of disaster."

Faith, thought Darroch, is a stronger and surer rudder, but he did not say so. Among Moderates it was better to say little and look modest.

Robert's four friends were the same age as himself. In his library they lounged in armchairs, loosened coats and collars, lit up pipes, and drank drams of whisky-toddy. Yet all were ministers of the Church of Scotland, though two of them, Mr Gordon and Mr Parker, did not at present have pulpits of their own. The former lectured on Divinity and the latter on Church History, at Edinburgh University. The two others were Mr Lindsay of Roslin, whose father owned land, and Mr Middleton of Temple, whose family was distantly related to Lord Hairmyres.

They regarded themselves as gentlemen first and clergymen after.

They talked about paintings and artists, in relation to an exhibition then on show in the city; about a recital of music by Handel and Bach that they had heard a week ago; about Mr Dickens's novel *Oliver Twist* recently published, and about the

242

subject of criminals in literature, mentioning books which Darroch had never heard of; about politics, British and European; and about economics.

The old George Darroch would have felt and looked out of place: his not smoking or drinking or smiling at the mildly lewd jests would have shown him to be not morally superior but intellectually and socially inferior. The new George Darroch sat at ease, except for an occasional fit of coughing brought on by the tobacco smoke, and said nothing but in such a way as to hint that his silence had its source in modesty and not in ignorance. Even when the conversation at one point touched on the importance of coal to the country's industries he, who had spoken to men who hewed it out of the bowels of the earth, did not speak. Everything they said, everything they were capable of saying, came from their heads. When he spoke it would come from the heart.

It took the form of a question meekly asked: "Do you think, gentlemen, that the Church should concern itself with the establishment of social justice?"

They pretended to be amused that the little dimpled oracle had at last given voice, and had uttered such a platitude.

"You must define your terms more accurately, Mr Darroch," said Parker. "Which Church do you mean? The Roman Catholic, the Anglican, the Greek Orthodox, the Muslim, the Buddhist, the Confucian?"

"Our Church, Mr Parker. The Church of Scotland."

"But at present it is split into two factions. Which of these do you mean?"

"The more compassionate, Mr Parker."

That was a counterblow they had not expected. They looked at one another, grinning, but they were plainly disconcerted.

"By the Church," said Mr Gordon "do you mean the institution or its individual members?"

"The institution, Mr Gordon. I am aware that individual members already perform eleemosynary acts."

They laughed at his use of the big word. It had been a trap. Their laughter showed they had fallen into it. They were not so clever.

"You said 'concern itself'," said Middleton, the only one not to have a Scotch accent. "That is also vague phraseology, Mr Darroch."

"And the term 'social justice' is also most vague," said Mr Lindsay.

Robert came to his brother-in-law's rescue. "Come now, gentlemen, most people would broadly understand George's meaning."

"Yes, Robert, but most people's thoughts are vague and inchoate," said Parker. "In the beginning was the Word, you know. Language must be scrupulously used."

"Perhaps we should ask Mr Darroch to expatiate," said Gordon.

"Very well," said Darroch "It was Mr Lindsay, I believe, who informed us that more than thirty million tons of coal are produced throughout the world, four-fifths of it in Britain. It so happens that in my parish of Craignethan there are several coal mines. I have often spoken to colliers and their families. I have visited their homes. I have urged them to attend my church. None has ever come. They think they would not be made welcome, and I am afraid they are right. We depend for our material well-being on these men, and yet we treat them like outcasts."

Did he really care about coal-miners? He had much self-exploration to do and many self-discoveries to make.

They could not make up their minds whether they were dealing with a booby or with someone who, through Christ's favour, knew things that they, for all their erudition, never would.

"This is an old question, Mr Darroch," said Parker. "You are not the first to ask it, you know. Because so many Catholic theologians were asking it Pope Gregory XVI issued his bull Mirari Vos about eleven years ago, forbidding the Catholic Church to ally itself with revolutionary liberalism."

Darroch had never heard of Pope Gregory and his bull, but he was not discouraged. On the contrary, he felt pleased that they were reduced to trying to belittle him with a display of pedantry.

"All Europe is in ferment, Mr Darroch," said Middleton. "Revolutionary forces are growing in power in every country. They claim that they desire to establish social justice, but any intelligent person knows that if they prevail the result will be repression and bloodshed, and the spread of atheism. You cannot seriously mean that the Church of Scotland should join them."

"The Church's concern is with Christ's kingdom," said Lindsay, "not Caesar's."

Such a remark from the lips of an Evangelical would have been laughed at by the staunch Moderate, Mr Lindsay. Small wonder he looked embarrassed.

"The conditions of the poor continue to be improved owing to the benevolence of many landowners and industrialists," said Middleton.

"At Glenquicken," said Robert, "Sir Thomas Blaikie has begun the operation of a model farm. Excellent houses have been built for the workers. Their wages are higher than average because the productivity of the farm is greater. I believe many other landowners are carrying out similar experiments."

"It is a matter of market forces," said Lindsay. "The poor will disappear when the country is more prosperous."

"Besides, many ascetics have proved, have they not," said Parker, "that destitution, measured by a lack of material goods and comforts, is good for the soul."

Darroch said no more. He had reduced them to puerile and cynical jests. A few minutes later he excused himself. All of them, he murmured, would need clear heads tomorrow.

As he went upstairs to his room, and afterwards as he lay in bed, he surveyed the two George Darrochs. That meant of course there must be a third.

There was the George Darroch who had wiped the blood from Taylor's face, held Mrs Cooper's hand, was grateful to Mrs Barnes for her faithful service, wished to throw in his lot with the poor, loved his children and sought to reward them by asking them to share penury and hardship with him.

There was the George Darroch who had lusted after Eleanor Jarvie, lied glibly about her letter, was eager to associate with rich and important men, loved his children and wanted to give them comfort and affluence, and brutally had dismissed poor Mrs Barnes. .

Both of them, and the third one observing them, would be in St Andrew's Church tomorrow.

As he lay, in a state of delicious suspension, he heard Robert coming up the stairs, on hands and knees it seemed from the noise. He heard too Bessie opening her door and in an angry yet tearful whisper caution her husband not to be so noisy.

There could be no doubt: Robert had consumed too much whisky-toddy and was quite drunk. He must have lingered in the library drinking after his friends had gone. Judging from Bessie's tone this was not the first time. Robert was not the secure person he seemed. He had deep stresses that he tried to overcome with drink. One must be his sister's death, another his wife's lack of charity; a new one could well be his attempt to manipulate his brother-in-law.

Tomorrow, every man present at the Assembly, from the Marquis down to the assistant doorkeeper, would have private anxieties and personal weaknesses, which would make them vulnerable and which the great public occasion would not dispel.

Anyone, like Darroch himself, who had passed beyond vulnerability, was at a great advantage.

PART FOUR

CHAPTER 1

On Thursday, 18th May, Edinburgh was a city of sunshine, flags flying, shops shut, ladies and gentlemen in Sunday clothes, and carriages glittering on their way to and from Holyrood Palace, St Giles, and St Andrew's Church, with cargoes of black-garbed grave-faced ministers and elders. One newspaper reporter was afterwards to compare the atmosphere to that which must have existed on 16th January, 1707, when the Scottish Parliament voted itself out of existence: except that, as he was careful to add, the crowds then had been turbulent and vociferous, containing as they did many members of the artisan class, who were not nearly so conspicuous on this later equally historic but less passionate occasion.

He might also have pointed out that in Edinburgh in sunny May tempers of persons of all classes are usually a great deal more amiable than in icy January.

Crowds gathered outside Holyrood, to applaud the distinguished guests arriving for the Commissioner's levee; outside St Giles in the High Street, where the pre-Assembly sermon was to be delivered by Dr Welsh, the retiring Moderator; outside St Andrew's in George Street, where the Assembly was to take place; and outside a certain warehouse at Tanfield, on the outskirts of the city.

In the course of the day the reporter, moving among the spectators, enquired of many how much they knew of the issue which was to reach its culmination that afternoon. What was the Veto Act? In what way had Auchterarder been a test case?

What parts had the Court of Session, the House of Commons, and the House of Lords played in the conflict? And for how long had it been going on?

He found none to whom he would have awarded full marks, but he was not surprised. It had always been his experience that the public seldom made the effort to keep well-informed. In this case, too, there was some excuse. Not only had it dragged on so long, ten years in fact, as long as the Trojan War, as he had once remarked humorously in an article, it had also been conducted throughout by both sides in a gentlemanly manner, which had been to everyone's credit but had not made for memorable drama.

Most people questioned knew that it had to do with whether or not congregations had the right to send packing unsuitable ministers presented to them by landowners, and that the Courts and Government had decreed no such right existed. One old gentleman, who had visited a grog-shop or two, judging by the redness of his face and the inclusion in his speech of some emphatic terms later excised, summed it up thus: "It's like this, you see, Mr Peel says that if the Scotch Kirk taks his siller then it's bound to obey his laws, and ane o' thae laws is that the man that owns the land on which the kirk stands can appoint as meenister whaever he wishes and naebody can gainsay him. So if the Kirk wants to be free o' that restriction it'll hae to tell Mr Peel to stick his siller up his jooks."

This summary caused argument among those who heard it. Some objected to the aforesaid emphatic terms; for instance he had not said "up his jooks" but rather "up his erse". Others objected to the implication that the stushie was all about money. They were sure it had to do with important religious and moral matters, but what these were exactly they could not say.

Many people wanted to be present at the proceedings in St Andrew's, but the accommodation set aside for members of the public was very limited. Mr Kerr, H.M. Officer of Works, in charge of the preparations, discovered on the evening of the 17th that the doorkeepers had accepted sums of money from people prepared to spend the night in the church so as to be sure of a place in the public gallery next day. A man of probity and resource, he had put on the doors padlocks to which only he had keys. Therefore members of the public wishing to be present had to queue up outside the doors before dawn to have any chance. They would have a long wait, for the Commissioner was not expected to arrive before two in the afternoon.

During the preceding months a warehouse at Tanfield had been prepared by the Evangelicals as the place where they would forgather after the exodus from St Andrew's. Those ministers who kept faith and went out behind Dr Welsh and Dr Chalmers would walk in procession to Tanfield, where colleagues and elders would be waiting to welcome them. They would then all join in thanking God for their deliverance and in deliberating how best to set up a new Free Kirk. If only a few came the paucity of their number would be cruelly emphasised by the great abundance of empty places, for the warehouse had been adapted to seat 3000.

CHAPTER 2

Arthur and James Darroch spoke to each other with the formality of enemies temporarily at truce. They had a common purpose, though they would have described it differently. Arthur wanted to be present in St Andrew's Church during the Assembly proceedings in order to give his father moral support. James wanted to make sure that his father did not go back on a promise given, not in words, but in many other ways.

It meant their having to wait outside the church all night.

"What if it rains?" asked James.

"Then we shall get wet."

"I would come home."

"That would be up to you."

"How do we pass the time? Sleeping on our feet, like horses? Or on the ground, like tramps?"

"I shall take a stool."

"We shall have a very long wait."

"It will discourage others."

"You are cool now, Arthur. You will not be so cool tomorrow afternoon, after sitting on a stool, all the fucking night. Why cannot Uncle Robert use his influence to have us admitted at a civilised time?"

"You heard him say four hundred ministers would like to have their friends and relatives admitted."

"Few of them are as influential as he. Even people with no influence expect those who have it to use it, since they hope to have it themselves one day."

"He has said he cannot help."

"I am not sure that I particularly wish to be present. Nothing unusual will happen. There will be no great rebellion. A paltry few will walk out."

"You seem to forget, James, that for years it has been Father's intention to come out. So if he does not he will be going against his will and his conscience. You forget also that he will be doing it for our sakes."

"For his own sake too. He hates the idea of returning to Craignethan."

"I have not heard him say so."

"No, but you must have seen it in his eyes. Still, you are right. Perhaps it is worth suffering hours of misery and discomfort for the sake of enjoying years of ease and happiness."

"I am thinking of the girls, not of myself."

"I am thinking of the girls too, but also of myself."

Creeping out of the house about one o'clock, after Uncle Robert had at last gone to bed, they hurried through lamplit, deserted, chilly streets and arrived at the church to find a number of people already there, twenty-one at the main door and fifteen at the small side door. They were mostly servants, keeping places for their masters snug in bed. James considered this inequitable, but there was no one to complain to except the servants themselves, who were in cantankerous mood. There were also some divinity students who had fortified themselves with brandy and therefore for a while were rowdy and cheerful.

As the Darrochs were setting up camp a middle-aged gentleman and a girl about Arthur's age, wrapt from neck to ankles in a thick warm coat, took up their station immediately behind them. She addressed him as Uncle Will, he her as Cathie. She seemed to be finding the adventure exciting, he foolish.

More and more people kept arriving. That they were respectable, Christian, and in a few cases female, did not prevent them from pushing and attempting to usurp. Cathie won James's approval by the spirited way she resisted these encroachments. As for Arthur he was so delighted with her that he asked himself if she was the girl he was destined to fall in love with and marry, although he had not yet had a good look at her.

253

He had always liked the name Catherine.

When at last he saw her face in the pink light of dawn he was at first disappointed, but then he remembered that Mrs Wedderburn had once told him that there were qualities far more valuable than physical beauty. This girl had them all.

Though she kept yawning she was eager to talk. Her name was Catherine Grant. Her father was minister of Craigielea Parish in the County of Selkirk. He was an Evangelical and would come out if a sufficient number of others did.

Mr Holmes, her uncle, roused himself to make enquiries. When he learned that Arthur and James were nephews of Mr Robert Drummond of St Magnus's, and grandsons of the late Very Reverend Robert Drummond, he was satisfied and went back to his dozing.

"Is your father coming out?" he asked. "Mr Drummond is on the Moderate side, isn't he?"

"Father would like to come out but my mother died just two weeks ago." Tears came into Arthur's eyes and his voice faltered.

Her nose might be out of proportion but her sympathy was beautiful and consoling. "Oh, I'm so very sorry," she said. "If my mother had died my father would not have come. Your father must be very brave and determined. Do you have any sisters?"

"Four. I have also a baby brother, Matthew."

James noted how Sarah was included as normal. He felt a great affection for Sarah then, though it was balanced by a great antipathy to the so-called normal people about him.

CHAPTER 3

Shortly after five o'clock the city began to wake up. Lamplighters or rather lamp-extinguishers, with their ladders and poles, appeared; street-sweepers with their carts and shovels; workmen with tackety boots and bags of tools; and convoys of boisterous charwomen. Though masters and mistresses might be taking a holiday that day floors had still to be scrubbed and chamber-pots emptied and scoured. Some of these raucous skivvies shouted improper suggestions at the divinity students and then shrieked with bawdy laughter which disturbed pigeons on roof-tops and reinforced James Darroch's belief that the female sex was more vulgar and lascivious than the male.

About ten o'clock, alarmed by the size of the crowd besieging the church, Mr Kerr ordered the doors to be opened. Alas, heathen Hottentots could not have behaved more disgracefully then than those top-hatted Christians.

Nothing enraged James Darroch more than to be bullied out of his rights by people stronger than himself. Therefore, after having his feet trampled on and his cap pulled down over his eyes he burst into a righteous rage, screaming like a pig being slaughtered and laying about him with Aunt Bessie's three-legged stool. As a result he won through to the church door, and in his wake came Arthur, Cathie, and Mr Holmes, all of them being shoved and pummelled, and shoving and pummelling back.

Safely seated in the public gallery they examined their

wounds and exchanged stories of the brief, frantic melée. Arthur had had his stool torn from his grasp and had received a blow on the eye, which was already swelling. Cathie had had her hat knocked off and her hair pulled. Mr Holmes had lost his hat altogether and had been kicked on the shin; by a woman, he said indignantly.

In spite of their injuries those who had got in bore one another no ill-will and put all the blame on those left outside. At least three noses were bleeding, more hats than Mr Holmes's were missing, and many bruises had been sustained which would tomorrow bloom black and blue. Nevertheless they all felt magnanimous, like soldiers who had taken part in a victory and were grateful to have survived to celebrate it.

Outside some people who had been waiting longer than some of those inside but who had lost in the battle for entry hammered angrily on the doors for a while. All their lives they would remember that day not because of any calamitous split in the Kirk happening or not happening, but because they had been shamefully ill-used by fellow Christians.

Mr Kerr continued to show himself to be considerate and resourceful. Since there would be a long wait and there were no adequate sanitary arrangements in the church he devised a system whereby anyone wishing to slip out for essential purposes was given a card, on presenting which to the doorkeeper he or she would be readmitted. The cards were the kind awarded to Sunday school children and had Biblical scenes depicted on them. Mr Kerr signed them, lest by chance someone outside should happen to have such a card in his or her pocket.

The church was larger than that at Craignethan but not, in James's opinion, much more impressive. Its pews were not so old and worn, but just as hard. It was circular in shape so that everyone had a clear view of the pulpit or, on the present occasion, the Moderator's table and, above that, the throne on which the Marquis would sit.

Mr Holmes snoozed, as did many others. Arthur and Cathie played chess with a pocket set Arthur had brought. James read Jane Austen's novel *Pride and Prejudice*, one of his favourite books.

It had been given him by Annabel Wedderburn. "You will be amused by Mr Collins," she had said. "He is a clergyman and a buffoon." But James did not find Mr Collins ridiculous at all. Needing a wife, as a condition of his new post, he had proposed. The woman had refused. Without any ado he had immediately asked another, this time with success. Where was the buffoonery in that? In order to keep on good terms with his aristocratic patroness he flattered her assiduously. What was foolish about that? What James liked most about Miss Austen's novels was that the characters were all well-bred, including the cads, and did not have to work for a living. Even the clergymen were gentlemen, who left the more vulgar aspects of their profession to lowly-paid curates.

About eleven o'clock James felt two calls of nature. He could hold out for another hour or so but not possibly till two o'clock, although it would be, he thought, an appropriate irony if, while he was witnessing "the most dramatic moment in the history of the Church of Scotland for over a century" he was in agonising need of a shit and a pee.

Consulting Arthur he found him in similar predicament, but unwilling to admit it lest Cathie be embarrassed. This pretence on the part of lovers that their beloved did not shit or pee had always exasperated James, but never more than then, when he was in pain. The sensible Mr Holmes had already been out and in again. Cathie herself seemed as yet undistressed, but then, as James knew from Agnes's feats of retention, females could hold out much longer than males, presumably having larger bladders or less urgent bowels.

In Arthur commonsense at last triumphed over false modesty. He and James, each with a card, hurried out. The problem was where to go. James suggested Uncle Henry's hotel which was close-by and had many privies. Uncle Henry and Aunt Annabel were leaving that day for a tour of Border towns but perhaps they had not left yet.

They were both bleary-eyed. It would be an even more appropriate irony, thought James, if at the climactic moment when Dr Welsh laid the Protest on the table of the House (if indeed he did) they were both sound asleep.

When they asked at the reception desk if their uncle Captain Darroch had left they were told he had not: he was waiting until after the Assembly. It was easy for them then to seek out a privy and use it most gratefully.

Going out of the hotel they met Cathie coming in, chaperoned by two ladies whom they remembered seeing in the public gallery. If she was embarrassed she did not show it. She had her mind on one thing only, and it was not Arthur's handsome face.

CHAPTER 4

After one o'clock ministers began to come in and take their places. They were all Moderates and sat on the right hand side of the church facing the Throne. It had been agreed among them not to attend the pre-Assembly service in St Giles, where Dr Welsh, as retiring Moderator, was to deliver an address. They did not trust him not to take the opportunity to urge the Evangelical case. Therefore they had had time to take some luncheon. They looked relaxed, confident, and content.

About half-past one Dr Cook arrived, with his staff officers. These included Uncle Robert. They smiled as they whispered among themselves and waved to friends.

Their assurance annoyed and worried Cathie. "Why are they so sure of themselves?" she asked.

"Humpty-Dumpty was sure of himself," said her uncle, laughing.

Uncle Robert turned his head to seek out his nephews. He waved. Dr Cook, told who they were, waved too. It was a benediction that James welcomed but Cathie did not.

Shortly afterwards Uncle Robert came to speak to them.

Introduced to Cathie and her uncle he was very courteous but could not hide his elation.

He conversed with his nephews in the aisle. He was amused by their having to suppress yawns.

"Well done," he said. "How are you feeling?"

"A bit tired," said Arthur.

"What's the matter with your eye?"

"It was hit by someone's elbow. There was a scramble to get in. I'm afraid I lost Aunt Bessie's stool."

"You all look very confident, Uncle Robert," said James.

"With good reason, James. Lots of long Evangelical faces at the levee. Dr Chalmer's one of the longest. The Marquis on the other hand looked very pleased. As a staunch member of the Kirk he would not have enjoyed presiding over its destruction."

"Did you see Father?" asked Arthur.

"Not only did I see him, I was able to introduce him to Sir Thomas. I think I can say that they took to each other at once."

"Did Father tell Sir Thomas he would accept Glenquicken?" asked James.

"It would not have been opportune to discuss it then, James."

James nodded.

"But it will be all right, I assure you. Do not be surprised if your father does not appear this afternoon. I advised him to stay away altogether."

James nodded again.

"Indeed, I think you will find that many of them will have decided that judicious absence is the best policy. Well, I must return to my post. As soon as you can go home and get to bed. I think we shall all be celebrating this evening."

He went off, walking with the ease of a man used to commanding a larger and more opulent church than this.

Nobody would have guessed that last night he had been drinking more than he should.

"Aren't you sorry for him," whispered James, "married to a woman like Aunt Bessie?"

When they were married, thought Arthur, had they been in love? Or had their parents more or less arranged the marriage? Had Uncle Robert consented because her father had been a well-to-do paper manufacturer, who had settled on her a substantial dowry with which Uncle Robert had bought his two most prized possessions, a painting by Rembrandt and one by Rubens, which hung in his library?

"I hope Father takes his advice and stays away," said James.

"That would be cowardly," said Arthur.

"But if he comes and if some of them are stupid enough to walk out he might walk out with them. That would be goodbye to Glenquicken."

"He would be keeping faith with his principles and his colleagues."

"What principles? Did you not once refer to them as 'fucking nonsense?'" He lowered his voice even more as he said those last two words, but it was possible that Cathie heard them.

Arthur was furious, especially as it was true that he had so described his father's principles.

About quarter to two the Evangelical ministers began to arrive. Friends would have called them grave and thoughtful. Enemies would have said they looked despondent.

Among them was Mr Fotheringham, accompanied by a white-faced colleague who had a handkerchief at his mouth. This must be Mr Somerville who was dying of consumption. Arthur was surprised that his father was not with them.

Cathie was on her feet, looking for her father. At last she saw him. Proudly she pointed him out. He was a thin bald-headed man of little distinction. James heard Mr Holmes grunt. Evidently he had no high opinion of his sister's husband.

Still their father had not appeared. The church was now quite full. A group of ministers then arriving could not find seats together. The only row still empty was that at the front, reserved for Dr Chalmers and other leading Evangelicals.

Soon these came in, a few minutes before two, and took their places.

They were quickly followed by Dr Welsh, in black gown and breeches, carrying his three-cornered hat and a scroll. Everyone watched him as he put his hat and the scroll on the table. The scroll no doubt contained the famous protest, signed by hundreds of ministers. He sat with his eyes closed, praying.

Few apart from his sons noticed the arrival of George Darroch. He came in by himself, discreetly but by no means furtively. He found a seat at the end of a pew. Its occupants had to move along to make room for him. He seemed the calmest person in the church.

Arthur was puzzled. What was his father up to, by coming in so late and so conspicuously alone? Had he wanted to stay away but lacked the strength of mind?

James was anguished. His father could easily be swayed by the emotion of the moment into doing what he would regret all his life. He was capable of throwing away the happiness and safety of Glenquicken for the sake of a minute of self-indulgence.

If he does, thought James, I shall hate him.

Arthur was pointing out his father to Cathie. Prepared to show the same interest in his father that he had out of politeness shown in hers, she looked and was visibly more impressed than she had expected. Seeing his father through her eyes, Arthur saw that in that great concourse of ministers his father looked strangely distinctive, not only because of his bright hair and beautiful poet's face but because of something else hard to name.

Cathie tried to name it. "He must be thinking of your mother," she whispered.

Yes, so he must be; and also of Matthew, Jessie, Agnes, Mary, and especially Sarah. Arthur's own heart had often sunk as he thought of his sister growing up to be a lovely woman with the mind of a child of three. He himself would not have to see her often, but his father would, every day. Arthur too as an atheist could explain it as a tragic accident on nature's part, but his father would have to say that it was, like everything else in the world, a deliberate act of God's.

But there was more to his father then than grief at his wife's death and sorrow at his daughter's misfortune. There was something new, something Arthur had never seen before.

CHAPTER 5

Outside the church were heard the tramp of soldiers and the shouting of military commands. The Anthem was played, announcing the arrival of the Queen's Commissioner.

It struck Arthur that the pomp and the loud arrogant music were warnings to those ministers thinking of abandoning the Establishment that if they did so they would offend their sovereign and flout their lawful government. Let them not forget that in spite of what they called their transcendental arguments about Christ's Crown Rights they were really unimportant people whose opposition to the edicts of the mighty was a childish impertinence.

His sympathy with the cause of the Evangelicals revived.

In a splendid red and gold uniform the Commissioner made his entry, escorted by aides similarly accoutred. After bowing to the audience which had risen, and to the Moderator who had risen too, he took his seat on the Throne.

With a noise like the ebbing of the sea those hundreds of people sat down, with sighs and shuffles.

Silence settled on the great company.

Dr Welsh stood up. Usually a hesitant speaker, he was today firm and collected, though very pale. With dignity he offered up a prayer to the God that they all worshipped. Then he resumed his seat.

There followed a still more intense and painful silence. If a man had shut his eyes he could easily have imagined that he was alone.

Dr Welsh rose again. His voice was steady and sounded clear to the furthest limits of the church.

"Fathers and Brethren, according to the usual form of procedure this is a time for making up the roll, but in consequence of certain proceedings affecting our rights and privileges I must protest against our proceeding further. The reasons that have led me to this conclusion are fully set forth in this document which I hold in my hand, and which, with the permission of the House, I shall now proceed to read."

He paused, while many sighed and some groaned, and the Commissioner smiled, with patrician fortitude.

"We protest that, in the circumstances in which we are placed, it is and shall be lawful for us, and such other commissioners chosen to the Assembly, as may concur with us, to withdraw to a separate place of meeting, for the purpose of taking steps, along with all who adhere to us — maintaining with us the Confession of Faith and standards of the Church of Scotland as heretofore understood — for separating in an orderly way from the Establishment, and thereupon adopting such measures as may be competent to us, in humble dependence on God's grace and the aid of the Holy Spirit, for the advancement of His glory, the extension of the Gospel of Our Lord and Saviour, and the administration of Christ's House according to His Holy Word; and we now withdraw accordingly, humbly and solemnly acknowledging the hand of the Lord in the things which have come upon us because of our manifold sins, and the sins of the Church and nation, but at the same time, with an assured conviction that we are not responsible for any consequences that may follow from this, our enforced separation from an Establishment which we loved and prized, through interference with conscience, the dishonour done to Christ's Crown, and the rejection of His sole and supreme authority as King in His Church."

As he finished the Moderator laid the Protest on the table, picked up his hat, turned to the Commissioner who had risen, whether in respect or umbrage was not clear from his face, bowed, and then walked slowly and steadily towards the door.

After the grandiloquent words the simplicity of his acts was very moving.

Almost at once he was followed by Dr Chalmers and the other leading Evangelicals from the front row.

It then remained to be seen how many of the lowly and obscure would follow the great and famous into self-imposed exile.

In Arthur's case with pride and anxiety, and in James's with dismay and anger, they watched their father rise, the first of the unknowns, and make for the door, without a falter, his head held high, smiling.

There could be no doubt that his example, as much as those of Dr Welsh and Dr Chalmers, gave courage to his colleagues, who began to rise up, one after another, more and more and more of them, and go out. Among them was Cathie's father. Here and there one would sit on while his neighbours left, still wracked by misgivings; but he too kept faith and went out.

The Moderate leaders, so many Humpty-Dumpties fallen, could not conceal their incredulity and chagrin. Dr Cook shrugged his shoulders, as if to say: "What can you do if people will not listen to reason?" but it was clear that he had suffered a severe disappointment.

Not a single one of those who had signed the Protest dishonoured it by remaining. The church was now more than half empty.

Uncle Robert looked towards his nephews and sadly shook his head.

The Commissioner sat impassively, staring straight in front of him.

In the old days, thought Arthur, orders would have been given, the soldiers would have arrested the intransigents or at any rate their leaders, and blood might have been shed. In these new days authority had learned to use its power more patiently and therefore more effectively. The Commissioner would report to his masters in London. They would note the part of the Protest that stated how the protestors had loved and prized the Establishment. They would be confident that the new Church, whether or not it called itself free, would still conform in all important matters and in time would be persuaded back into the fold.

"Let's go out and see what's happening," cried Cathie.

In her eagerness she seized Arthur's hand. They hurried out. They would follow the procession all the way to Tanfield, where they would applaud the jubilant speeches and witness the signing of the Deed of Demission.

Mr Holmes got up stiffly and went out after them. He said he was going straight to bed.

James sat on by himself. His face was white with despair. He knew what had happened: given the best opportunity of his life to show off his father had not been able to resist it. For the sake of a minute's vanity he had sentenced his family to years of hardship.

The divinity students were gleefully congratulating one another. Was it because they loved spiritual independence or because a large number of comfortable livings had suddenly come on the market?

CHAPTER 6

When he came out of the church James was in time to see the last of the procession of ministers and elders making its way to Tanfield. Hundreds of spectators were cheering, with men waving their hats and ladies their handkerchiefs. Everybody was discussing with animation what they had just witnessed, which they regarded as an event of great spiritual significance. One greybeard, to the approval of all who heard him, cried that they should be proud of their country, for so noble a sacrifice for religion's sake would happen in no other.

James felt like screaming that they were all wrong: what they had seen was a demonstration of the disastrous divisiveness of the Scottish nation, which had kept it materially and spiritually impoverished in the past and was still doing so today.

Isolated by his despair he did not know where to turn or what to do. He had been left with no destinations, no hopes, no affections, and no loyalties. His father's betrayal had stripped him bare, like a tree in winter; and spring, with its fresh green leaves, would be a long time coming for him. Without his fully realising it, Glenquicken had represented the place where he might learn to love without selfishness and find his own happiness in that of others. Now it was lost to him forever.

He dreaded having to go back to St Magnus's manse. Aunt Bessie would rejoice at his father's treachery. Isa would think of something hurtful to say and then say it, with enjoyment.

Something tapped him on the shoulder. He turned, irritably. It was Aunt Annabel's parasol. With her arm through his

267

uncle's, she was her usual vivacious, excited self. She was dressed in the green dress and hat which she had worn on her visit to the manse.

"Isn't it wonderful, James?" she cried. "You must be proud of your father."

He shook his head. His eyes were hard as stones.

"Well, you should be. He was one of the very first to come out. He got a special cheer all to himself."

"He broke his word."

"On the contrary, your uncle and I think he kept it, very bravely. Do not look so despairing, James. Everything will be all right. You can all live in my house till a new manse is built. You see, I shall be sailing off to the Orient with my husband. In any case, your uncle and I think your father will become minister of Mr Jarvie's church in Cadzow. Mrs Jarvie told us it would be offered him."

He had not known that. It was much larger than Craignethan and was conveniently situated in town. The stipend would be more generous; and the congregation was not quite so unenlightened. Though never a compensation for Glenquicken, it should be an improvement on Craignethan. Unfortunately it would allow his father to devote more time, devotion, and money to his Paupers' mission, and to have himself appointed chaplain to the prison, where he would carry out his duties with absurd seriousness. He would become busy, ambitious, and false; whereas at Glenquicken he could have been content and sincere enough.

"You can't keep your eyes open," cried Annabel. "Arthur was telling us you have been up all night. We met him with a delightful girl. They have gone off to see the fun at Tanfield."

"He's going to have a black eye," said his uncle, with a chuckle.

Suddenly Annabel, giving James no chance to avoid her or ward her off, kissed him on the brow. It was an aunt's kiss, of sympathy and affection, but it was also a happy young woman's, teasing and challenging.

"Poor James," she said. "You'll have to find a delightful girl of your own. Won't he, Henry?"

His uncle nodded. He was enjoying James's blushes.

"Keep an eye on Maud for me, will you, James?" asked Annabel. "See that she and Agnes don't squabble all day long. They won't listen to Mrs Maitland or Mrs Barnes, but they will to you. We should be home in about ten days."

Then they strolled away, as delighted with each other as he was disgusted with himself.

All the same, she had reminded him how he might after all find a fruitful purpose at Cadzow, or even at Craignethan. He could keep his promise to his mother to look after his sisters.